south

Book 2 of the Morningstar series

LJ FARROW

For YKW², for reasons too numerous to list in this lifetime.

Table of Contents

Author's Note

Among the Visually Identifiable Minorities (*i.e.* persons of color and those with the visible stigmata of disability), Persons with Albinism (PWA) are especially striking. Because of the arresting features of their condition, they are readily singled out and historically have been demonized, objectified, and even more rarely, deified. In those parts of the world where PWA are persecuted, maimed, raped, and murdered, much of this violence is ascribed to the residual tenets of superstition.

To that end, the association of PWA with magic is problematic, and it has been a pervasive way in which they are portrayed in popular culture, including in this story. The four superhero protagonists in this series are meant to be supernaturally extraordinary, gifted beings, and in this book, you will meet Kusini, perhaps the most extraordinary of them all.

But PWA do not seek to be exceptional. Their lives are predicated on an inability to blend in, to be part of the mainstream of society, to be able to carry out daily activities in peace, to assume an unassuming existence. Superstition has traditionally robbed them of equal consideration for education, jobs, and even their personhood. Rather, they seek to be seen first as persons, and long to see the day when their own lives can be as mundane as any other teacher, engineer, physician, soldier, politician, preacher, or businessperson. They yearn for normalcy, ordinariness, and peace from oppression and prejudice.

Because Kusini's giftedness is breaking from a necessary proscription, I hope her story teaches as much as it entertains, and I am going to blame the Morningstar for cursing her with abilities that could worsen her persecution.

The prevalence of albinism worldwide is about 1 in 20,000; in Tanzania the prevalence is estimated to be 1 in 1,400 (with 1 of every 19 persons a carrier of the gene).

KUSINI PAUSED NEAR THE LONG shadows cast by the stand of acacia trees, and absentmindedly shook the dust from her feet before she crossed the short distance in the clearing to reach the hut that sheltered there, out of sight of the grasses on the high plateau from which she had just descended.

Her husband, Ambakisye, waited patiently inside. He knew she was there; she could feel his secret smile in her heart.

She felt the familiar sensation of goosebumps on her flesh when she encountered the boundary that was placed around the home using love and magic. The protective spell had held over the years. Despite her worries, she was relieved to feel it close around her. She breathed a sigh of relief each time she returned and found it intact.

She needed this oasis, needed it to remain free of the terror and violence that sometimes threatened her very sanity.

The woven red and yellow door hanging always made her smile – next to the spell it seemed such a silly, insubstantial thing that she and 'Kisye used to separate outside from inside. Considering all that comprised their long and complicated history, it seemed almost frivolous.

But many long years ago 'Kisye had made her help him collect rag materials in these azo-dyed hues, and had insisted they weave it together, one row at a time. His work had been much tighter and more regular than hers, because it was one of his exceptional skills. The project was a labor of love, and a symbol of something that neither of them had ever believed could happen, and that neither of them would ever take for granted.

It had been a collective creation; at the time she had not realized what it was for. But he had cajoled her through it, insisting she continue when she failed to make her strands lay down in lovely, orderly progression like his, telling her that those things were not what was really important. Likewise, he refused to allow her to use any magic to complete it, when she was past all patience and didn't care if she never saw another strip of weaving cloth in an eternity.

When it was finally finished, he'd told her it was a wedding gift.

She was slow to understand what he meant, so he'd patiently draped the cloth around her to make her see. She had been the one who stopped breathing, afraid to let herself have such happiness.

As Kusini closed her hands upon it, she felt the crackle of its magic anyway, but it was nothing she had deliberately done. Nor did it surprise her; strong emotions could be trapped within everyday objects more often than people realized. This common magic went mostly unnoticed but had significant power nevertheless.

The wooden hut was round, with a capped roof that had originally been thatch, but which 'Kisye had replaced with overlapping triangles of corrugated tin. He had built a shallow cupola at the peak that helped with ventilation but prevented birds and rain from entering. He had shaped the walls of modified sandy adobe to replace the mud they had started with, an upgrade that kept the temperature inside comfortable whether in extreme heat or on those rare few cool days that one could experience on the elevated steppes of the Serengeti.

Beyond the entry was a small, domed hallway where she ducked her head to remove her hood before discarding her linen djellaba. She could smell grated cinnamon and fresh goat meat mingled with the scents of burning incense and tallow from many candles. There were hundreds of rounded niches purposely created in the adobe wall, many with candles and other treasures that they two had collected, such as beads and pottery, and the flocks of lovely wooden birds that 'Kisye had carved for her.

She hesitated, thinking about the long weeks she had been away, and thought to smooth her abaya, and considered the state of her hair, but he caught her there before she could really primp, because he was too impatient to wait for her to decide to fully make herself present in their home. It was an awkward thing for her, to resume the person she could only become in this private place in the space of the few seconds she had to herself once she entered it. After all the suffering she had witnessed while she was gone, at a necessary emotional remove, the transition still took some time.

She sensed his presence at the inner door, and when she looked up, 'Kisye was leaning casually against the archway, his smile the most beautiful sight in all of Africa.

They were nearly matched in height, she approached two meters in stature; he had surely achieved it. She had to stretch up just so, but not quite on tiptoe, to look him in the eye. 'Kisye was lean and muscular, beautifully formed, with the build of an athlete. His platinum curls were cropped close to his scalp, and the freckles that scattered across his nose and cheeks reminded her of nutmeg sprinkled on cream. His eyes were pale gold, only slightly darker than the impossibly long, giraffe-like lashes that ringed them. He had a passion for modern clothing in the Western style, and wore soft cotton blue jeans with a mustard colored t-shirt.

He took the single step he needed to close the distance between them, grabbing her up in his strong right arm, his laugh inviting hers. It was a luxury she only indulged in with him.

Kusini rested her head against his chest, listening to the still silence where she should have heard his heartbeat, where she knew it had once sounded, but no more. She could never keep herself from reaching out to his opposite shoulder and his missing left arm, the reason for his absent signs of life.

Not that she was surprised; she and the lost arm were the only reasons he was here at all. She merely needed this repeated reassurance that he was really here, not lost to her as she'd feared on that long-ago day. He patiently waited while her hands moved over his form, confirming its substance, understanding her need for this ritual. Only when he felt her relax fully in his embrace, sigh out all the anguish from her travels, and, he suspected, her fears of losing him, did he move again, allowing himself to feel the pleasure of having her body against his own. Only then did she let him lead her into the house, to the meal he had prepared for her, to the warmth at the hearth, and to the love that sheltered there.

IN THE FIRST DAYS OF the Ulimwengu, Ngai Mwathani stood atop the mountain and surveyed the beautiful lands spread out beneath his feet. The majesty of all he surveyed pleased him greatly, but he needed companions on his journey through time, ones who would help him care for this paradise, grow plants for food, harvest fish and beasts, and protect the sacred cattle that he had sent from heaven to graze on the vast grasslands of the valley.

To the Maasai he bestowed his cattle, to the Ildorobo the right to hunt the beasts of the land and harness the power of the bees to feed themselves with meat and honey, to the Kikuyu, he provided the seeds and grains to cultivate crops across the landscape.

Because these people were beloved of their great Mwathani, he dispatched a herald, the chameleon, Kenge, to travel into the world and tell the people that they would possess eternal life, that they would share the immortality of their creator.

But the Nyota ya Asubuhi, the Morningstar, eavesdropping on Ngai and Kenge, devised a mischief by which it could rid itself of the pestilence of humanity. It took the form of Lizard, the Mjusi, and set out in the direction that Kenge had gone.

Kenge walked slowly, stopping to eat along the way, while the Morningstar, wearing its lizard skin, traveled with all haste and arrived among the human-kind before Kenge. The Mjusi announced to the people that they would indeed die, and because it reached them first, this sealed the outcome of their fate. They would forever be mortal, subject to death. Because they were thus convinced of their own mortality, nothing the great Ngai could do would change it.

Ngai Mwathani could not change this undoing caused by the Mjusi, but he could promise humankind their rebirth in the cycle of life. Poor Kenge is to this day regarded an ill omen for his failure to deliver the message of life to all the Mwathani's people, and his little brothers and sisters are often destroyed today in payment for that ancient mistake. It is believed that this is why the chameleon has learned to hide himself so well.

As for the Mjusi, its interference did not end there. It whispered all sorts of nonsense into gullible human ears, making sure that it dictated their fears. It made them suspicious of other tribes, intolerant of differences, ensuring long and pervasive suspicion of the unexplained.

It brought forth the second of its great warriors, this one a sorceress who would stand apart from her own people. Her otherworldly appearance and magical talents were unmatched among the humans, and the Mjusi hoped that the price she paid for both would ensure that she would gladly stand beside it for the Reckoning.

1

KIZUWANDA EXAMINED TUMPE ONCE MORE, finally convinced that she could not be saved. With sadness she could see that the young woman would not survive the birthing chair. Tumpe was too weak; it had taken too long.

Kizuwanda hoped that Tumpe had enough strength left to deliver the child; it would pain Kizu to have to tell her brother, Suhuba, that both his wife and child were dead.

As if reading Kizu's mind, Tumpe lifted her head, eyes fever bright and unfocused, and cried out in pain. Kizu whispered urgently in her ear, repeating her earlier exhortations that Tumpe must help her, Tumpe must push, and silently praying enough of Tumpe was still there to assist in the birthing.

Tumpe threw her head back, and Kizu felt something strange — like a gust of wind through the hut, although the night had been still, and dawn was quietly approaching. She listened for the birdsong that would confirm it, but all was silent.

When she checked again, she could see the crown of the baby's head, but it was far too pale, and she was struck with a new fear. But she had no time to dwell on this, because things were happening fast.

Kizu saw the whole head emerge, and sensed that Tumpe was fading quickly.

"*Mara moja saidi*, one more," Kizu begged, but Tumpe's head slumped forward, and she could no longer hear her, would never hear anything again.

Kizu sweated in frustration, gently rocking the baby back and forth, and when the shoulders finally came free, a long girl-child slid out onto the ground.

Kizu's fears were confirmed. The child carried all the proper lovely features of Mother Africa save one – her luminous white color.

2

KIZU FELT THE COLD BEGINNINGS of true fear as she cleaned and wrapped the baby. She could not allow herself to be distracted by the beautiful little face of her niece; she knew that the infant's appearance alone was a death sentence. The people's law was clear; any child with such features was to be turned over immediately to the tribal witch doctor. Kizu shuddered. These babies were murdered, their bones used to make potions prized by many for their powerful and valuable magic.

She thought of her brother, Suhuba, but was unable to fully convince herself that he would help her. They had been close as children, but in the *Maasai* tradition, once a boy reaches the age of maturity, he is separated from women and children in his quest to become a hunter. He had lived with the other warriors in the wilderness, feeding on blood and meat, as he learned how to become a man. Kizu had to admit to herself that she did not know just how he would react to his daughter's appearance. She also knew that many men would disclaim such a child, often accusing the mother of some infidelity, which in some tribes could justify divorcing her, or killing both mother and child. Suhuba had loved Tumpe desperately, and Kizu could not bear to hear cruel words about sweet Tumpe fall from her brother's mouth, so she abandoned any thought of seeking him out.

Kizu had little time; she knew her brother awaited word of the child's birth. Gently, she arranged her dear friend on a woven leaf mat, placing a red blanket around her legs. She laid the child at Tumpe's breast, knowing it was distasteful, but the baby knew what to do, and Kizu had no other easy choice. She was going to have to take the baby away from the village, and she did not yet know how she would next feed her. The child's first meal was the nourishing early milk of her mother. Kizu knew Tumpe would not mind what seemed an invasion of her peaceful rest, and she whispered loving prayers for her dear friend, thanking the great god *Ngai* for blessings.

Kizu used a second red cloth to enshroud Tumpe's torso and her head, delaying long enough to remove one of Tumpe's many beautiful earrings from high on her earlobe. She quickly pressed the small hoop through the baby's left ear; for this intrusion, the child gave a small cry of protest and then fell silent, soothed by its feeding. Kizu smiled in satisfaction; the baby would have something of her mother. She then lovingly covered Tumpe's face before gathering the child in her arms and making her way silently into the night.

3

KIZU COULD FEEL THE DAWN, even though the birds were not yet singing. In the distance, she saw the signal fire away off in the bush, where the men held vigil. Suhuba was with them, waiting for the young boy that Kizu would surely send as a messenger when his child was born.

But the village children slumbered on, and even the hunters at the distant fire were likely to be sleeping yet. Instinctively, she looked over her shoulder and all around. It was rumored that the *Watende* could see the feelings of his people, and she had to admit she felt watched in a way she never had before. She shook off the chill she felt, most likely related to the fact that Kizu had never strayed from the teachings of her people, had never disobeyed their tenets, had never any cause that she could be judged for. Stealing a child was a grave misdeed; keeping such an omen from the witch doctor threatened the safety of the entire village. It was what she had been taught, what she had witnessed before, but this time was different, she was ashamed to discover, if only because now the baby was one of her own family.

Even more than that, she knew that Tumpe would have done this same thing, but she would have fought them without running, at the peril of her life and that of her child. The outcome would have been the same.

Kizuwanda, Kizu the meek, who had never even raised her voice to another, believed that she could write a different history, shape a different ending for the lovely child she clutched to her shoulder. So she snuck down the dusty path between the huts and away from the distant fire.

As the eastern sky lightened almost imperceptibly, one of the cocks crowed, which caused the goats to stir. It gave Kizu an idea, and she paused long enough to slip a halter over one of the fat females that had recently kidded. Kizu herself had attended the birthing of this one, and she knew it to be a docile matron nearing the end of her life. She was still milking, which was a blessing, and Kizu knew that when the time came, the goat could provide meat and blood to the outcasts. But she barely dared allow herself to think that far ahead, and when she clucked her tongue softly, the animal followed her and the baby without protest.

4

BY THE TIME THE UNFORGIVING sun rose into a sky so hot it appeared white, Kizu had taken shelter in a stand of acacia. She knew they had not traveled far enough to avoid being found by Suhuba and his group of hunters. These *Maasai* warriors were experienced trackers, and they knew the territory on this part of the western plateaus better than anyone.

But she knew the child's delicate skin could not stand any exposure; she would surely burn and blister terribly in the direct rays. Kizu was thankful it was the dry season, as the unrelenting heat was too much for the lions and other predators; she hoped at least that one of her many prayers would be answered, and that they would have time to reach the river and find more permanent shelter. The plains of the *Maasai Mara* were harsh and dangerous always; a woman, a baby and a small goat would attract the kind of attention that Kizu knew could prove fatal.

But the great *Ngai* watched over them; neither baby nor goat made any noise to give away their hiding place, and after the long night, Kizu herself drifted in and out of consciousness throughout the worst heat of the day.

Kizu took milk from the goat and collected it into a small gourd whenever the baby needed to be fed, repeatedly dipping her finger into it and placing the tip into the child's mouth so she could drink. The goat protested mildly in disdain, but the baby made not a sound. She never cried. Kizu worried, but the little one seemed normal in every other way, robust and wriggling, with so many facial expressions that Kizu was utterly enchanted within hours.

The stand of trees was a small island on the lee side of the hill, and the *nyasi nyekundu* there grew tall and thick, obscuring the three of them from view, but Kizu knew that her efforts to rearrange the grass where she had entered the sheltering enclosure would not well disguise their passage. Certainly not from experienced hunters, not from the keen senses of the *Watende*.

As the afternoon lengthened, and the light outside their hastily chosen shelter changed, Kizu heard the low humming of the hunters as they made their way across the grassland. She knew they were spread out in a protracted line, covering more ground, and it was a strategy they used to flush out game. They were not as concerned with silence or stealth when they hunted in this way, because their aim was to incite their quarry to startle and run, giving itself away.

The baby, who had been sleeping, shifted slightly in Kizu's arms and opened her eyes. Her eyes seemed knowing; their amber color was jewel-like and startling. She stretched her arms wide and yawned, then turned her head toward the sound of the approaching men. Even the goat stood up, rolling its eyes and stamping forward and back, and Kizu despaired of any escape. She knew it would be impossible to keep both baby and goat quiet, and the animal was ready to bolt, already recognizing the sound of the approaching men.

Kizu considered letting the goat escape the stand of trees, thinking that it might distract the men from her hiding place. But the goat carried the mark of the village, and that would surely lead to careful examination of the space between the trees. Its presence here would serve as a clue to her whereabouts, since the hunters surely knew the goat was missing.

It was then that she heard an even more ominous sound, that of the *Watende* chanting softly among the men, perhaps singing some spell that would help find her, or more likely the baby. There were signs he could have discerned from Tumpe's body, and it was certain that he had secured a talisman with which to locate them. Thus she was helpless as the hunting party came nearer and nearer; discovery, she felt, was a certainty.

She had to admit she felt a certain relief in that thought, as her confidence in sustaining a fugitive lifestyle was lacking. But fast on the tails of that relief was the grief of failure, for she knew that the fate of the child would be far worse than her own. Even if her life was forfeit for her betrayal, the child faced torture and suffering before she would know the peace of death.

As she instinctively clutched the baby closer as the men drew near, she felt the infant struggle silently, and looked down to discover that she was trying to free her arms of Kizu's embrace. Kizu set the babe down on the soft cloth she had placed on the ground, and the child reached up toward Kizu's face before putting her tiny hands together and locking them in place by crossing her thumbs. The air felt charged, and a gust of wind found the small space among the acacia, although the day had, like the night before, been still.

She could hear the hunters outside the stand of trees, see flashes of the red of their garments through the leaves, and the goat was shaking and dancing in terror. There was even stealthier movement near the entrance of their hiding place, and Kizu could hear the grass move as it was examined by someone now very quiet and purposeful. Sure and steady footsteps circled the trees slowly; the group of hunters was still.

Kizu saw the scarred bare legs of the *Watende* when they stopped near a gap in the vegetation closest to where they were hiding. In the silence that followed, she could hear the steady flick-slap of the zebra tail he carried always. He had stopped chanting. Then he relieved himself where he stood, and the pungent smell drew a bleat of terror from the goat, which could no longer remain silent.

Kizu braced herself for a rapid extraction from the trees, but none came. The men were silent. She glanced down at the baby, and saw that her eyes were closed tightly, her plump lips clamped shut, her beautiful face almost fiercely concentrating. Her hands remained clasped together, and Kizu reached for them, concerned that something was wrong. But when she tried to touch the child she received a sharp shock, truly painful, which caused her to draw back immediately. The goat screamed again, but there was still no response from without.

The *Watende* had not moved, and the zebra tail dangled near his leg. He was silent for a moment, then Kizu clearly heard his soft whisper.

"*Nyonyeshe*," he breathed, and she felt a chill. She could feel his magic, dark and dense, reaching out. He was asking the spirits to show him where she was. The goat was bucking against her lead rope, and delivered a sharp kick to Kizu's side, causing her to gasp in pain and surprise. The baby remained silent, her expression of strange focus completely unchanged.

When Kizu looked up again, through the small window in the grass, the face of the *Watende* was on the other side, peering in at her, seemingly looking right at her. She could scarcely draw breath her terror was so great. But she quickly realized that he could not see her there, whether due to the dark depths of the shade or otherwise, but even that did not make sense with all the noise the goat was making. In response to Kizu's stress and her fear, the goat's bleating was now constant, and crescendoing, but still there was no response from the men outside. Kizu shook her head at the impossible thought that the screams of the goat were not being heard. She suspected that the men were just waiting her out. Yet although the witch doctor's suspicion was evident on his face, he gave away no indication that he could confirm they were there, and finally he moved away from the stand of trees that hid them.

After what seemed a very long time, but could only have been minutes, the men resumed their humming progress onward and away from the three souls in the trees. Kizu listened until she could hear no more of them.

When she returned her attention to the baby, the child was now sleeping peacefully on the ground, arms stretched over her head. Kizu gingerly reached to lift the tiny form into her arms, anticipating that terrible jolt, but none came. The child nestled against her bosom and sighed contentedly in repose. It was full dark before Kizu heard the soft snore of the goat beside her, and it was many hours more before she herself succumbed to exhausted slumber.

5

DEEP IN THE NIGHT, LONG after the hunters had moved on, a lone figure crossed the selva, headed for the stand of acacia, under an orange moon. The sudden gusting wind of the night before had stirred up the red earth from the hills, and this fine dust cloud bathed the moon in color.

It also blunted the moonlight, unhelpfully limiting his already poor night vision, adding to his disadvantage to the large predators who surely roamed nearby. Their vision was affected little, if at all, in the nighttime gloom. Their other senses were more acute than his as well, although he was not without his advantages. Suhuba was an expert tracker, one of the best among the *Maasai* who had achieved warrior status, and he was armed with a hunter's senses, years of experience, fearlessness borne of time, and a wickedly sharp spear.

He had remained in the village that first day, ignoring the insistence of the *Watende*, who came to him to lead the group of hunters in pursuit of the missing child. The man came with his false prayers and an exhortation to take up his weapons and come among the searchers, but Suhuba was so immolated in his grief that he gave these efforts no attention. Suhuba knew the interest in his child was born of some malign intent, and when the witch doctor reached toward Tumpe's enshrouded form to speak some ritual, Suhuba turned a baleful, murderous look upon him; this arrested the *Watende's* hand in its path. Suhuba had to swallow his rage, knowing that it was mostly born of grief, but he had tolerated this false concern for the people for too many years. The *Watende* was a dark and selfish man with too great an appetite for sacrifice.

He had also shooed away the women who came to attend his young wife, sitting alone with her for many hours, remaining unconcerned about the preparations for a search. He pulled the linen shroud from Tumpe's face, smiling at the loving way that it had been done; his love for Tumpe had been shared by his younger sister and her care in this was evident. He looked at her face for a long time, grief and love warring in his heart. He was not ready to let her go, but knew he must bow to the wishes of the great god *Ngai*.

He stared at her, his mind trying to piece something together, until finally he caught the break in the pattern — one of her earrings was misplaced. It was one that had been placed as part of her wedding adornment, if he was not mistaken, it had been a gift from Kizuwanda. He smiled. The gesture was deliberate; it was a message just for him. Kizu had taken the child for reasons unknown, and the removal of the earring could have been for only one reason. It had been bestowed as a gift to their child; Kizu had effectively told him the infant was a girl.

Finally, he covered Tumpe's lovely face, and backed out of the hut they had shared. The elder women waited patiently with blood and fat to prepare her for the next part of her journey. It was time to get answers to his questions, time to confirm that he and Tumpe had succeeded in ensuring their immortality. He had to find the tiny descendant, find sister Kizuwanda, and he knew she would have a very good reason indeed for abandoning her home and taking the child.

Whatever that reason, he hoped to find them before the others. He knew better than to trust the corrupt and greedy motives of the *Watende*. So he abandoned the body of his bride, knowing that she would be left out for predators, returning her to the circle of all life.

But even that ritual would expose the refugees to more danger, as it attracted greater numbers of carnivorous beasts.

To Suhuba's knowledge, his sister had never even raised her voice in anger, much less had to defend herself physically. If she was traveling abroad with an infant, the danger increased. In addition, the day had been hot and close, and there was little shelter from the sun.

When he overheard one of the village women lamenting the loss of one of her nanny goats, he allowed himself a small private moment of amusement. It was unlikely that the animal had been stolen away by a predator; his sister was showing more ingenuity than he might have expected. *Maasai* culture exalted cattle, but their milk was poorly tolerated by infants, where goat's milk could be a source of nutrition.   He was proud of his sister's thinking, but the nanny was unfortunately not a subtle animal, and could be a noisy nuisance, increasing the risk they would be a target for lions or more easily located by the hunters.

He had to admit that neither he nor Kizu were the children they had been; when he had left the village to live with the men, she had still been very young. They had maintained a mutual affection because they two were the only surviving siblings in their family. Kizu had served as a sort of maiden aunt to Tumpe, her chaperone, and he had to credit his sister as a champion of his cause when he pledged his intentions to the elders to finally marry in his advanced age.

Suhuba tracked the hunters, but abandoned their trail early on when he found no signs of a directed approach. They lacked the clues he carried, and were at some disadvantage as it appeared they had failed to learn of the missing goat. Suhuba had always had a gift for tracking; a near-fatal mistake as a young man had honed it. He heeded any and all signs he could find, and paid attention to missing pieces of a pattern as well. He was the eldest hunter in the tribe, which contributed to his patience.

His efforts brought him to the stand of acacia, just as it had the *Watende* and the hunters before him; unlike them, he recognized its importance to Kizu. It was an obvious oasis on the nearby plains, and would have accorded shelter from the sun. Here, the red grass grew thick and tall around the stand of trees, but there were subtle disturbances in the undergrowth where it thinned across the base of two leading trees.

The breeze carried to him the musky scent of goat, and the perimeter of the enclosure was also marked by human scents; the acrid smell of urine was the most predominant. Suhuba dropped down to push his way into the small clearing, noting that the dusty soil and short scrub grass was disturbed within, tamped down. It was too dim to discern footprints, but he could smell goat droppings and knew that this was where Kizu had waited out the day. He knew from the freshly broken grass near the trees that she had only recently abandoned the site. He ducked out and stood tall, stretching his spine, considering the options.

Knowing that their need for water and additional shelter would be great, he turned in a circle, trying to imagine what Kizu would do next. He sensed, more than saw, the great void in the darkness where the Kilimanjaro stood in the distance. Between him and it were the great crater and its foothills, which would afford many hiding places. Also, the *Mbulumbulu*, the site where the river flowed between Nguru and Eyasi, slowing to a bend marked by a small watering hole protected in the lee of the rock face on the eastern slope of the gorge. There were tales of the wildebeest gathering there that Kizu would recall from childhood, and she would try to find the spot that their mother told stories about, that place where the great *Ngai* placed the first persons, the cradle of all life.

He crawled back inside. He stretched out in the space to wait the coming day. Whatever his sister was attempting, he was unlikely to find her or catch up in time to protect her in the dark. Although he had not planned to sleep, he did, and dreamed of his wedding day. But instead of recalling Tumpe as she had been, he dreamed of a golden goddess with her face, bright as the southern sun, with a radiant halo of platinum curls. He couldn't know that he was seeing into the future.

6

THE SKINNY FIGURE NEAR THE water's edge moved slowly, keeping near the reeds that grew up onto the bank, almost completely camouflaged by the red clay mud that covered her, head to toe, protection from the equatorial sun. She watched the woman upstream beat clothing on the rocks to clean it, laying the brightly colored cloth out to dry on clean woven mats of grass.

The activity upstream drove small fish and toads downstream to hide in the reeds, and she impaled them on a long sharp stick she carried, stacking them one atop another as she plunged the weapon repeatedly into the shallow water and the sticky mud of the riverbank. When she was satisfied that she would catch no more, and her ears told her that the washing was finished, she crept through the reeds and peered out at her *Shangazi*, Auntie Kizu, who was draping their linens over reeds and tree branches.

"Kusini, come here," Auntie Kizu called, not bothering to take her eyes off her work, and Kusini wondered how Auntie always knew where she was, even when she thought she was hidden. She sighed, knowing what was to come, and trudged out of the reeds and up the riverbank, dropping down to squat next to the water's edge where the woman waited to take her homemade spear.

Kizu smiled at the small creatures that Kusini had caught; they would make a tasty stew with the root vegetables they would gather before they returned to their shelter among the hills. Then she turned her attention to the child, who was, as usual, in desperate need of a bath.

Now six years old, Kusini had achieved the stature of a child twice her age, with long, gangly limbs that were nonetheless graceful and strong. She had a lovely, straight neck that would have been coveted among other *Maasai* women, because it would need little stretching with coils to achieve the ideal length that a prized bride would want to attract the most prestigious of husbands. Kizu smiled at the irony of this thought, since Kusini's appearance was proscriptive of any possible betrothal she would otherwise have had as a young *Maasai* maiden.

But at present her long hair was matted with the red mud that was applied daily to protect her delicate skin from the sun, and she was completely enshrined in several layers of it. Branches, dust, and leaves were stuck to her skin, and even her morning wade in the shallows had not washed the residue of several days' application from her calves and feet. She looked like some mythical creature that had climbed up from the depths of one of the many claypits nearby.

Although Kizu usually kept the girl's ordered blonde curls tamed in thick braids against her scalp, Kusini would sometimes protest too much fuss, and escape Kizu's firm grasp. Such had been the case the time prior, and despite Kizu's efforts to cajole her, Kusini had steadfastly refused to allow Kizu to touch her, crossing her thumbs in defiance, knowing that Kizu could not touch her without sustaining an uncomfortable jolt of energy. The energy had grown with the child, and the last time Kizu had tried to capture her when Kusini had not consented, it had knocked her from her feet. This had resulted in tears from Kusini, who was afraid she had injured her auntie. Kizu knew that the child neither understood nor wanted this terrible gift of power but could not help but use it as a defense.

While it often frustrated Kizu's efforts at maintaining grooming and hygiene, she was secretly glad that Kusini was thus protected, for reasons that were kept to herself. She knew in her innermost heart that the *Watende* still searched for the two of them, after all this time, and she knew if they were found that she, Kizu, would be useless to fend him off if he caught them.

Kizu set the long stick aside, placing it near the grass mats that were drying in the sun, and held out her hand to the child. Kusini sighed deeply, as though terribly put upon, and her thin shoulders slumped slightly in defeat, but she allowed Kizu to lead her into the shallows under the trees, where the shade provided protection from exposure.

Kizu washed and washed, clearing mud from toes, ears, and even hair, revealing the glowing and lovely girlchild beneath it. She smiled, because Kusini remained an ever so slightly orangey-pink color from the ochre pigment in the clay which stained her skin and hair after so many years of its application. She could still lift the child; even though Kusini was nearly as tall as Kizu, she remained slight enough in build to carry. Kizu placed her on the dry ground under the trees and dried her off with the hem of her skirt; this time Kusini tolerated the placement of a single quick braid encircling the crown of her head, after which the heat of the day had begun to intensify unbearably. Kizu wrapped her in an *abaya* with a large hooded *djellaba* of tightly woven red cloth, finishing just as the child's wandering gaze began to narrow, signaling her impatience with her auntie's attentions. She helped Kizu gather up their belongings, taking the smaller bundle atop her head before setting out up the long hill to their home on the rocky face of the plateau.

Kizu did as she always had, asking the same questions as they climbed into the shadow of the rock face, a ritual exchange repeated almost daily in the child's short life.

"What happens if the others come?"

"I stay hidden."

"What do you do if your *Shangazi* tells you to run?"

"I run, and I do not stop running," the small voice answered.

"What if auntie is not with you?"

"I run, and I hide." Kizu could see the distress this caused each time, as she watched the stiffening, and the exaggerated straightness of the narrow back climbing up the hill ahead of her.

"What if they come calling for you? What if they offer you food, or water?"

"I must be quiet and still until they go away."

"What if you hear your auntie calling for help? What if I am crying out?"

"I must – keep going." Only the small break in the answer gave anything away.

"What must you do if you see, or hear them, hurting me?" This question was always met with the same stubborn, angry silence. This alarmed Kizu more as the child grew in strength and stature. There was some immutable power within Kusini that emboldened her as she matured, and Kizu did her best to teach Kusini to be circumspect in spite of it. Whatever power the child carried within her, she was still no match for the hunters, and certainly no match for the *Watende* should she be captured. Kizu's plan was to train the child to escape, though it was clear that a part of her wanted to fight, and Kizu knew that Kusini had inherited Suhuba's fearlessness along with her mother's beauty. Kizu was thankful that her own timidity had not overly influenced Kusini's development.

They traversed the remainder of the long hill in silence, Kusini steadfast in her refusal to respond, despite Kizu's pleading that she must not turn back in response to such a challenge. She explained that Kusini must keep herself safe from harm and under no circumstances try to help, but it was as though the girl was deaf to her entreaties as they climbed.

Kusini ducked down to enter the opening in the rock face that admitted them to a modestly wide defect in the hill that was large enough for a cooking fire and sleeping area. She unrolled the bundle she carried and leaned her stick against the far wall. She shoved the hood off her head and discarded the djellaba roughly near her woven sleeping mat. She sat in one quick motion, crossing her legs as she sank onto it, her back to Kizu. She crossed her thumbs in her lap.

Kizu untied the bundle she had carried, thoughtfully returning their few belongings to order. She quietly cleaned the small animals and fish that Kusini had speared, preparing them for the stew. She stepped out of the rock enclosure to dispose of entrails and returned with a gourd full of water and a few of the vegetables that grew nearby. These she set down near the site of their cooking fire before coming around to sit stiffly on the ground in front of Kusini.

Kusini resolutely closed her eyes, and Kizu noted her crossed thumbs and determined posture.

"I know you want to be left alone, and I will not try to touch you," Kizu told her, wary of the protective power those crossed thumbs invoked. "But you must understand that since the night of your birth, the only reason, the only purpose I have in this life, was the one the great *Ngai* bestowed upon me. I am to protect you for as long as I can, even if I must pay with my own life to do so. It is a fate I accept, and a cost I am willing to pay.

"But it would be wasted if you were to be captured, hurt, killed, because you could not understand the importance of your own life and its protection to me. I have prayed for strength, and I know you have a bigger purpose in this world than you can know, a value beyond this place, for which the *Ngai Mwathani* has clearly blessed you. To fulfill that purpose you must survive, and that may mean you, yes, *you*," Kizu repeated as Kusini finally opened her eyes, "must someday leave me behind."

A small sob of despair left Kusini's lips, and she let her hands fall apart, the palms upturned on her lap, and Kizu watched a tear track down her lovely face.

Kizu took that face in her hands, gently, and continued to speak. "And you must never think of this as a failure, no matter what happens, it will not be your fault. You will do me a great honor in living, in using your gifts for good, in helping those who cannot help themselves."

"So now you must answer me, darling girl, what must you do if you see, or hear them, hurting me?"

In a voice made small with pain and defeat came the answer Kizu sought. "I must run, and keep running, and not look back."

7

SEVERAL MOONS LATER, KIZU AWOKE in the dark of the night and sat up on her bedroll, listening for whatever might have awakened her from fitful, disturbing dreams. She reached across her body toward Kusini's sleeping mat, but the child was not there.

Shadows danced on the rock walls, but they were familiars of the shelter. Appearing and disappearing with the strength of her cooking fires, they were old friends by now. Kizu rubbed her sleepy eyes and shook her head to clear it. She confirmed that the child was indeed not asleep in her customary place, and she felt the beginning of panic. The child was adventurous, but she never willfully left Kizu's company, and she had been repeatedly cautioned against wandering abroad in darkness.

Panicked, she jumped up and pulled a wrap about her shoulders and head and stepped out of the rock. The ground was softened from the daily rains and she could see Kusini's small footprints on the ground near her feet. Her own feet sank slightly into the earth, and she was unable to decipher which direction the child had taken.
The air was hot and close despite the hour, expectant with humidity and insects. Frogs sang proudly from the river, their throaty croaks drowning the song of the cicadas.
The rainy season was upon the land, and it had stormed since day's

end, but now high clouds pulled away to the east, revealing a bright moon. The pungent smell of the wet plants carried on the warm breeze, and she could clearly see the hilly path ahead. There were fewer numbers of bats than usual, as the moisture in the air could build up on their tiny wings and render them flightless. Their erratic flight was almost dancelike, and in large numbers their wings made a whispering rush that was one of Kizu's favorite memories from childhood.

Pulling her wrap closer around her head to discourage the biting flies, she followed small clouds of them down the hill toward the river, hurrying faster as she reached the scrublands that rose up to meet the lower slopes of the plateau. She resisted the urge to call out for the child; there were still predators about, and although they were less desperate during the rainy season, when more animals congregated near the swollen river, they were no less a threat to a little girl alone on the floodplain. She neither wanted to alert predators to her own position nor wanted Kusini's answer to identify hers.

The river was swollen with rains, and there were more animals about, both due to the abundant water and the time of year. The mighty wildebeest was beginning its migration, and Kizu shuddered, hoping to avoid them; such beasts spooked easily, and she and the child could easily perish beneath their trampling hooves.

When she reached the slippery bank, she waded in a few steps to clean her feet, sticky with clay from her descent from the shelter. She remembered to thank Ngai for the cool relief the water provided, and for the lack of crocodiles in this part of the river. She despaired momentarily, realizing that the child may not have come that way at all. But she had no time for such weak nonsense, and actually smiled to herself, recalling that she had been teaching Kusini different bird calls, many for birds that did not live in their region.

It was one of these that she chose to mimic, as she could be certain that if an answer came, it would be the child, and not another bird responding in kind. It also decreased the likelihood that the sound would be readily identified as prey by the local predators. She wandered up and down the bank, giving the soft call.

In lieu of an answering call, she was rewarded by a loud rustling in the reeds, and Kusini emerged, filthy from the water and the mud. Kizu nearly wept in relief.

"Thank the gods!" Kizu exclaimed softly, reaching out to pull Kusini close to her. But the child took a step back and crossed her thumbs. Kizu sensed more than saw the abrupt shake of her head.

"No, Auntie, don't make a fuss. I will tell you the story. I was on my way home." All this a declaration rather than an apology, as if nighttime forays were normal. Kizu had to smile; she was still quick to remember her childhood impatience with the fussing of her own mother and the many aunts in their tribe.

Gladness and relief were her predominant feelings, so she stepped out of the water and led the way. She could sense the child climbing along behind her, using her fishing spear as a walking stick. It was odd, Kizu had not noticed the stick when Kusini had emerged from the reeds, but she had half-learned to ignore certain unexplained events where this extraordinary child was concerned.

They reached the shelter without incident, but when Kizu turned and saw the child in the firelight, she gasped. Kusini looked as though she had been dragged through the mud and debris in the river, and her clouds of platinum hair were clotted with leaves, twigs, and long grass. Her skin was daubed with the rosy clay of the river bottom, and one arm was injured, clotted blood and filth streaked it along its length and some of the blood had run down onto her leg.

"What in the name of all that is good?!" Kizu shrieked, reaching carefully for the arm to examine it, pausing for a moment until it was clear that the child was going to allow it. Using warm water from the gourd next to the fire, she cleansed the arm carefully and saw two arcing half oval patterns, both atop and below the wrist; on closer inspection, she could see that the lines were made up of several small, relatively deep punctures, and the skin around these was already an angry red color. The pattern was so regular that Kizu's mind searched for its cause.

"It was the lizard," Kusini explained, as if it all made some sense that Kizu could not grasp. Her look was knowing and all too wise to provide Kizu with any comfort.

"The lizard?" Kizu repeated, still not understanding.

"The *Mjusi*. It comes into my dreams. Tonight, when it bit me, I awoke to find it here in the shelter," Kusini replied. "I asked why it would do that, and it said it would give me something to keep forever. Maybe this was before I woke up. But it scurried out into the night, and it appeared to be growing, so I followed it down to the river, where it hid in the reeds.

"But I *knew* it was there – I could see its eyes. When I pushed into the reeds, my fishing spear was in my hand, even though I was sure I had left it on the back wall of the cave when I came out into the night. It ran again, and it was still growing, in fact it was enormous, and I had to chase it through the reeds as I followed. It was thrashing and splashing about, but then it backed into a thick stand of acacia shrubs upriver and refused to emerge. By that time, it was larger than I and I thought it had started to walk upright on two legs, but I could still see its scaly wet skin.

"Then it spoke to me – '*next born, witchborn, child of sun*' – and its voice was soft and thick. I didn't understand the words, yet I knew what it said. I asked it to come back out, so I could see it, but it refused, saying it was afraid of my sharp stick. I had never seen it before, but now I do not think it was really a lizard at all.

"I reached in to try to touch it; I even set my spear aside and moved slowly. I leaned in to push apart the reeds and a horrible stench rose up. The lizard was gone, but a half-eaten rotting calf was stuck there. It must have been carried downstream on the swollen waters.

"I had to leave that place, but I lost my balance, and I fell backward into the water, and I could hear the lizard whispering my name. The chilly water on my face made me fully awaken, and I heard a large animal splashing up the bank on the other side of the river. I think it was the same lizard."

"The same?" Kizu asked, feeling cold fingers of fear wrap around her pounding heart. The wounds were explained; it was clear they were the marks left by the sharp teeth of an animal – the pattern confirmed the force with which those jaws had closed over the child's arm.

"I have dreamt about it before. Always the dream comes, and it talks sometimes, and sometimes I only see its eyes, shiny even in darkness. It shows me things from far away."

"Far away?"

"Either far away or not really real," Kusini was precociously contemplative for her age. "I feel coldness like nothing we have here, with an entire world covered in white, like that at the top of the Kilimanjaro, and I can hear an animal breathing loud, running and running in that white, white world."

Kizu finished wrapping the child's wrist in silence, and then pulled her close, hugging her in relief as much as to tame the gooseflesh that had arisen on her own arms and legs. She was afraid to speak the legend aloud and give it any power, but she knew it was important to teach the child some of the old lessons. And this child especially, with her inner power, her *magic*, could certainly attract the old gods. And if this lizard was in fact the mischievous *Mjusi*, he was not to be trusted, because he robbed humankind in his jealousy over their importance to the great *Ngai*.

Kusini did not protest the embrace, she seemed to welcome it, and Kizu told her the ancient tale of *Kenge* the chameleon, how he dawdled on his errand and was overtaken by *Mjusi* on his way to tell the people of *Ngai's* great plan to deify them, make them immortals alongside himself. She talked of how *Mjusi* had stolen the people's belief in their own God-given destiny simply by speaking to them another fate, but the first message was the one the people accepted as their truth. When the unfortunate *Kenge* arrived, the people had been seduced into mortality and mistrust by the lizard impostor, and *Mjusi* had been causing much mischief ever since.

"You must be wary of any lizard that appears, because it might be *Mjusi* trying to cause you trouble. It speaks in riddles and can trick us into believing things that are not true. Its aim is confusion, despair, and division. It has brought great misfortune. Our warriors call it the Ghost and the Darkness. The Darkness is the well of all that is evil, and the Ghost comes with it to do its bidding. They are separate, but they are one."

Kusini absorbed the story and was so quiet and for such a long time that Kizu was sure she had fallen asleep. But just as suddenly she crawled off Kizu's lap and stretched out on her sleeping mat. She turned away and simply said, "It always comes back."

8

"THERE'S A MAN ON THE other side of the hill," Kusini whispered, squeezing her narrow frame through the gap in the rock shelter. At ten, she was nearly as tall as a man, but still inconceivably lean. If she grew much taller, she would be unable to fit through the opening to the shelter, Kizu thought, looking up from her weaving.

Kusini had been out since morning, gathering water, capturing toads and fish, and exploring the surrounding grasslands. Kizu had been amused that the child had become such a wanderer, curious about what lie beyond the boundaries of the small life they had created, but she was not amused now; she was afraid.

"Were you seen?" she whispered back, leaning in to say the words directly into Kusini's ear, grateful that she had not started the fire for their meal.

"I was not seen," came the cautious reply. "But they don't have to see us to find us, you said. He was one of them, Auntie. He had a spear, but not like mine. A real one."

"Kusini, it is time," Kizu said gravely, strangely calm although the fearful certainty of her demise was upon her. "Time to go. Time to hide."

"But what of you, Auntie?" the child inquired, "You must come, too."

"I will gather a few things and follow behind you," Kizu replied, hoping her words did not betray the falseness from which they were spoken. "Now you must go, and hide in the place we agreed upon, and wait for me there, where you are safe."

Kizu knew not what Kusini saw in her expression, but she was pleased that with only the slightest hesitation she was off in the direction of the gorge, traveling nimbly over the ground, in that leaping run that Kizu had before associated with her older brother. The girl disappeared from sight seconds later, and not a moment too soon, for the next face that appeared at the gap in the rock was preceded by a heavy, dark shadow that felt like a living thing.

The wizened, frightful, leathery countenance of the *Watende* appeared opposite the opening of the rock enclosure, and he smiled with an eerie pleasure that struck terror in Kizu's heart. The only relief she felt was that he showed no sign of having noticed the retreat of the child over the shoulder of the hill ahead of him. He was accompanied by his special guard, warriors without conscience who did his bidding and asked no questions. For their service they were rewarded the spoils of the witchdoctor's power.

In the late-day sunshine, his eyes were bright spots sunken deep in his skull, and his yellowed teeth were sharpened from years of grinding. Kizu knew he could not fit through the entrance of the shelter, and she pressed herself tight against the back wall, where she should have been securely out of his reach. She felt not at all safe.

He flicked his zebra tail wand against his leg, and began to chant softly, softly, so softly that the wind threatened to carry the words away. But Kizu did not have to hear them to feel each one touch her like a lash, burning under her skin, and although his language was unclear, she understood each word, because he called her from a dark fount of power. It was a power that she had feared, and suspected all her life, and believed in, because it was her religion. The *Watende* was authority, the father, the healer, the decider…and her flesh grew cold with the knowledge that he controlled her.

"Kizuwanda, my daughter, you will come and submit your flesh unto me and mine. You will tell me about the child you stole from me, and answer for your crime against your family." Although she did not move from her place, stubbornly refusing with her mind, her feet began to move, carrying her forward, and she saw the place where he had changed her as a child, the ritual that had gone so wrong those many years ago, when instead of entering womanhood, she had been made sick, been made less, been robbed of her fertility and her chance to marry. She recalled the nightmares of him, and realized that she had never been dreaming, that what she feared of him had been part of the way he now controlled her, because he had stolen her flesh on that long-ago day and kept it for his magics.

And when she realized that she must never betray her niece to this monster, this one who wanted only sacrifices and stolen power, she saw with certainty that this time of her own suffering and death had been foretold. Her arm thrust forward violently, and just as forcefully the wizard's strong hand closed over it, pulling her right to the defect in the rock, and even though she no longer resisted, he bent it double, back against the outside face, slowly cracking first one and then the other small bones of her arm, relishing her screams. Her other arm joined its fellow, and was met with the same fate, and Kizu thought she could hardly stand it, and feared she would tell anything to avoid any more pain.

As they dragged her from the shelter, she saw, on the arched roof of the enclosure, the tiny green flash of movement as the lizard withdrew into a crevice high in a shadowy corner and was lost to sight. It gave her the strength to resist, knowing the *Mjusi* worked through the old witchdoctor, and she prayed for the strength to withstand the great pain and humiliation that was to come.

The old man whispered to her, as they held her for him to violate her, that she could end it all by giving him the child, but she knew such an ending meant only a quicker death and the same treatment of the girl prior to her own dismemberment and death so that her bones could make his potions and increase his power. She stubbornly refused to talk, and told herself she would not cry out, but they took immense pleasure in eliciting her screams, and it seemed it would never end. Those screams chased Kusini up the final elevation of the rock wall and onto the grassy plateau.

Kusini kept her promise only until she reached a place where she could hide in the shadows of the great rocks and then she peeked out. Too young to fully make sense of what she saw, she knew only that she was afraid, and she was angry at herself for not knowing how to save her beloved Kizu, angry at herself for being too afraid to help, too afraid to look.

Just then, she felt, rather than saw, a small movement near her face on the surface of the rock and she sat back, startled, landing hard on her tailbone, and barely stifling a cry before noticing it was only a small lizard running down the rock. It stopped and looked at her, then it started to speak, describing, between the screams on the hill below, the acts causing those screams.

Much to her distress, it described the dislocated and broken limbs, the serial rape, as she flinched and stifled her moans of distress at this fracturing of her childhood ignorance. It kept talking, even when Kusini snatched it from the rock and squeezed it. She felt it grow in her palm, and it was increasingly difficult to generate any force as it did so, but she wanted only to silence that calm, sure voice, telling her the very things she wanted to avoid, the whole terrible event described in that eerie, unfamiliar language. The hissing whisper that accompanied the sudden silence which heralded her beloved Kizu's terrible death.

Then, angrier than she could ever remember being before, she flung the small body far away from her in vengeance, wanting to punish it, hurt it, crush it. As soon as Kusini heard the tiny squeak when it hit the ground, she felt deep remorse, knowing she had murdered little brother lizard, because as soon as she had let go, she felt something else with certainty. The *Mjusi* had departed, abandoning its fleshy familiar to her wrath.

9

SUHUBA EXAMINED THE TRAMPLED GROUND in the acacia shrubbery carefully, then walked in circles outward, looking for other signs. He did not hum, but remained silent, listening to the song of the river nearby.

When he heard the buzzing of flies, he followed the sound to a stand of juvenile acacia and red grass, where he found the remains of a small calf, now mostly bones but with enough residual putrefaction to attract a small crowd of carrion insects. The ground here gave away nothing; there had been too much rain to erase prints. He could not tell whether the calf had been killed there or elsewhere, but there was also a chance that it had drowned. There were fewer teeth marks on the skeleton than he would have expected; the bigger predators often broke the bones for the marrow inside, and the carcass was still relatively intact. He suspected drowning, with later predation by the small animals and insects along the riverbank.

He kept looking for the better part of the afternoon, keeping mostly to the dappled shade beneath the trees that grew beside the water. All creatures had to drink, and if he were going to find what he was searching for, it would be here.

As the sun dropped down to the west, the day softened, although it did not cool. He found some telltale droppings upstream of the calf's remains, on the opposite bank. There had been some effort to hide them, he was pleased to see. They had dried in the equatorial sunshine, and when he crushed them with the toe of his sandal, he saw something that encouraged him.

He squatted down to take a closer look, pushing through them with a stick, and then stirred the dried particles and sniffed. He identified a trace of the scent of his mother's root vegetable stew, one of the oldest and best memories of his youth, and he smiled.

When it was time to take a break, Suhuba rested with his back against one of the older acacia trees and watched the landscape. He had repeated this task once a year for the past nine years. Occasionally, he stopped to brush flies away. At one point he wandered back by the river to fill his gourd with water. He placed another handful of the red mud in his hair, grateful for the brief coolness it provided, and returned to his spot under the trees to wait and watch.

He sipped water and watched the sun sink ever closer to the earth, patiently observing the riverbank. He didn't miss the emergence of the strange, mud-covered figure from the reeds on the far side. It looked around briefly before scooting quickly up the hill and over the ridge. Suhuba smiled, recognizing the gangly, loping stride as his own.

He didn't follow; he had long ago discovered the now-abandoned shelter among the rocks. He rethought that assumption. Although the fire inside had not been lit for several weeks, and no food had been prepared or eaten there, he had no way to confirm that it had been completely abandoned, because he was too big to slip into the space. His sister and the child had been able to squeeze through the crack in the rock face. It was an excellent refuge for the two of them, but its disuse and his sister's absence were related, he feared.

Sadly, he had also discovered signs of a struggle on the hillside. The ground was disrupted by many feet, and there was blood still staining the broken grass, despite the recent rains. The place stank of fear, and the blood carried a human scent, but it was the work of cruel men, not lions. He had no evidence that his sister was anywhere about, and this saddened him. Kizu's absence was what had drawn him to watch and wait. His fear of her loss was confirmed, but he had enough faith to hope. The clay-stained figure was an answer to his prayers. His daughter had survived.

10

KUSINI KNEW THE SHELTER WAS a useful decoy. Anyone following her or searching for her would readily assume that the space was occupied. She encouraged this illusion by moving objects around and occasionally making new fires at the small hearth. The pattern of the soot staining the roof changed only subtly, but she knew an expert tracker might notice and settle the idea that it was where she continued to live. If any of the men who had taken away her beloved *Shangazi* might return, they would watch the shelter, which predicted the possible locations from which they could watch. This, in turn, would allow her to plan how to watch *them*.

Thus, when she noticed him, she gave no indication that she was aware of the hunter who watched by the river, leaving him to believe that he could not have been seen. She continued the camouflage taught her by Kizu, using the river's mud to cover herself and to hide among the reeds.

She kept to a meager diet of insects and the small animals she could catch in the shallows. For reasons not entirely subconscious, she refused to eat the flesh of lizards. She also determined that a cooking fire was the easiest possible locator of her position, so she stopped cooking her food, existing entirely on a raw diet. While not the most pleasant of lifestyle changes, what it lacked in aesthetic it more than made up for in safety.

When once she made a slight exception to her lizard-free menu and consumed a salamander, it made her violently ill, and she rued the decision. She was unable to keep down more than a few sips of water over the next several days and determined that the animal must have carried some sickness. She subsequently avoided that creature as a source of food, but would later watch a skinny, abandoned hyena pup try to consume one and spit it forth in a spasm of foamy saliva, so perhaps the thing was poisoned.

Suhuba observed many of her efforts to survive, and smiled to himself at the practical ingenuity of his daughter. Yet a child, she was finding her way. Africa was a harsh mother; her children persevered and found a way to survive or they were consumed.

Kusini had learned in the most base and terrible of ways that sometimes the things that were relied on the most could pose the greatest danger. The shelter was a useful place that had proven to be a very deadly trap for Kizu. A fire brought warmth and cooked food, but it was a beacon for predators, four-legged and otherwise.

Suhuba, for his part, was patient. He knew that this child had to be special for Kizu to risk everything, and whatever had become of her, it had scared the child into a state of caution. She had essentially returned to the wild.

So he watched, knowing that he was long overdue to return to his village. The season to hunt was upon them, the long dry hot days stretching out in endless succession into the future. The *nyumbu* were on the move, and only small high clouds sat over the Kilimanjaro.

The lion prides were also on the move, and he could hear their coughing calls from the grasses of the plateau above the gorge. Bone-chilling to some, the sound called to him, making his blood sing, beckoning him to exact further retribution for his own losses.

But rather than return to the only home he had ever known, or join his tribesmen in the hunt, each morning he watched as a mythical being climbed up from the reeds, covered in clay from head to foot. Its hair was a snarl of mud and plant debris, fearsome and yet strangely beautiful to behold. It cautiously emerged to the shelter of a small stand of acacia where it would surreptitiously consume a small amphibian or fish it had caught. It would cleanse its mouth with water from the shallows, ever vigilant, secretly aware it was watched. Then it would return to the shallows and move upstream within the cover of the reeds, apparently constantly in search of something while fishing with the small spear it had fashioned.

And when the man with the hideous eye rose up from those same reeds in front of her one day, Kusini protected herself in the only way she knew how, the man's scream of surprise and pain startling the birds from the trees, the sounds of their panicked wings heralding her escape up the rim of the gorge to the shelter of the rocks.

Suhuba sat for hours in the shallow water, recovering from a profound shock that left his muscles weak and sore, feeling the age of his many rains as he never had before. When the sun began to settle in the west, he was finally able to pull the sharp end of her rudimentary spear from the large muscle of his shoulder. He found his feet with difficulty and promised himself he would stop being such a foolish old man, charging in when he did not fully understand his quarry. She had defenses he had previously been unable to discern.

But the old hunter was a survivor, determined to find another way to approach his child. He gave no indication that he knew her location at the rim of the gorge, where she had returned to watch him from among the rocks as he struggled up the riverbank and retreated back along the floodplain. He disappeared from her sight just as the sun sank below the horizon, and she was too disturbed to leave the spot in which she had wedged herself, finally falling asleep, in the morning discovering that the mud had dried, temporarily incorporating her form into the landscape.

11

THE MAN RETURNED SEVERAL DAYS later, bringing more supplies and provisions than he'd had before. He moved slowly and purposefully, and though he tried to hide it, his arm was bothering him; Kusini could tell it in the way he favored it. He appeared ignorant of his surroundings, and made no effort to disguise the fact he was setting up a rudimentary campsite right on the riverbank. He undertook these chores in plain view of the walls of the gorge, and the old shelter itself, where she had retreated, feeling safer there than out in the open following their encounter.

Suhuba knew the child was not savvy enough to abandon the area entirely; although she must have recognized it as a place of incomplete safety, her entire life had been lived in the shadows of the rock face, and the world beyond was uncertain. It was also unsafe, and he admired her cautious prudence.

When the medium-sized lizard that clung to the arched overhang started to speak, Kusini was unconcerned. She had become used to *Mjusi* and its mischief; it appeared at will. She had long ago stopped scrutinizing every lizard she saw, realizing that it was a waste of her time – its appearances and disappearances were seemingly random, but this time, she correctly assumed it had been summoned by the unusual happenstance at the water's edge.

Of late, its voice was not one but many, overwhelming in its timbre, as if her very ears might split open when it spoke. The language remained unfamiliar and unknown to her, yet she understood every word.

"We suggest you kill him before he kills you," it advised, and Kusini remembered enough of what Auntie Kizu had taught her to be suspicious. She also remembered it had taken too much perverse pleasure in Kizu's death, ensuring that she had heard every horrid detail. In similar fashion, as if in answer to these thoughts, it repeated to her in agonizing whispers what use a man might have for such a girl as she, just as those soldiers had used her Kizu, killing her in pain and humiliation.

Kusini did not give away any of the emotions she felt as it spoke to her in that insistent, buzzing voice, hearing again Kizu's screams, too clear to be a memory, supplied by this creature for whatever its own twisted purpose. She remained unmoving, as if unaffected, until she could somehow sense it was distracted with its own description of degradation and suffering, and she leapt into the air, plucking its leathery body from the rock, feeling her power course through it. She noted with pleasure its distress and surprise, this time certain that her touch had trapped the *Mjusi* in the flesh of the small creature, beyond immediate escape, and she sensed something else – was it fear? Its struggles increased as it enlarged in her hand, loosening her hold, and she felt something dark rushing in the air around her, and several small disturbances rocked her body, and the *Mjusi* departed, leaving brother lizard to awaken in her grasp. Panicked, it hissed at her, and she released it, gladly, watching it shrink before her eyes prior to disappearing into a crack in the rock wall of the shelter. Slowly, the screams retreated from her ears, no longer just Kizu's own, but a dark chorus of many. The silence was a relief.

It was soon replaced by another sound, one that was familiar to her. The man was humming, and it was a tune that was known to her, part of a song that Kizu had sung or hummed while deeply engrossed in her chores. The sound beckoning, she slipped out of the shelter and down the hill.

Kusini could no longer see him, but followed the sound of his humming to the reeds. She remained under cover and crept upstream, peering out into the clearing where Kizu had done her washing.

The man had a red cloth tied about his slim waist, and he had tucked it up to protect it where he had waded into the water. His body both fascinated and repulsed her; his skin was so black it appeared blue in the shadows, but it was marked by patterns of tiny scars that crossed his torso, both arms, and the bridge of his nose. These markings were almost beautiful next to the scars that transformed the left side of his face, several deep gouges ran from his temple to his chin; that eye was clouded over, sightless, with a lid that sagged downward grotesquely. A piece of curved bone pierced his nose, and his earlobes were stretched to his shoulders, similar to her Kizu. His were decorated with red threads and his hair was stiff with red clay.

Although fierce, his face had a noble appearance; his cheekbones were stark and high above hollowed cheeks. His mouth was prominent, but his lips were thinned over very white, even teeth. It was an ugly and arresting visage, and he appeared very aged to her young eyes. There was something familiar about that face that she couldn't place, something almost comforting.

He appeared to be bathing, washing the dust off his skin in the shallows. She watched as he cupped a handful of the water and laved it over his shoulder. His humming was interrupted by a grimace as he pressed the edges of an ugly wound there, the wound she had created, and he grunted as he pressed the flesh and thick pearly fluid spilled out. He did not stop his ministrations until the fluid was thin and bloody, and then he washed the area again. Once that was done, he dipped his face to wash it, and Kusini was surprised when he spoke to her, first in a language that was unclear to her, and then in Kiswahili, "*Jambo, upepo wa Kusini.*"

She was doubly surprised, as she was certain that she had made no noise, and she was sure she could not be seen among the reeds, but he had known her name. And he had divined that Auntie Kizu had taught her what she had called a universal language, rather than teach her the *Maa* language of their people. Kizu had wanted her to be able to communicate with other tribespeople, and thus had instructed her in the broader common language of the region. And this man knew it somehow.

When next she peered out between the reeds, he had advanced to her location, his face only inches from hers. She shrieked, losing her balance and splashing down on her backside in the shallow water. She scuttled backward quickly and dashed downstream as fast as her feet would carry her, but when she looked back, she was alone. He had not chased her.

She stood up on tiptoe, peering over the reeds, but could see nothing. She crept partway up the hillside to get a better vantage point, and saw that he had returned to the riverbank, where he was calmly building a fire in the shade of the trees.

The ridge rose up behind her, shielding her from the sun's afternoon rays, and she sat among the rocks next to the path, but the man made no move to follow her. Instead, he took something down from the trees, and she saw it was the body of some small animal. He separated the hindquarters with a small sharp blade, and tore away hunks of its flesh, skewering them on a stick and placing them near the fire. She stood up and saw that he was using the hottest rocks next to the fire to cook the meat.

Soon, the scent of his meal reached her, and her treacherous mouth began to water. She watched helplessly as he checked one of the skewers and deemed it done. He tested a small piece of meat, chewing enthusiastically. Her unfaithful stomach was the next to rebel, protesting loudly. She was unable to resist standing tall to see whether he had more.

Without looking up from the meal, he finished making another skewer and placed it next to the fire to cook. She heard the sizzling of the juices and turned away, ready to retreat up the hill, but a movement of his arm caught her eye. He had pulled another finished hunk of meat from the stone, and held it out in her general direction, clearly making an offer. He gave no other indication that he paid her any mind; continuing to focus on his preparations.

When she made no move to return to the riverbank, he stood up long enough to deposit the meat on a large rock several paces from his fire and returned to his work, turning his back on the offering, and her. Finally, her legs rebelled, and rather than carry her to safety, they led her straight back down the hill. The sun was steadily slipping away, and as the sky darkened, she scooted ever closer to the fire. The meat was waiting in front of her; she could see the fats darkening the rock, and her mouth watered more. She swallowed, took a deep breath, and plunged forward, snatching the meat, barely taking possession before taking flight up the hill and away. She slid sideways into the shelter, scraping her shoulder in her haste, and wolfed down the meat hungrily, watching the figure at the fire carefully.

The man never interrupted his tasks, keeping his fire burning into the night, long after her exhausted mind could no longer elude sleep. Knowing he was too large to get into the shelter, she allowed her eyelids to slide shut. She slept so deeply that she was entirely unaware that hours later, in the deep dark of the night, he lit a torch and climbed up to the narrow opening in the rock, and watched over her until the sun returned.

12

SUHUBA WENT ABOUT HIS DAILY tasks and occasionally smiled at the irony of the situation. He had been blessed in his old age with a child, and had been content to watch her progress from afar, trusting beloved Kizu to teach her the ways of the *Maa*. Of course, that had been impossible outside the village, and rightly understanding this, his sister had taught the girl the language they had learned of their mother, an *Ildorobo* maiden stolen in a dispute over hunting lands. Their mother had been a translator and a cook for the men she traveled with, because their maternal grandmother had been from a faraway village to the south and spoke the common language among the tribes of the eastern coast. The child was prepared for life off the *Maasai mara*, which Kizu had assumed was to be not only a necessity, but a certain eventuality.

With Kizu lost, he recognized that it was very likely hunters from his own village and the *Watende mabaya* that had taken her. For whatever reason they had been unable to capture the child, he suspected there was still great danger in remaining in that place. Whatever the interest of the *Watende*, it was not in sister Kizu, especially now that he knew this child had some special magic. He was unable to tease out the extent of it, and he was aware that his continued absence from the village would necessitate some degree of searching. They did not need to find him here; they knew the place, and his presence would only confirm the suspicions of the witch doctor that the child could not be far off.

So he ignored her, and went about his business, paying her no heed. Children, he knew, were naturally curious, and this extraordinary child was no exception. Within a few days, after continuing to feed her, she began to shadow him, so he obliged his fears and led her out of the *Oldupai* and across the high plains toward the great *Ngorongoro*. The crater was large, provided many options for shelter from both elements and predators, and was far enough from the village to be disregarded as a possible destination for a wandering hunter.

The trip took several days on foot, and he began to show her how to survive, realizing that he was teaching her the ways of the warrior, those lessons he would have taught a son in preparation for manhood rites. They slept out under the stars, used cooking fires only during the sun's high point, and he taught her how to catch small game by trapping it in tight thickets and dispatching it on the point of a spear.

The child watched all with those golden eyes, and resolutely refused to speak. She kept her clay mud covering; despite it drying and flaking in the relentless sun it was too thick to fully shed, and its cracked and peeling appearance transformed her into another kind of creature, traveling in her own small cloud of dust several paces behind him. He did not try to approach her, and she in turn maintained a prudent distance, said distance decreasing accordingly when the sun went down, which gave him both a sense of relief, as her protector, and a sense of pride at the wisdom she displayed.

She was most outwardly distressed when they crossed large unbroken stretches of plain, preferring when able to keep to the shade, moving under trees and shrubbery when possible. He supposed it some tenet of caution given her from her time with Kizu, never suspecting there was a more practical reason. When they found water, she patiently reapplied her mud mask, showing no qualms about her appearance, working until she was satisfied with its thickness.

She began to mimic him, carrying her sleeping mat and spear as a makeshift sling for her gourd and linens. If he came too near, he noticed that she put her hands together, and he began to understand that it was some sort of distress signal, because she did so seemingly without conscious thought, and it happened, he saw, whenever she was apprehensive or afraid. He recalled the shock of his first encounter with her, and never pursued the issue.

One cool morning, the child slept more deeply than usual, so Suhuba went about his chores, building up the fire to warm her. He slipped the lion hide he wore off his shoulders and placed it gently over her sleeping form.

After consulting the sky, he was satisfied there would be no rain, so he backtracked to the small spring they had passed the previous afternoon and refilled their water gourds. He heard the morning calls of ostrich hens in the distance, and on his walk back he surveilled the low grasses carefully.

He was rewarded in his efforts, finding an abandoned egg in one of their burrowed nests. He remained still and contemplative for several minutes before attempting to secure it. While his stomach relished the idea of bringing such a delicacy back to camp, his mind recognized that an angry ostrich could easily run him down and disembowel him, and he was wise not to forget this.

When he returned to the campsite, Kusini was beginning to stir, her movements suggesting she was shaking off the vestiges of her dreams.

Suhuba cleared space for the egg at the edge of the fire, nestling it among cooler ashes and pushing the hotter embers away from it, hoping to keep the shell from cracking before it could cook. He squatted near the warmth, stretched his legs and arms, and said his prayers.

He must have dozed briefly, enjoying the warmth, because her soft voice startled him awake.

"How did you know my name?" she asked from across the fire. She was peering at him curiously from where she sat atop her sleeping mat. She held the skin closely about her shoulders, and it dwarfed her, making her look like a much younger child.

"I gave it to you before you were born," he replied, concentrating on the fire. "I whispered it in your mother's ear."

The child was silent then, the only sounds coming from the crackling of the embers between them and the world around them.

Suhuba watched her considering these statements. He checked the egg, and satisfied it had cooked enough, rolled it gently away from the fire with the blunt end of his spear. He doused it with a handful of water, ducking his face away from the steam.

A small muddy head popped up, peering at what he was doing, but despite her curiosity, she was resolute in her refusal to ask. He obliged her anyway. "Once the egg cooks it will stick to the shell. If you pour cool water on it right away, the edible part pulls away from the shell, making it easier to free it for eating."

The golden eyes watched him as he cracked the egg and broke it into halves. He set one next to her feet and claimed his own, showing her how to drink the softer yolk from the center. Then he demonstrated how he scooped the firmer part from the shell with his hands.

She mimicked him, and he enjoyed watching her pleasure when she tasted the yolk, one of the richest meals to be had on these vast plains.

"Are you my father?" she suddenly asked.

"I have that honor," he replied between bites of his meal.

She continued quietly eating, but finally spluttered out what she had been holding onto, exclaiming, "But you are so *old*!"

Suhuba couldn't stop his grin, but upon seeing her perfectly earnest expression, he set his face as seriously as he could manage, adding, in an ironic tone that did not quite manage to hide his amusement, "That is so. I am ugly, too."

He saw the tiny spark of surprise in her eyes that told him she was now wondering if he could read her thoughts. Then, when her surprise turned to worry, he added, very sincerely, "It is a blessing that your mother was young and beautiful. Surely you look like her." Then, because Suhuba loved to tease, he peered closely at her, as if trying to see through all the caked-on mud she wore. "I think."

Then he purposefully began to gather his things and pour sand on the remnants of their fire, ignoring the indignant rise of her small shoulders as she shrugged out of the lionskin.

He handed her the gourd he had refilled for her, and she surprised him by coming close to return to him the hide. Her hand even brushed his briefly and she paused. Suhuba was very still, but asked, "Are you warm enough?"

She nodded then, letting go and turning away to roll up her sleeping mat. When they set out walking once more, she remained close by his side, seeming to take shelter in his shadow.

13

IT WAS WARM ENOUGH, COMING on summer, the end of the dry season ending, so Suhuba kept on eastward, well past his original destination, right to the forests that marked the approach to the base of the Kilimanjaro. Here there were lush, green trees, and Kusini seemed fascinated with the quiet, shady dark beneath the canopy.

They found their way along animal footpaths; any other way through was impossible without a method of clearing the dense brush. The birds and animals here were different than those of the vast, dry plains, and to Kusini it was like discovering another world. Some of their calls were frightful in the dim, dappled green of the afternoons, causing her to draw closer to her father. If he noticed her fearfulness, he gave her no notice, finding frequent reasons to stop and gather her nearer to him for water or a bite of fruit. She began to understand that he had earned the name he had been given, for *Suhuba* meant 'friend' in the Swahili tongue that Kizu had taught her. Her father was kind, indeed, his personality in opposition to his frightful appearance, and she could understand the hope his parents must have had in bestowing it.

Although she could acknowledge that he must not have been so frightful once, she had the difficulty faced by all children – they lacked the imagination to see their parents as anything other than what they experienced through a lens of authority and distance.

They followed a goat path for several days and finally arrived in a bright clearing, where a small break in the expanse of the treetops allowed abundant blue sky and sunshine to emerge over a crystal blue pool fed by a small waterfall.

Suhuba did not hesitate to climb up onto the rocks to enjoy the cool spray – it felt good to wash after weeks crossing the dusty dry plain. He closed his eyes and let the water pour over his form; so engrossed was he that he did not immediately notice that Kusini had chosen to join him.

When he finally opened his eyes, the golden goddess from that long-ago dream emerged naked from the waterfall beside him. Suhuba stared at her, seeing his Tumpe in the lovely girl he'd never doubted was his daughter, and finally he had all the pieces of the puzzle. Although her beauty was the literal negative of her mother, there was something about her that was even more arresting.

She was as white as he was black, and where a creature of the earth had accompanied him over the long, high plain, the woman-child that stood before him was as radiant and luminous as sunlight. Although nudity was commonplace among the people, Suhuba turned from her, wanting to preserve her dignity. He knew that she had shed her clothing to bathe, but it was also a gesture of trust.

Now he understood the risk Kizu had willingly taken, the risk for which she had paid with her life and breath, and perhaps more – he would never know for sure. Those afflicted were believed to lack souls; believed to be mere ghosts, and as infants they were ritually sacrificed for power. Hence the *Watende's* interest in his child. Hence the murder of his sister – Kizu had given her own life to save this one.

Suhuba had never seen a person like his lovely daughter older than an infant. In tribal life they were consumed by witchdoctors for magic and did not survive early infancy, the time of their slaughter. The witchdoctors justified this by using their magic to make powerful potions in the name of helping the people, in the name of warding off evil.

And this one had some immense, unheralded magical power; he had experienced it firsthand.

He pulled his cloak about him once more, and glanced back to see her wrapping her rosy garments around herself. She peered back at him shyly, and he could see that his sister had discussed some of the old ways and superstitions with her – had taught her wariness about her appearance in the eyes of others. Her expression held a question, and she waited for a response. This was also a great leap forward for the two of them. She had shown herself, a gift to tell him she could trust in him.

He reached for her hand and helped her down off the rocks. He reached to help her tie the garment at her shoulder, and said gently, "I was wrong. You are *more* beautiful than your mother." The child responded by looking at her feet, but he could see that she was smiling.

They sat together on the flat rocks near the shallow pool and shared a meal of fruit and dried meat while the sun warmed them. He noticed the sun drove her into the dappled shadows long before he noticed its heat. He assumed she was bored, not realizing the discomfort to her delicate skin. She crept down off the rocks with her spear and cast about in the nearby shrubbery, hunting for small game.

He spread out on the rocks and fell asleep in the sun. Her screams pierced him awake and he ran into the jungle with his own dagger at the ready, her transmitted fear settling in his skin.

A short way down the path through the trees, she emerged at a sprint, her eyes like moons of fright. She nearly knocked him over, practically leaping into his arms and then trying to force him backward and away. She screamed and screamed, seemingly without even seeing him there, about the lizard and the head, and he could not comfort her or even calm her. So distressed was she that he could sense the energy coming off her in waves, and was ultimately forced to separate himself, as her touch was becoming painful. When he was finally able to extricate himself from her grip, he noticed that a trickle of blood had flowed from his nose, quite spontaneously. Despite her protests, he crept forward into a dark, dense glade within the forest, leaving her sobbing on the path. He was inexorably drawn into that dark heart, into the quiet where he could hear and feel the silence.

There was something here, some terrible magic that silenced the songbirds and the bullfrogs, where the heat of the day did not reign. The scent of blood and death met his nose, and he followed it to its source. When he arrived, at first, he could not be certain what he was seeing, and it took some time for his eyes to adjust to the gloom. At the base of a poison arrow tree was the remains of a man. The remains he identified as those of the *Watende*, by his ritual scars, and the pattern of the ceremonial threads that crisscrossed the base of the zebra tail he carried. He knelt to examine the body more carefully, and saw that the cause of death came from the effects of the bite of a poisonous snake; by the appearance of the skin surrounding the wound and the bruised swelling of the corpse, it was likely the work of a mamba. But that didn't explain the signs of struggle in the clearing, or the fact that the *mganga* was missing his head.

14

IN THE DEEP DENSE GROWTH beyond, he discovered the scattered remains of those *Maasai* warriors the *Watende* kept as a guard. They appeared to have been mutilated, but Suhuba recognized the pattern of their injuries - having once seen an unfortunate zebra caught beneath the trampling hooves of the wildebeest. But that meant that this carnage had not happened here, where there was barely space enough for a man to pass between the trees, so Suhuba's blood ran cold when he considered the dark magic that had brought the witchdoctor to this fate.

Whatever had committed this atrocity dared to place the sacred cow head atop the corpse. Suhuba searched in ever-widening circles for the man's head and the rest of the remains of the stolen cow, but without success. Heads were captured in pagan battles, but these were the province of legends, stories passed down by the ancestors to the elders, and this was a practice that had apparently been outlawed by *Ngai*, as the theft of heads was associated with significant transfer of power - the capture of the soul of its owner, and worse, the possibility of continued manipulation and corruption of the magic of the lifeforce, a magic that connected all to the sacred circle.

But Suhuba knew that such a theft would bring the potential for very dark mischief, a terrible omen indeed. Whatever had brought this to pass was powerful and dangerous, and he could not shake his distress when he thought of the nearly impossible task of transporting this tableau from the place where it had occurred. It had been placed here deliberately, placed here to be seen. It dawned on him slowly that this message was for one person and one person alone. His daughter. Her distressed flight from the jungle shadows meant that the message had been successfully delivered.

No sooner had the thought come and gone, but he heard and sensed movement behind him. By force of habit he reached for a spear that he had not carried from his place near the stream, and caught the quickest of movements from the corner of his eye. He turned, knowing he was too late, already anticipating the sting of the fangs, and the knowledge that his survival was uncertain. But the mamba writhed uselessly in undulating loops, impaled on a cruder implement, his daughter's reflexes so quick she had arrested his death mid-strike. Not knowing it was dying, it still tried to bite, uselessly, at the ground near it, at anything too close, and it remained a danger.

He gently moved her away from it as she shuddered in her shock and fear, and he turned her away from that terrible place, relieved that she leaned into him for comfort, and that he could at least tolerate her still-stinging touch.

Because the message had been for her, and the message had been received, he hoped that eventually she would speak with him about it, for understanding could only come through her interpretation of what she had seen. He led her back beside the waterfall and sat quietly with her in the waning sunlight until she stopped shaking altogether. He considered his plans to escape that same hunting party by leading her off the plains and into the lush foothills of the mountain. Somehow, his intentions had been anticipated, guessed at. Or was it that she could be tracked, followed, somehow created this magic from her own raw talent unknowing? When she spoke, her tone did nothing to warm his icy blood.

"It is my fault," she lamented quietly. "I wanted this, I imagined it, and they followed me here."

Suhuba was quiet, but only a few moments, then he said, "No. This did not happen here. They were trampled by wildebeest, likely somewhere near the gorge, near the bend in the river where I found you. I just do not know how they got here."

"The *Nyoka* brought them." Kusini's tone was sure and strong, but her eyes were unfocused and far away. "The *Nyoka* is the serpent, the servant of the lizard. The *Mjusi*. The *Giza*."

And Suhuba, who had made himself a stranger to fear, realized that it was wisdom that reacquainted him with it now. "Who told you of this?" he asked quietly, already sure he knew the answer.

"Auntie Kizu," the child's whisper followed his lead, and Suhuba realized that a hush had fallen over the clearing. "When I told her the lizard spoke to me. It spoke to me before she was killed. It told me what happened to her when they…" Kusini bowed her head and a tear dropped into her lap just before an anguished sob escaped her. She did not continue.

The Ghost and the Darkness. It was an old Maasai legend, that evil could roam the land and where you could fight off one badness, another would happen elsewhere. Suhuba had heard of many things he could not explain, and it was thought that if the *mgangas* were foolish in their use of power that they could be seduced to darkness and destruction. It was also said that the Darkness expected sacrifice for its gifts, that no part of its power was borrowed without later call for some terrible price, and the Ghost was the bone collector who came afterward, with a taste for flesh. Greed and corruption was said to unleash it.

Some of the elders still believed that *Ngai* had a brother that had been his rival for the hand of *Olapa*, the moon goddess who became his wife. When *Olapa* chose *Ngai* over his brother, he split into two in his rage. He did so to try and overmatch *Ngai*, but he was then unable to exercise the proper control over both parts of himself. One twin could not tell the truth, no matter how mild, but his actions were predictable, and the other twin could tell only the truth, no matter how horrific, and his actions were unpredictable. Thus, the

Ghost and the Darkness, though it was said that the Darkness ruled the Ghost, who was manipulated to wreak havoc among the people.

Now his child was at the center of something much greater than either of them. The collector had come for the *Watende's* head, and had nearly had Suhuba in the bargain. If not for Kusini's speed and bravery, he might have been lost. He told her, "It was brave to take on the *Nyoka.*"

Kusini shook her head. "In the end, it leaves the snake. I cannot trap it inside the flesh, and it knows I must destroy its host. If I could…then, perhaps…" She shook her head slowly. "It came for you to punish me, because you are pureflesh."

"I cannot be such," Suhuba protested. "I have hunted, and killed. I have even killed other men in battle. I have not been pure for many, many moons. There must be another reason."

"There is only one other reason," Kusini lamented. "To punish me."

"Punish you? For what offense?" Suhuba demanded, afraid of what she might tell him, but never expecting what she said next.

"The lizard knows that I love you."

15

SUHUBA THOUGHT IT BEST TO return with her to the plains. While they traveled, he got her to tell him everything that had happened. He considered his options. She, meanwhile, proved to be a gifted hunter and tracker. These were talents that his sister could not have helped develop, and he recognized a natural aptitude in her that many learned hunters did not start with.

Against the teachings of his father, and his father's father, Suhuba broke with *Maa* tradition, and began to train his daughter in the way of the warrior. He did not have the *mganga*, or the village, to perform the rituals. There would be no circumcision ceremony. She could not be asked to prepare as a wife – he had no authority that would overcome her lack of standing in their society, therefore, he could never find her a husband.

Neither could he leave her without the means to survive. She had the rudimentary instincts, and the coordination. She was often fearless, recklessly so. He knew what such an impetuous approach to hunting could lead to.

So he taught her, just as he would have a son. She watched, and learned, and did not question. He showed her that her spear was also a stick that could be used for fighting, for defense, and how to use an opponent's momentum or inertia to move them with it. He showed her how to make *munono*, and taught her why cattle flesh was sacred. He explained ceremonial rituals, and the way that cow's blood was mixed with milk to make the *motori* used in celebration. He instructed her how to make mead from honey, and when to drink it to give oneself courage before the hunt.

And she performed, as he had known she could, as if her survival depended on it, which of course it might. There were many perils for one who had to exist without the help of a village family, and special dangers for a girl abroad in the wilderness. He did not lie to himself about the possibility that all he had taught her would have any effect on her survival facing the dark power of the *Mjusi*, but there was something profoundly powerful about *her*, something he could sense when she was feeling any strong emotion, and he watched that power develop as she grew.

Seemingly overnight, she was becoming a woman, and Suhuba realized that several years had passed. She was less introspective, somewhat more confident, and ever more circumspect about certain of her rituals.

But if she was ever more modest around him, her trust of him grew in other ways, enough that she began to ask questions of him, some of which he could tell she had been holding onto for a very long time. One evening, after they had eaten and put out the fire — the first night after the big rains had ended, he was startled to look up from the remnants of his meal and find her studying him intently.

"*Baba*," she began, and he smiled to himself as he did every time she called him Father. "What happened to your eye?"

Her bravery always impressed him. Of course, while many others may have guessed at what had transpired, none had ever been bold enough to ask it outright. He was well aware of the fierceness of his countenance; that and his age had long discouraged idle talk.

"Ah. I was a young man, and foolish, perhaps not really a man yet at all. My father and his father had blessed me with the wisdom of their generations, but I thought I was grown enough that I no longer had to listen. I had already shown some talent as a hunter, skill in fighting, and great courage in the rite of manhood. I assumed that there were no further lessons to learn."

Suhuba paused here and sighed. "Daughter, the best possible lesson I can teach you is that wisdom is earned over a lifetime in which the learning should never end.

"I was tending cattle with my cousins one overcast day. After midday, we took turns out in the heat, so the others were napping beneath a baobab tree at the edge of the pastureland. Several of the cows were refusing to approach the trail that led to their watering hole, and were trying to climb down over a rocky hill, where they were getting stuck on the bluff. I thought it unusual that they were avoiding the water, and I was suspect that something had changed, but I failed to pay proper attention to these signs, and I failed to trust my instincts. I was impatient, and just wanted to get the animals – and myself – to the water.

"The cattle had been nervous most of the afternoon, and they weren't really grazing, either. I decided to force the issue by securing some of the calves to a rope and heading down toward the water. The calves' distress drew their mothers behind us, and they fought me all the way down the hill, but I was determined to exercise my will. I saw it as making sure I was caring for them, but really, I was ignoring all the lessons I had been taught about nature and watching the signs. Animal instinct is powerful, and one is wise to pay attention to their behaviors. The closer we came to the water, the more they balked. There was a wild, coppery scent at the bottom of the hill, sweet, like decay, but this, too, I ignored.

I was both lucky and unfortunate that I had taken the lead that day. I did not see the lioness until she rose up from the red grass at the edge of the water, but her ambush caught me, and spared the sacred beasts in my charge. For my foolishness, the gods made me pay with half my eyesight, and all my good looks," Suhuba injected this bit of humor, but there was no response from Kusini, which did not surprise him. Her intense and serious demeanor was rarely distractible. "I should have lost more than that. She knocked me onto my back, and would have finished me, but I had a knife in my belt and stabbed her in the flank, holding the knife in place when she tried to run. She dragged me down by the water, where she had an aging kill, the source of the scent of decay. I pulled the knife through her flesh, and she let me go. I could not see through the blood running down my face, and did not yet realize that I had lost my eye.

"The cattle scattered back up the hill. I did not know where the lion was, and I was acutely aware that she could return for one of my cows, or worse, attack my tribesmen as they slept, a just punishment for my foolishness. Not knowing where my blood ended and hers began, I followed her trail for what seemed like miles; by the time I reached her we were both crawling and weak. It should have occurred to me that she would head back toward her sisters, but I could only try to fix what I had started.

"The hurt I had given her was fatal; the one she had given me was not. I overtook her far from the grazing hill and finished my duty before I collapsed, ensuring she could not return. It was nearly dark before the warriors from the village reached me. They thought me a hero, and they harvested the claws from the beast. The loveliest maidens from the village turned those claws into a tribute necklace, and offered themselves to me, but I refused these gifts, knowing that my wounds were the result of my arrogance and disdain for my lessons.

"I went back to that place with my warrior brothers, and we tracked down the sisters of the lioness I had killed. There were seventeen capable killers in that pride, and we watched them for three or four days, until we were sure that they were not tracking her, which would have led them back to our herds, and our village. Had my actions led to the escape of that single lioness, I could have been the cause of great destruction for my people.

Kusini waited, but for Suhuba, there was nothing more to be said.

16

KUSINI GAINED WHAT KNOWLEDGE SHE could. Life with Suhuba brought daily lessons, some of caution, some of bravery, some of practicality, but all of survival. The lesson of the serpent he observed, and being cautious as they crossed the grasslands, he taught her to search among fruit trees and acacia stands for discarded snakeskins that had been shed in transformation.

When he discovered them, particularly the skins of the boomslang or the mamba, he showed her how to chew these into a bitter paste and spread the paste on her legs. "It is some protection from them," he explained. "If you stink of snake, many creatures not prudent enough to flee you will do so, and the snakes will think another larger snake is about, because your walking legs will disturb the grasses more violently than usual."

He kindly, and pointedly, discovered and revealed to her the many other examples of albinism in nature, showing her the bright leaves of the albino palm growing up from the floor of the selva, in the foothills of the mountain range, the striking whiteness of a tree toad otherwise identical to and just as lethally poisoned as his brethren, the stark contrast of a white giraffe or zebra running across the plains within its herd, even the glistening beauty of a milky cichlid swimming in the great lake to the West among a school of its azure counterparts.

"The great *Ngai* meant for these things to be so, or they would not be so," Suhuba observed sagely. "You will find your condition among plants, animals, insects, and fish. Preserved in nature, there is a purpose for all things. These differences persist throughout, and across, the spectrum of life. Why they are mystified, feared, and not respected, I cannot say, but it is not for me to say. There is some greater reason you are here, and one should not question the Great One in this matter."

The fact that Suhuba was also frank enough to explain the people's biases and superstitions to her, and the practices that accompanied the birth of a child with albinism, was his way of instilling a pragmatism that she would require to survive. He was unapologetic and graphic in his teaching, making it clear that she would likely be hunted, coveted, persecuted in some way throughout her life. For the first time, she understood the bravery and sacrifice of her beloved Kizu, who had defied the teachings and mandate of the people to save her life.

"But why didn't Auntie ask for your help?" Kusini protested.

"She was wise not to trust me," Suhuba explained. "These practices are ingrained in societal norms, and she was sure that I would willingly have turned you over. She left me a clue that you had been born, and a clue that you were a girl, but we had not lived closely together since childhood, when I left her and our mother to go into the wilderness to learn to hunt and become a man.

"Surely, you would have helped her," Kusini persisted.

Here, Suhuba merely shook his head. "To say it with certainty would be to taste a lie in my mouth," he admitted. "I cannot promise what I would have done. Kizu's actions gave me a separate set of circumstances with which to consider what was right. Even she had never defied authority in such a way. I wonder if the instruction came from your mother, as Tumpe had her own mind about things, but we can never know, because she did not survive."

This truth both hurt and saddened Kusini, but she respected and loved Suhuba even more for treating her as an equal and always being unfailingly honest. She felt some guilt about whether it was her fault that her mother had died, but could not bring herself to speak of it, then or ever. She was afraid of what he might say.

These, and other pearls of wisdom were bestowed. When teaching her to fight, he spared her nothing, to her great surprise. He allowed her no excuse; no protest of childhood would he hear, saying only, "Mother Africa is listening, but she will not answer your pleas. You must learn to fight off this old man, so that you can fight off ever greater enemies. Yours may not always present as fleshly beings, so you must be strong, and cunning."

He cruelly exposed the weakness of her feelings for him when stick fighting, and put her on the ground repeatedly, drew blood repeatedly, which was cause for early resentment on her part, until she realized that he wanted to train that weakness out of her. She learned to fight back voraciously, and her stick fighting lessons ended only when she consistently spared him no mercy.

And when the *Mjusi* came, it came alone, as lizard familiar, whispering doubt into her ears and her dreams. It told her of helpless scenarios of death for Suhuba, for herself, speaking a language that she did not know but nevertheless understood. And increasingly, as she matured, she felt the slinking, slithering, slow crawl of the creature on her skin, even when it was not there. She awoke often to the sensation, clutching madly to catch the creature, but as her power grew, it knew to avoid her increasingly potent grasp.

Finally, finally, Suhuba taught her the secrets of the lion hunt. The ritual fires and prayers over several nights prior to departure. The lies that each hunter told one another, each one more outrageous and fantastical, to inflate the ego and convince the other of outlandish bravery.
Ultimately, the mind-numbing foray itself, across hot plains, for long days, tracking their quarry, and when identifying it, herding it into dense undergrowth, or flushing it free, using that eerie coordinated humming.

She accepted these challenges willingly, and performed as he expected her to do; but when these lessons, too, were finished, she made her own adjustments to suit her. She did not - could not - well tolerate the long days of sunshine, and had to paint her skin in heavy mud and cover herself in linens. Suhuba was impressed that she was bold enough to hunt at night; it removed the discomforts created for her by the sun's direct rays, but gave her a distinct disadvantage over the great creatures he taught her to hunt. He began to realize that her eyesight and her gifts gave her advantages that he did not have. Coupled with her instincts, she was a formidable opponent to these great cats.

Indeed, in her thirteenth year, she impressed him with prowess and cunning she had not learned from him. She wedged herself on the first low limb of a large tree and fell asleep there, using herself as bait for a cheetah that she knew lived in the territory. She sent Suhuba away to set up camp outside the area, insisting that this was a test she had to face alone. Her voice trembled a bit when she told him to leave her, and he was proud that she was using and mastering her fear.

The animal was bold enough to jump onto the branch next to her, thinking her easy prey, but she had weakened the limb just beyond her perch, causing it to crack, which awakened her at the time the animal lost its purchase and balance, and her spear and strength did the rest. She disdained the use of her magic in hunting; she felt it dishonored her prey. This last made Suhuba proud.

She fashioned a hood and cloak from the head and skin, which provided her good cover from the equatorial sun. She had long since left Suhuba behind in stature; thus, her height and this hunter's trophy gave her a fierce visage, as she stared out on the world through the eyes of the beast she had conquered.

17

ONE MORNING, SHE WAS AWAKENED by a strange feeling. It was the sense of some distress. But it was not her own distress, seemingly it originated outside of herself.

The air was cold, colder than usual for the high plains, and Kusini glanced across the remains of the dead cooking fire and noted that Suhuba was in his usual spot, fast asleep. The immediate reassurance she gained from this observation did not offset the odd unease she felt. Her heart thrummed in her chest.

Kusini got to her feet and looked around, but could identify no clear disturbance in the near surroundings, and saw only gently waving grasses in the distance. The sky threatened no storms, and the sun was rising in its usual place, but the animals were quiet.

Unable to rid herself of the strange feeling of dread, she set out toward the watering hole nearby. She was somewhat surprised to find that her premonition lessened as she continued in that general direction. Her feet wanted to carry her past the watering hole and beyond, onto an old path created through the trees, in the direction of *Oldupai* Gorge. She stopped and when she did, the desperation increased, and the need to continue onward strengthened. She was rightfully wary of the sensation, and did not want to leave Suhuba behind. But when she tried to turn back, her heart pounded within her chest, and she doubled over in pain.

She was immediately suspicious that this too was the work of the

Mjusi. When she was able to stand again, she set her teeth in determination and returned to the makeshift camp she shared with her father. This short distance cost her a great deal of distress, but she fought through the physical pain to get there, hoping that her wise father could help her sort out what was happening.

When she was a mere few steps short of her bedroll she collapsed. Her pain rose to a crescendo. Her pulse sounded in her ears, and she felt so dizzy, she could no longer hold her head up. She managed to bring her thumbs together and cross them, and while the feeling did not subside altogether, it did lessen considerably; it was enough for her to gather her wits and call softly to Suhuba. His answer did not come, and she knew perhaps he was sleeping too soundly. She called again more insistently this time, using his name instead of the familiar *Baba*, and this time she heard him rousing.

She made it once again to her feet, swaying precariously, but able to keep her balance as long as she kept her hands together. She could see her father a few feet away getting to his feet, sensing her distress. She tried to speak to him, but she could tell he was unable to hear her. She saw only distress on his face as well, and when he tried to approach her, something unseen drove him to his knees. He placed both hands on his head and grimaced in pain. Kusini watched helplessly as blood spurted from his nostrils and ran down his chin. Suhuba looked up at her in disbelief and shock and waved weakly at her. He clawed at the air for some relief and gestured wildly in her direction.

Kusini looked down at her hands and realized she was the source of his distress. She immediately separated her hands, and this seemed to provide him respite. It did quite the opposite for her. She was unable to keep her feet, and she felt crushing pain in all of her limbs, and a suffocating pressure in her chest, spine, and head. She could do no more than look to the sky blankly. She sensed a lightness, a falling, and a terrible impact that incapacitated her. Finally, the pain reached the limits of her conscious suffering. Before the world slipped away from her, a crescendo of voices in an unknown language howled away in her brain.

18

SHE SCREAMED HERSELF AWAKE SOMETIME later, imagining the vultures eating from her flesh, her arms flailing to scare them off, hearing their indignant screams as they departed. But this, too, was a vision, and she could not shake the feeling that it belonged to another, elsewhere. She had no understanding of this, simply sensed it.

She glanced across the ashes of the cooking fire, and saw Suhuba lying on his bedroll, watching her closely. He had cleaned the blood from his face, and she wondered if she had imagined that too. His expression told her she had not.

"Daughter, are you well?" he inquired carefully, and she saw that his spear was very near his hand. Another glance told her that his knife was tied at his waist, which was unusual when he was at rest.

"*Baba*..." She began to speak but was unsure what to say to him. He was afraid of her. Or perhaps he rightly thought, or guessed, that she was being influenced by something else.

"You have been asleep for two days," he told her. "Or something like sleep. I cannot say it was not something else. I wanted to help you, because at times you were obviously suffering hurts, but I could not – you would not...so I prayed to *Ngai* for your recovery, and kept watch.

"Somehow, when I tried to rid myself of the suffering, I passed it to you," Kusini spoke slowly, unraveling the part of the mystery from which she could make any sense.

"And each time I tried to touch you, I felt it anew," Suhuba informed her. "And once, a shock even stronger than that you gave me down by the *Mbulumbulu* long ago."

She sat quietly for some time, struggling with her feelings.

"You should go down to the water hole and wash up," he advised. "It may help." She gingerly put a hand to her own face and felt the crust of her own nosebleed. She nodded quietly and slipped off down the path.

The day was dawning bright, and she was easily able to follow Suhuba's tracks down to the small water hole beneath a stand of giant acacia. This water had been left by the heavy rains of the earlier part of the year, and may have been connected to the river by what was now a dry stream bed. She suspected that there was likely a natural well here; the heat should have otherwise caused it to dry up as it had the stream bed.

There were signs of animal activity, but much of it was old footprints left in the mud before she and her father had camped here. She gulped several handfuls of the water before washing her face, and stretched her stiff limbs. She stood for some time with her feet in the water, staring off into the distance at the great *Kilimanjaro*, thinking of nothing in particular, until she heard an odd sound behind her. She did not turn, wondering if her father had come for her, realizing the danger she posed and the magic she possessed but could not control. She had seen his posture and remembered the closeness of his weapons.

A quick downward glance allowed her to peer through her lashes, and she saw that there was nothing behind her. Whatever had made the sound was gone, perhaps a small creature, and she dismissed her concern. She shifted her weight in the mud slightly, and felt a stickiness between her thighs. When she pressed her hands to her body, they came away bloody, and she gasped in horror.

Behind her came now the deliberate sound of something moving in the grass, and she turned in a full circle, but still was unable to see anything. The dry grasses began to sway rhythmically, and a whispering, hissing voice reached her ears. A grotesque figure with shiny orbs emerged from the grass, and she saw it was the *Watende*, flicking that terrible zebra tail against its legs and smiling. She knew it was a vision, the man was long dead, but the *Mjusi* was still using his flesh. She shuddered, wondering if she could keep her feet. She was strangely rooted in place. The creature waded into the pool with her, and she felt battered as if by gusts of wind, odd enough, but quickly realized there were unseen things about her, and she was unable to bring her hands together.

She tried to scream, but the voices howled up around her, and these were accompanied by the *Mjusi's* terrible words. Angrily, it swore at the heavens, and said, "*Nextborn, witchborn, child of sun* – you are mine and shall *not* be fruitful." It came close to her, and it stank of death and decay, and when it placed its hands on her lower belly, she felt overwhelming pain and sickness so profound that it brought tears to her eyes. "*Ngai* shall not cheat me and try to redeem you. You are *not* pureflesh."

Kusini had never sensed such distress from it before, and felt the effects of its anger. The voices howled away, and suddenly fell silent. The absence of sound was even more disturbing, as if she was out of the world, sucked into a vacuum, to a place that looked like her Serengeti home, but was over-bright and absent the natural signs of life. The moving grass undulated rhythmically, and the blades were coordinated in their sway, hypnotic. She watched as the grass became thousands of serpents, stretching up their silvery necks, with eyes black as the night sky, watching, and waiting.

The monster's hands left her belly, and she turned to take hold of its flesh, but found only empty air. But the water at her feet churned and roiled, and she was rocked again by invisible beings as a creature far worse lifted itself from the muddy bottom of the watering hole. It was covered in greyish scales and was long and slippery, twisting about her legs as its form split, and its girth thickened as it slithered up her body and out of the pool, trapping her arms at her sides and constricting around her form. From this primitive serpent-like body, it grew arms and legs, using these to maintain its hold on her, keeping her close in its embrace, its scaly flesh moving against her skin. Its jaws opened to reveal fangs that dripped with venom, but it twisted and turned as its head changed shape until it had completed its transformation.

The creature holding her was so much both man and snake that she could not discern where the end of one became the other. It turned black eyes on her face, and she could still see the needle-like teeth. Its forked tongue darted out, back and forth, touching her face, and she recoiled when its sibilant voice sounded close to her ear.

"Ah, you truly are pureflesh, you taste of it. Much as I want to enjoy you, I have other priorities, and there are bigger plans for you," it whispered. Then its eyes changed, becoming amber bright, with a dark slit at the center, and it let her go, quite suddenly, so that she lost her balance and fell into the water with a splash.

She panicked as she felt its tail curl around her, holding her beneath the surface, and fought for her life. Her struggles seemed only to allow it to bind her more securely, and she realized that it was toying with her, allowing her to breach the surface for a sip of air before plunging her back in. She sucked dirty muddy water into her mouth and swallowed so much she was certain to drown, but still the struggle continued.

And just as abruptly as it had all started, it was over, and she was being dragged up the far bank by it, its strong hand fisted into her hair, and she found her voice to scream but had no air, so she was barely able to squeak out a moan. It pulled her into the sea of snakes, which struck repeatedly, biting her face, limbs, and torso, envenomating her with what she was sure were fatal amounts of their poison. The pain was excruciating, and she was soon unable to move more than her eyes.

She sensed, more than heard, a disturbance among the serpents, and through a haze, saw her father, making a path for himself to reach her, his eyes afire with vengeance, and his spear at the ready. She reached out a hand to warn him away, realizing that coming to her rescue meant certain death for him, but the darkness flowed over her, and she could do no more.

19

CONSCIOUSNESS, WHEN IT RETURNED, WAS not a gift. She had transformed into some grotesque parody of herself, swollen, weak, dying but denied the respite of death. Pain was the totality of her existence, and she could not objectify it or escape its reach in sleep. She felt it screaming in her brain if she so much as moved her eyes.

But it did not matter. Kusini could see nothing but bare earth and the white sun above her somewhere. She was out of time and place, and her landmarks, including the great mountain, were all gone.

It did not take long to realize that this was a place of suffering, of punishment. There was no respite from the burning sun, and the earth did not turn from light to darkness. Her skin burned and blistered and peeled, but there was no end. Consciousness came and went, but the death she prayed for did not find her.

Sometimes she woke to a new torture; the lions found her, but were not interested in eating her. They slowly and methodically licked off her skin to get to the blood beneath, one type of pain superimposed on another.

In between, the lizard scurried over her form, sometimes whispering to her of things she cared not to remember, sometimes taking its own liberties. And the vultures and other raptors could manage to take a bite here and there. Somehow, she eventually found a way to bring her hands in contact with one another, and used what little energy she had to send them away.

And the *Nyoka*, the serpent-man, crawled over and around her, lamenting falsely on her behalf, tempting her to ask for things she didn't want, to earn reliefs she knew it would never grant. And she realized that it enjoyed this plight, that it was tasting and savoring her suffering, and that the *Mjusi* had unleashed it on her.

When she managed to burrow into the earth upon which she lay, which had been softened by her blood and waste, she held her thumbs together tightly and began to heal. Her thoughts coalesced into coherent plans for revenge and destruction, thoughts that frightened her, so uncharacteristic were they.

They let her believe she could escape, and then sent the fire ants. When the ants were done, she no longer knew who she was.

When the lizard next came to visit, it assumed that the shapeless form there in the red clay soil was irreparably broken and feared it would serve no purpose. It had been wrong about the strength bred into her. It was distracted with anger and disappointment in its serpent familiar, who had never been unsuccessful at training monsters and so it did not notice the glittering golden eye that watched it with cold detached interest. The thing that reared up from the ground lunged for the lizard, catching it in her teeth, and the Morningstar barely escaped the small body before its animal host was swallowed whole.

The woman who eventually climbed out of the watering hole had grown back the flesh she had paid to their torture, but this woman had no mother, no father, no anchor to her humanity. The red mud that clung to her body and hair dried rapidly in the midday sun and gave her a gruesome appearance, but it was the pulsating energy she radiated that sent the small creatures on the ground scrambling to escape. Many were not successful, and their carcasses littered the undergrowth where they fell. Birds dropped from the air, but the woman did not seem to notice.

She climbed the hill, searching in the grass until she stumbled over the remains of her old campsite. She kneeled, examining the disturbances in the ground, sniffing the air carefully, tracking. She found her feet swiftly when she heard a sound nearby, but her other senses could not help her locate the source of it. She was distracted enough that her foot caught on something discarded in the grass, and she nearly tripped. She picked it up, turning it over and examining it slowly. Her mouth broke open into what did not qualify for a smile, her teeth gleamed white against her clay-coated flesh, before her lips went slack again. The pieces of the memories failed to fall into place, but she donned the cheetah skin and wandered off toward the majestic mountain at the edge of the world.

Behind her, the old hunter followed at a prudent distance. He recognized the Sorceress that climbed up out of the hole in the earth, the place where he had witnessed her disappearance, and any less experienced tracker would have failed to notice the change in her scent; he did not. He doubted love would be enough to save him if he faced her now, and he knew she need carry no weapons to kill him. Absent her considerable power, he had taught her just how to do it.

20

THE WORLD SHRANK TO ONE tiny cave, cleverly hidden above a steep stone crevasse, where wind, water, and the remains of an ancient glacier had culminated in a spectacular rock slide, splitting the side of the mountain open like a wound. Spread out many thousands of feet below, its foothills boasted lush greenery, flowering wild coffee plants that had yet to be tamed, and spectacular wildlife.

Far away to the east, the coastal cities and islands of Unguja and Pemba (whose names were unknown to the cave's single dweller) were increasing trade with the Arab world, India, and China. The Portuguese were rapidly gaining control of the coast, but had difficulties infiltrating inland due to strong merchant ties to the Arab world that were held by the Swahili city-states, as well as the strong tribal forces to the west that held the changing world at bay. So strong were these warriors that they managed to keep out the Arab slave trade that would eventually invade the coast of east Africa, despite the Arab merchants that had managed to establish trade as far inland as Dodoma and Arusha. Such efforts would persist to the modern era, when European settlers tried to colonize the tribe lands of the northwest. Roads were built, and cities grew up in the wilderness. Eventually the post roads would reach to the Great Lake to the west of the Rift Valley, where a brisk fishing trade thrived, sending fisherman back east to the markets along the route that ran south of *Oldupai* and *Ngorongoro.*

None of these things diminished tribal infighting. Superstition and belief in the tribal *mgangas* remained central tenets of tribal peoples that were native to the region, and some of those foreigners who aspired to power and success were willing to try anything, even appealing to the dark arts to assist them with their greedy desires. Even as civilization advanced, the demand for talismans persisted, and the different and the misunderstood were ready victims of this industry.

The Sorceress kept to herself, and the legends grew of the magical woman who lived in the mountain. She was included in an oral history of the elders, semi-deified by those who recognized the value of fear. Her power was lauded as the reason she had survived birth as a 'ghost,' and was used as an excuse to hunt others of her kind. But to all of this she remained blind and deaf, despite her many dreams and visions of the evils humans perpetrated upon each other.

She was unaware of the lone wanderer who traversed the foothills, both a watcher and a guard, and had she known of these happenings, would not have recognized her father even if he were brought before her and relayed the history of her childhood. She would not have given him the chance.

Animals who wandered too close to the aerie did not survive, because the Sorceress had no sense of self, she had nothing upon which to draw for control. Those persons curious enough to search for her became ill, and wandered on the mountainside, either succumbing to the elements, or falling down the stone face to their deaths, without her even being aware they had come.

But the boldest of those medicine men who sought to capture her power or gain it from her suffering met a different fate. They were tracked, hunted, and killed by a fierce specter with a face that seemed pulled from the depths of the now dormant volcano he patrolled. The Sorceress was no more aware of these efforts than she was of the weather.

She lived as she had as a child, eating the tender roots of the hardiest mountain plants. She disdained flesh, and grew so tall and thin that her appearance became otherworldly. She climbed in darkness up to the snowfields and glaciers to collect snow and ice, which she ate, seemingly ignorant of the cold and the thinness of the air.

In her dreams she left the cave for lands unknown, running in the still white forests she had dreamt of since her childhood, knowing that this was not her life that she experienced, but the life of another. And new dreams found her leaping through the green sticklike trees of a different forest, in another place, curling and dancing about, sometimes with the not-unpleasant taste of blood in her mouth. And more often than not, the lizard clung to the stone walls and roof of her dwelling, and she watched it carefully, but it had apparently lost any need to speak. It was waiting, but she was not. She had no independent sense of time, and no longer had any conscious knowledge of a single reason she existed.

21

THE ONE WHO FINALLY SLIPPED past the sentry did so because he was pure of heart and was himself a brave and talented hunter. He climbed the mountain gradually, avoiding the sickness that comes from altitude by scaling laterally, back and across, ascending by no more than a few thousand feet each day. He had to improvise against the cold, which he had not been entirely prepared for, but eventually he reached the cave and braved the ledge above the life-ending drop to the forest below. He avoided the bones of the animals that had lost their lives there, knowing that the sounds of them breaking beneath his feet would carry farther in the still air.

The cave appeared abandoned and he cursed himself for the risks he had taken to seek out a legend that he should have guessed was untrue. He stood at the mouth of the dark space and mustered courage to face his fear. He had the too-acute sense of being watched, and he examined the signs around him that seemed to confirm that the cave was being used. There were footprints of varying age, both entering and leaving the cave, the newest perhaps no older than a day or two, and others that were nearly eradicated by the elements.

The picture that emerged was less than encouraging that he had reached the proper destination, as these appeared large enough to be the prints of a tall man, and he sought a woman. He moved slowly across the opening, careful not to move as one who feared for his life, conscious that his progress might be observed. Taking as much time as he dared to linger without some sort of light to assist his entry within, he looked carefully about for a source of tinder. He discovered some desiccated rock lichen of significant thickness and used his flint to ignite it. Apparently, it held some dampness that he had been unable to discern, as it burned very slowly, but this was to his advantage, as he was unsure how long he might need this makeshift torch.

When it was of no value to delay further, he stepped into the cave and jumped at his own shadow wavering on one of the side walls. He frowned; he was rarely anxious, but here he found that he had some sense of deep foreboding and he was a superstitious man who paid attention to his instincts. This feeling definitely originated from the cave, and he noted that his heart pounded loudly against his ribs. Despite the draftiness of the space, he was sweating, and his head began to ache and throb. He took a few more steps and stopped when his nose began bleeding. There were many shadowy corners in the cave, and it seemed much bigger inside than he had expected. It was as though his light was being consumed by the blackness.

He thought he heard a soft sound, but it could have merely been the slightest movement in the air near him. He took a step backward, but found he could retreat no farther, his legs were no longer under his control. His torch dimmed further, going out on its own although he was certain there was more than enough fuel left to sustain it. The blood from his nose was flowing faster, and he could feel it dripping onto his feet.

"I mean no harm. I come to seek aid from the Sorceress," he explained to the darkness around him. "I ask protection for my unborn child. The *mgangas* have had signs, and I come here because I go against their wisdom that my child must become a sacrifice…" To his great surprise, a sob of desperation and grief escaped him. He dropped to his knees, unsure how to combat the weakness this place extracted from him.

It was then that he heard a voice, soft and raspy with misuse, speak a few words that he thought were *Maa*, but he could not understand what was said. In the space of a few moments, the cave was ablaze with light so bright he was unable to see anything. He had been shown her inadvertent power, so he continued to kneel and bowed his head, showing respect and submission.

The voice came again, just as soft and sandpapery, and its quality rose bumps on his skin. The voice seemed to be all around him, inside him, somehow. This time it spoke the common language of the plains. "It isn't safe for you here. I am not safe. I cannot help you."

Nothing more was said, and after a few minutes his eyes adjusted to the blazing light which, like the voice, oddly seemed to have no direct source. He lifted his head slowly and looked up. When he saw her, he nearly screamed, both because of her appearance and her proximity.

She had settled directly in front of him, squatted on impossibly long legs, so pale and gaunt he was unconvinced of her humanity. She looked out at him through the eyes of a cheetah skin and studied him with calculated interest through eyes that were golden as the sun, with centers large, deep and dark. They glittered with intelligence and blazed with power. The jaw of the animal shadowed most of her face, but he could see that she was beautiful. He was suddenly aware that the blood from his nose was slowing, but she was so close that he had soiled her feet with it.

"I apologize," he started to ask forgiveness, but there was no more to add. She was clearly the cause of the bleeding, and she had warned him off. She did not seem overly affected by this intrusion to her person, and his bleeding had stopped, although he doubted the danger had passed.

"I come from the valleys north and west of this mountain. Our medicine men examined my bride and predict the birth of a *ghost*."

She flinched away at the term, and he paused, and continued. "She has been watched over since she came with child, and the elder women were barely allowing me to see her. The *mgangas* have told us that it is our duty to our people to submit our child for sacrifice, since such a child is an omen.

"Worse, I defied them, because I hear the lie on their tongues. They want the ritual for power, and I fear for the life of my bride, because they will not care for her in the birth – they are greedy for blood, and now all our lives are imperiled.

"I stole my bride away from her family during the night, and we have taken refuge in a neighboring village. Our own tribesmen will be hunting for us, and we endanger those who shelter us, because they do not know the truth of our plight.

"The village *mgangas* have a network, and they have ways of finding us. I am a simple man, but this is wrong. I want my family safe."

"Even if your daughter is like me?" she countered.

He answered without hesitation, but his voice trembled. "I did not say they predicted she was a girl." He paused a moment more, clearly discomfited by her clairvoyance. "As the great *Ngai* wills, I shall accept. She shall have no less right to my love and protection."

The Sorceress stretched her limbs and stood at her full height, which was head and shoulders taller than he. "You must go now. She is coming, and your brother cannot hold them off," she predicted. With that, she turned her back and the cave plunged again into darkness.

He backed toward the entrance to the cave, knowing he'd best not defy her in this, and desperately wanting to return to see his bride. He could not protect her from here.

As he stepped back out into the world, he ran his forearm across his face to dry it. "I dreamed also of *you*. You came to us as a healer, the deliverer of our destinies. Only *Ngai* sends such visions. I am Mnatoa, and my bride is Ak'ili," he whispered into the wind, but he was sure he was heard.

22

SHE SET OUT ON A moonless night. There was no breeze, and she did not look back at the cave as she navigated the ledge and started her descent down the mountain. She did not recall climbing the mountain in the first place, but had seen it all in some remote dream and did not worry about getting lost. She let her feet lead where they would.

She traversed the foothills and entered the dark enclosure of the jungle growth at the base of the mountain. She leaned against the trunk of an ancient oleander and inhaled the scent of the greenery around her before pushing off and continuing down an animal path through the undergrowth. She frowned as the birdsong ahead of her died away with her approach, and at the sounds of the animals scrambling from her path.

She paused for a moment, trying to draw a fleeting memory, but it eluded her. She stood up on tiptoe and made a few bird calls. She was still unable to place just how she knew them, but the birds answered, which gave her hope, so she walked onward through the trees and out to the sloping foothills that guarded the mountain.

At the point where the grasslands met the hills, on the last rise facing west, she discovered her sentry. The site of him perched there flooded her with memories, and she knew he had kept watch over her even though she had not known he was there. He was sitting, slightly slumped, and appeared to be sleeping. She approached quietly and reached out to him, but when she touched him, he toppled over gently, and she realized that he had refused to leave her, even as he rejoined the circle of life.

Lovingly, she draped the cheetah skin over him, and whispered a prayer to the heavens. "Farewell, *Baba*," Kusini whispered, before slipping away into the long grass that would lead her back into the great valley, and the *Bantu* village where her feet carried her.

Linking her thumbs briefly, she whispered a soft command. "*Cover.*" Soft linens whispered over her flesh, and she pulled the long end of a scarf over her head and across her face without slowing her stride.

23

KUSINI DID NOT KNOW WHERE she was going, but the strange inner compass she possessed led her onward. To the north and west of the great valley, she was surprised when she encountered a road. Where the old migration route of the wildebeest had been in her childhood, there was now a cart path stretching east and west as far as she could see.

She went west, detouring from the path only to find water and to seek cover when sleeping. Termite mounds sloped off to the south, and she passed zebras grazing lazily on the dotted landscape that was shadowed by high clouds. The peaceful rhythm of the late afternoon was disturbed when she startled a small herd of female kudu with last year's calves, and they leapt suddenly from the red grass, fleet and strong, soaring easily over her head before bouncing gracefully away.

When the red sun became a shimmering ball disappearing over the far horizon, a shape coalesced, silhouetted at the crown of the road. It was a man in ceremonial dress, holding an upright spear that was half again his height, and as she approached, she saw it was Mnatoa. He nodded once when she came near, but prudently did not speak. He studied her eyes for a moment, which were visible between the folds of her headscarf; she was otherwise obscured within the voluminous red gown and cloak. Kusini was amused – he knew enough of magic not to trust that it was really her. He had learned that eyes cannot lie. When satisfied, he turned resolutely and began walking, leading her onward to her destination.

They skirted a small village and he led her into an orchard of custard apple trees that were cultivated into a makeshift farm. He was vigilant for snakes, as was she, and he used the cover to slightly change direction before emerging on another grassy plateau to the north. Here he waited for the sun to complete its descent below the edge of the world. When the darkness enrobed them, he called out in a bird's voice, and after a few long moments, somewhere out ahead in the grass, his call was returned in kind.

Mnatoa made to continue onward, but Kusini placed a flat hand near him, and he had to hold. Bringing her hands together, she whispered, "*See us not.*"

Only then did she allow him to continue onward, and when they reached the midpoint of the clearing, there was another man, waiting. His appearance was like Mnatoa's, and she knew him to be the brother. She uncloaked them, and the man started in surprise, which he mastered carefully, loosening his grip on the spear he carried only when Mnatoa reassured him. Kusini waited for the two men to continue ahead of her, following only when they were far enough ahead that she could fully see their movements.

They continued walking north before abruptly turning to the east to follow a dry creek bed that led them into a false canyon between two hills. A rocky outcropping had allowed the water to carve a tall broad hollow into the sandstone bottom, and here there was a camp. Three women waited near a banked cooking fire, one heavy with child. Her frame was slight, and she was about the same age as the other two. She wore a simple shift of cotton in a light-colored fabric, and her head was wrapped in a colorful turban. One of her companions could have been, and probably was, her sister.

They all stopped the work they were doing to prepare the meal, and Kusini paused outside the circle of soft light from the coals. She could feel their eyes on her, and sense their wonder and curiosity. The pregnant woman left her tasks to greet Kusini in a language that she did not understand, but then she switched to *Kiswahili*, and welcomed Kusini, thanking her for coming. "I will be grateful for your help with my baby." She could not help but peer up at Kusini's pale face with open curiosity, probably imagining the appearance of her own child. She smiled suddenly, and her slightly crooked teeth did nothing to mar her beauty; indeed, her smile was open, radiant, and sincere. The expression betrayed her youthfulness; she appeared barely out of her adolescence. "You must have a great deal of experience with this?" she asked, but before Kusini could answer, Mnatoa spoke up.

"She is very skilled, indeed," he assured the woman, and then said to Kusini, "This is Ak'ili. And there is my brother Inatoa, and his two wives." He gestured awkwardly in an attempt to hide his lie, but his wife knew him well.

Her eyes downcast, she said, "We shall have no more lies, I think, husband."

"He lies out of love," Kusini interjected gently. "I am no midwife, nor am I a medicine woman. But I will use my skill as best I can to help you."

"And why should you do this?" Inatoa challenged, because he was afraid of her, and he was one who needed to show dominance, especially in front of his wives, whose posture and expressions were far less welcoming. They were obviously repulsed by her appearance, the whiteness of her face and her great stature disturbed them.

"Brother, you disgrace yourself," Mnatoa spoke sternly, and Kusini realized that he was the elder of the two. She slowly approached the fire and nodded at Ak'ili's gesture of hospitality, taking a seat to appear less a threat. She slowly unwrapped her headscarf, submitting herself to their scrutiny, trying to reassure them that she meant no harm.

Ak'ili nodded again and herded the other women back to their tasks, serving Kusini first, before her husband, leaving Inatoa to his wives. She made a point of coming to sit just to Kusini's left, her skirt in contact with the folds of Kusini's cloak, and shared her bread and mead, talking of nothing of significant importance. It was a gift of acceptance and understanding, and Kusini was grateful for it.

24

"WILL I SURVIVE THE BIRTH?" Ak'ili asked, reaching for Kusini's hand to assist her to balance as she squatted beneath the overhang of the rock. Ak'ili felt a shock when her hand encountered the Sorceress's, but Kusini settled her own emotions and accepted the contact.

Mnatoa had been happy to relocate the campfire and their companions to give the women privacy. Kusini had asked Ak'ili if she did not want her sister to attend her, but without explaining, Ak'ili gave a small frown and shook her head gently.

"Would you like me to remain?" Mnatoa asked, and Kusini smiled. He was sweetly protective, and she allowed Ak'ili to decide.

"Husband, we will not need your fretting," Ak'ili responded firmly. "We will do better if you keep the watch." She left unsaid, but Kusini sensed, that she shared Kusini's mistrust of her brother-in-law.

So the two women had been left to their respective work of bringing a child into the world, and Ak'ili was afraid as only a first-time mother can be, not knowing what to expect other than what she had seen, and looking for reassurance.

But Kusini refused to lie. "It is possible to die in childbirth. I am certain you have seen this in your village, perhaps among your family." She herself had observed it in nature, sad and resolute, since the offspring of those born to this harsh place rarely survived without a mother. She thought of her own mother, and the name came unbidden to her mind, the only part of Tumpe that she had known. Had Tumpe been this afraid?

"I want to live. I want to see her," Ak'ili explained. "I have already seen her in my dreams, and I know I already love her. Does that sound foolish?"

Kusini shook her head gently, and Ak'ili continued. "I look at you and imagine her as a young woman. It brings me hope – you bring me hope." To this, Kusini had nothing to say, and they lapsed into a concentrated silence.

When the labor pains grew terrible, Ak'ili sweated but did not cry, and gasped for breath as she continued to work. Kusini adjusted the woven mat beneath Ak'ili, and wiped her clean, and soon the infant's head appeared, pale and round, and Ak'ili gasped weakly.

Kusini sensed the urgency of this moment, and briefly let go of Ak'ili, but only long enough to bring her own hands into contact. "*Settle*," she breathed, and she felt Ak'ili's desperation disperse, and the woman put her head down once more and groaned out in the effort, and onto the mat slid a girl child, white as the snows of the *Kilimanjaro*, tiny, lovely, and miraculous as no other thing in nature can be. Kusini scooped her up with the scarf and wrapped her, handing her to Ak'ili, who sobbed in her pleasure. "Oh, look how perfect is she!"

She eased Ak'ili onto her side and placed the baby at her mother's breast, in that moment reliving her own birth by proxy, imagining her beloved Kizu and Tumpe sharing this same event. Kusini waited the afterbirth and secured the cord. The child gave a healthy cry, and Kusini felt triumphant.

She arranged the two of them for sleep. When they were settled, and the baby was feeding, she stepped out of the enclosure, considering in what direction she should turn to locate Mnatoa, but he had heard the cry and came on the run, unable to contain his joy.

He stopped only to look directly into her eyes, for as long as he dared, saying, "Sorceress, I am your man for life."

Then he ducked inside and shouted his joy to the heavens at finding his family intact and well. Kusini gave them privacy, turning up the creek bed a short way before sitting down in the shade of the rocks and taking a rest. She remained there until twilight, and without returning to the hollow, or speaking another word, she lifted her frame from the ground, crossed her thumbs, and whispered, "*Keep them.*" Then she turned away from them and followed her feet back across the plateau to the cart path.

25

INATOA STOOD IN THE CENTER of the road, and in the diminishing light, she could see that he was not alone. A line of *Bantu* warriors stretched from the grassy plateau to the fringe trees at the edge of the orchard, all in ceremonial dress, wearing elaborately beaded *shuka* and carrying their spears. Beyond Inatoa stood a very old man, covered in bone necklaces and wearing a shortcloth, holding a sharpened circle of shale.

"Do not do this," Kusini murmured, and her voice was around them all, and inside them. It was a terrifying effect of her power, but the men held their ground.

"I knew my brother would bring you here," Inatoa spit out his words in hatred. "We will take your power and then sacrifice the child. My brother is a fool."

"You are no brother to him," Kusini observed, and slowly unwound herself from her garments, dropping them on the path. She stretched up to the heavens, and said, *"Prepare."*

Ostrich feathers fluttered down from her waist engirding her in a skirt of armor, and a stiff short headdress made of the mane of a lion spread away from her face, leaving her breasts and arms free for the fight. Her father's long spear came to her hand in response to her command.

"This is the spear of Suhuba," she warned. "It has memories of many kills. The king of beasts has given a hundred lives to its might. Come if you must, for it is ready." She bent her knees in readiness, taking a warrior's stance and inviting their attack.

One by one they came, and she spent no magic as she incapacitated them one by one, fighting them off repeatedly with the stick until she could see that only death would end their struggles, and dispatching them on the end of the spear, until only the old man and Inatoa remained. Kusini stood up straight and tall. "Enough," she gasped from the effort of the battle. Her torso was slick with sweat, her thighs and back marked by stick strikes, but her breathing was still steady and strong.

The old man smiled, toothless, and he laughed and sang a short song in a language she could not decipher, but which was strangely familiar, and jerked with some unseen force, summoning some evil, and she felt it reach its fingers out toward her. His chant was distracting, but it was she who felt the serpent's approach from behind as it came in close to strike, and without turning her head, dropped the spear down and through it, impaling it, noting with satisfaction that the *Nyoka's* energy had not escaped it, and hearing the screams of its familiars swirling about her like a hot wind as it experienced the fate of its earthly host.

And this arrested the spell of the *mganga,* because there was only one other for him to call, and Kusini knew he feared the *Mjusi* more than he feared for his life, so he abandoned Inatoa and slinked off into the grass.

She turned back to Inatoa and squared her shoulders, but could see he did not want to fight her, his boldness a front; he had not expected to have to engage her in combat with so many reinforcements, and, of course, he had watched them all die by her hand. So she repeated her warning, "Enough of this." As she feared, although he had not planned to have to engage her, his hatred and pride were so strong that he would not back down.

He fought like one who had everything and nothing to lose, and she suspected that he had allowed himself to be corrupted by the *Mjusi* in exchange for power, but Suhuba had taught her well. When he rolled on the ground as if injured, she moved in, but he had recovered the shard of shale and lashed out at her, opening up a long gash in her thigh. Her blood spilled out over him and onto the ground and her anger rose up with the pain as she fell.

He was unwise enough to stand over her and heap further insult instead of going for the kill, but she had passed into a quiet rage, and she felt *it* become alive, larger than anything she had ever felt. It was then that she realized that his hatred and her spilled blood had activated what the *Mjusi* had planted within her, but it was too late to draw back the anger and regain control.

Inatoa witnessed a terrible event as the Sorceress rose up over him with eyes that blazed with the light of the stars, and her voice carried to the ends of the *Ulimwengu*. *"Kutosha!"*

It crashed into him, and blood spurted from his nose as the power passed through him and beyond, and he coughed up even more blood as he left his feet, and death arrived before he reached the ground. His eyes stared an accusation to the heavens, and Kusini was left in a terrible silence, racked with tremors that she could not control.

With a cry of anguish, she sprinted back across the plateau, down the stream bed and stopped short of the camp, sensing no life ahead. Dreading what she would find, but already committed to seeing the worst of it, she crept forward and discovered them. None in the camp had survived, and the lifeless body of the infant lay where it had been flung when Ak'ili fell. She had come to rest at the end of her mother's outstretched arm.

Kusini backed away in horror, knowing she could tolerate no more, afraid of what could happen if she did not regain control of herself. But the worst was already done, none had survived. Not just those she had come to protect, but as she wandered in the days ahead, she encountered dead animals and birds, and villages where the occupants had all fallen, razed by the power she had not known she had, had never wanted, had been unable to control. She even came upon the *mganga,* and although he hung from a tree, his neck twisted grotesquely in his bone necklaces, his face was covered in blood, and trickles of it had dried in odd lines where it had run from his ears. She knew these to be the stigmata of her power, which had likely killed him in stride as he took his cowardly flight from the site of her battle with Inatoa. He had later been placed for her to find, a grisly reassurance that he would cause no further trouble. It was not lost on her that this was also the way to let her know that the *Mjusi* had made the offering, to show her that his power was not to be invoked without a price.

She shrouded herself once again in long robes, in mourning for lost hopes, a lost childhood, her own damned soul. And she wandered, in the world, but unmindful of it, refusing to engage with humanity, with the lizard in her ear, whispering its pleasure with her deeds, and two hundred years slipped by uncounted.

26

KUSINI BECAME A PART OF the landscape, so quiet and removed that she could walk among the grazing herds, sometimes traveling with them as they searched for water. She had passed, truly, into legend. She found that her feet still carried her where she needed to go – to stranded travelers, a young mother sobbing over a child stung by a scorpion, a difficult birth – and she followed them, knowing that to give aid was her small and singular atonement for the great destruction she had wrought in the centuries now lost to time. A plague, it was told, had nearly wiped out the northern tribes of the *Bantu*, had laid waste to livestock and predators alike, and only she knew the truth of it.

One particularly hot afternoon, no different really than thousands of others, she found herself drawn onward by a keen sense of need. A family of meerkat screamed at her when she came too close to their dwelling while following the old antelope trail down into *Oldupai*, but after that the quiet and peace of the gorge soothed her.

She sank down gratefully at the base of a prickly thorn tree to rest, but her soul was weary, not her limbs. Something in the place was calming, and she was not surprised when the tears came, and did not cease. She had experienced a similar emotional effect each time she visited the gorge.   She cried still for Kizu, Suhuba, Mnatoa, Ak'ili, and their child. Silently, reverently, the tears flowed, but her guilt was lodged within, and it refused to come free.

"Cry for yourself, too," the voice came, that of an aged woman, directly into her, and that voice quieted everything else, and she felt her pain lessen.

She looked around, but the only creature nearby was a small white chameleon, clinging to a branch of the tree, chewing determinedly on a leaf. She was startled when the voice came again, though the creature did not appear to notice her. *"Child, do you not know who you are? Tell me why you came to this place."*
Kusini sobbed it out, feeling slightly foolish to be speaking to a chameleon, who was surely not the source of such a voice. "I let them all down. They loved me, they protected me, they trusted me, and I killed them all. Born with one curse, I beget another."

"Until you can see it as a blessing, you will never control it."

Kusini ignored this and stretched out on the ground. She closed her eyes, and it was so peaceful that she considered staying. She imagined never getting up, just wasting away in this ocean of calm, slipping out of the world.

"You cannot die here," the voice replied to this unspoken wish. *"This is the spring of all life, where* Ngai *set down humankind, and it calls to you because it is your home, more than any other. It is the source of all concerns, and you are the one they wait for, the one they will need to survive the coming storm."*

Kusini could not decipher these riddles, but she did open her eyes when she felt something on her arm. The chameleon stepped carefully from the branch, swaying awkwardly as she placed a split-toed foot on Kusini's arm. It pinched her to gain purchase before slowly transferring the rest of its legs in kind. She sat up, seeing its struggle, and placed it in her hand, where it seemed to settle gracefully, its distracted eyes turning asynchronously as it examined her.

"The lizard delivered the wrong message to them, but never shared it with

you," the tiny creature observed. "*I have waited to deliver my own message, but was thwarted, until now. It seems I have found a way to redeem my tardiness. And so, you shall live, as do the immortals, and redeem yourself by taking up the legacy of Ngai's first and most important message.*"

Kusini could parse nothing from the chameleon's words, but there was no more to come. If the voice really had emerged from this minute sage, she had spoken her part. The quiet sounds of the grove returned, and Kusini watched the pattern of the leaf shadows shift and flow hypnotically as the breeze stirred the floor of the gorge.

And then, she noticed something curious – sensed something fed to her mind unspoken. Impatience, and the rumblings of hunger in her belly. She smiled.

Gently, Kusini lifted the chameleon back onto her branch, close to a cluster of young leaves, where she settled contentedly and appeared to forget Kusini was there. It no longer felt appropriate to remain, so Kusini got to her feet and listened for her own voice, the one deep inside, that had set her wandering without direction. After a few moments, her feet knew where to go, but when she started, it was with a purpose that had eluded her before. She had debts to pay and refused to lose any more time. She was to respond to her visions of distress, and follow them to their sources, and provide what assistance she could, to the limits of her considerable power. She was to live up to the name she had earned of legend and embrace the Sorceress to pay her considerable debt to humanity.

ambakisye

27

EVERY FEW YEARS, WHEN HER wanderings brought her to Dodoma, Kusini would spend at least one or two afternoons exploring the marketplace, admiring the many varied textiles and artwork on display. Over time, tribal motifs had been joined by Arabic design, which was becoming more evident in the architecture of the buildings as Muslim families migrated inland from Zanzibar and the eastern coast. They brought with them new foods, and the scent of exotic spices, brightly colored silks, and the call to prayers from the mosques at day's end.

She loved the varied sounds and smells she encountered, especially the delicious scents from the many food vendors that made a living there. It was a world so entirely alien to her life on the high desert plains, and her voluminous clothing and the deep cowl of her abaya did not seem so out of place. This was especially true following the influx of the Arabs; their women went about covered at all times, albeit for reasons vastly different from her own – or perhaps strangely similar to her own. They were deploying these coverings to protect them from the sight of men not their husbands. Kusini supposed that, ironically, her reasons for covering herself did not diverge far from theirs.

Over the years she had even adopted a *hijab* and veil in favor of a deep cowl when in the greater cities, because there was actually the rare Arab woman with pale skin and eyes, and absent the giveaway her close-cropped curls would have been if exposed, she could pass relatively freely in these crowds without drawing a second glance. If she darkened her brows and lashes with the kohl crayons favored by these same women, the effect was even more anonymizing. Thus, she could spend time in this great city hiding in plain sight.

There was one stall that captivated her, one unlike any she had ever seen before. It was tucked away down a narrow side street, among other small goods merchants that seemed to have overflowed the main square and spilled around twisting, turning paths that led off the central marketplace. One could get lost in these meanderings; there were so many lovely and exotic things to look at.

But this vendor was different; while most of the other merchants sold spices, food, dry goods, or other household necessaries, this stall was filled with thousands of small carved birds of such exquisite workmanship they seemed alive. One almost expected them to sing or take wing out over the fluttering multicolored canopies and into the blue sky that could be glimpsed between the rooftops.

Kusini's curiosity about the place quickly turned into a habit of browsing there at least once a week during her stay in town. The proprietor was often carving or painting during daytime market hours, but she assumed he did most of his work of an evening, or even in another location, his home perhaps, given the sheer number of sculptures he displayed. She imagined him setting out before first light, on little sleep, transporting the exquisite flocks in a pouch or a cart.

Because his wares seemed more decorative than useful, not being essential to any household function that she could discern, Kusini wondered how he was able to sell enough of them to survive. Yet she passively witnessed a brisk business as she took these casual strolls, blending into the flowing crowd around her.

One quiet afternoon, when the doves settled sleepily in the

arches and alcoves of the surrounding stone buildings and nestled in the shady corners where the awnings of the stalls overlapped, the merchant, although he had not previously given any notice of her lingering there, beckoned her closer. She was surprised, but secretly pleased, because it was a rare opportunity to get a closer look at all of those beautiful birds. Best of all, there were no other people nearby.

The proprietor himself kept covered, with a scarf that covered his head and wound across his lower face, as if he were about to travel the great Saharan sands at a moment's notice, and what appeared to be winding bandages on his arms, with wrappings on most of his tapered, ochre-stained fingertips. The upper part of his face was also obscured by similar bandaging. He wore long colorful tunics over loose trousers flecked with what appeared to be multicolored dyes, which Kusini assumed were stigmata of his artistic vocation. Although he wore sandals, she noted that his feet, too, were wrapped in dressings soiled by the rosy street dust. He was so utterly covered, and so standoffish with his customers, that she suspected he was ill. There was always a faint medicinal odor about that stall, one of bitumen and pitch. She associated these scents with him, rather than as coming from the goods he sold, and she came to suspect that he was a leper covering his disfigurement.

Kusini drew closer, noticing as she came near that he inclined his head as if he were listening to her approach rather than watching it. But she felt perhaps he was being kind, not wanting to make her uncomfortable, sensing her general reluctance. When she reached the entrance to the stall, she could see that the stool he was perched upon was very low, creating the illusion that he was small of stature. Now she could see that he was, in fact, long-limbed and tall.

He dipped his head in greeting and then tilted it toward the interior of the space behind him, effectively inviting her inside with all those gorgeous birds. She had to admit to herself that she was intrigued, but she was also a bit tentative, reasonably worried about being discovered for what she was and getting trapped within the space. But her intrigue bested her caution, and soon she was engrossed in the happy task of close examination of the many marvels contained there.

Each sculpture was a tiny, lifelike replica of a natural creature. Their most arresting features were their eyes and their wings. The eyes bore every semblance of life, the painted light spots perfectly executed. Their downy feathers were carved with such graceful detail that each was a masterpiece on a minute scale.

So absorbed was she that she neither heard nor sensed anything unusual until the proprietor was right behind her, so close to her that his outer garments were in contact with hers.

In a gesture so gentle it was almost intimate, he grasped one of her hands, turning it palm up to place a tiny sculpture upon it. The small blue bird was lighter than she expected, surprising her almost as much as the fact that he was able to touch her without triggering her defenses.

This bird was the loveliest she had yet seen, and Kusini reached out with one questing finger to stroke the smooth wooden head. In one swift motion, the man enclosed her hand in his own, covering up the little bird on her palm. When again he opened his hand a moment later, she felt a fluttering tickle on her palm, and the small blue bird took flight, soaring out of the stall and away into the blue beyond of the sky.

Kusini started in surprise but could not hide her delight. She turned to look into the vendor's eyes, but he had averted his face such that the deep shadows of his cowl obscured his expression.

Her upturned hand still rested in his. She could feel the rough texture of the bandages but strangely had no urge to pull away. Reverently, almost reluctantly, he let go of her, and she felt strangely bereft of that touch. It took her several moments more to move a step away from him, and he mirrored her movement gracefully, as if they were sharing a dance.

He returned to his stool, giving her space, and eventually, when she realized he had withdrawn to his previous state of reserve, she resumed her perusal of his carvings. He left her to it, and she enjoyed the luxury of being allowed to explore the many treasures he had created. She felt safe and almost normal alone there with him.

She left some little while later, when she was surprised that the light had changed, and the first bells were ringing from the towers of the mosque. By the time she returned to the rooms she had rented, dusk had settled over the city, and a few bright stars shone from the eastern horizon.

As she removed her cloak, she felt something trapped among its folds. She hung the garment carefully and unraveled the irregularity, hearing a soft sound as something small dropped to the tile floor at her feet.

She lit the small oil lamps in the alcove and bent down to investigate. The lovely perfect carving of the blue bird he had placed in her palm stared back at her from between her sandaled feet. Kusini picked it up, knowing its false fever was most likely from her own body heat, but somehow strangely certain it still carried the warmth of his hand.

<h1 style="text-align:center">28</h1>

KUSINI DID NOT HAVE A name for the type of pleasure that the little bird brought her. It was more than just the fact that she had never been given a gift; it was perhaps that the possession of something so frivolous, so totally unrelated to any basic need, made her feel connected to the world in a new way.

She had no manner in which to articulate her thanks to the man, and the idea of even attempting to do so made her impossibly, awkwardly discomfited. So she avoided the market stall at the depths of the maze, and when in a few weeks it was again time for her to make her rounds to the local villages, she left without returning to that place. She tucked the tiny blue treasure into her travel bundle and set out as usual.

She drew the bird out in the deep quiet of the night, by the fire, to reexamine the details. The bird was ever and always lifelike, a tiny companion with a constant curious look, as if it watched her no matter at what angle she held it.

The wood was soft to touch and light in her hand. The carving was even more exquisite than she had initially appreciated, down to the tiniest feather at the tip of the wing and the miniscule talons at the end of each delicate foot.

Near the end of her yearly circuit, she was summoned in secret

to attend at a difficult birth. The mother and father lived in hiding –
several steps into the forest at the back of their families' village –
where, surprisingly to Kusini, they were fiercely guarded and had
been raised with love and understanding rather than suspicion.
Kusini felt a rush of gratitude for these villagers for putting family
before the dictates of superstition, for the two young expectant
parents were both affected by albinism. She was also aware of her
own regret that such filial love was lost to her.

The young mother labored long and weakened much, but Kusini
showed the family how to sustain her with chopped goat's meat and
blood meal with water. Much to Kusini's surprise, the extended
families lingered for the delivery; it was an unusual tribute and show
of support that she had never before seen. It was only when the
child was fully delivered, as gloriously luminous as his parents, and
she heard their collective gasps of surprise, that she understood their
fascination; they had not expected the child to have albinism.

Kusini welcomed their surprise, and even, to an extent, their
disappointment. In such a loving, close-knit group, she knew they
could accept this outcome. She knew they could absorb the lesson
she gave them, the one she often gave – that even though unaffected
parents could have an affected child, in cases where both parents
were affected, *all* of their children would be so affected, as such
parents had no other legacy.

Even when the grandparents took her aside, feeling some
burden of guilt for passing on a trait they never knew they had, all
she returned to them was her unwavering patience and reassurance.
There were always so many questions, whispered fervently, and she
often remained for hours, answering them all. She was asked
whether it was wrong that the couple had been allowed to marry, but
Kusini explained what should have been obvious – for those that are
so different, there is a comfort in kindred that cannot be found
elsewhere. It would never be obvious because of the overwhelming
cultural taboos created by the existence of the condition, and the
reliance of these families on the advice of their medicine men and

witchdoctors, which dictated an alternate set of rules to live by.

She stressed that love and protection were even more important now that the child had come. An albino family would have been a coveted prize indeed for the *mgangas*, and she shuddered, hoping that her distress would not attract the *Mjusi* and its mischief to that place.

Kusini remained until she ensured that the child would eat well, and a few days more to assure herself that the young mother was thriving. On the day she was to leave, she was remunerated with a gorgeous heavy melon that was still some days from full ripeness. She set off with the fruit, her destination not a continuation of her ongoing desert circuit, rather the rooms for rent in the city, and the tiny stall at the back of the market where the birds and their mysterious maker waited.

29

KUSINI FOUND SHE HAD A growing irrational fear on her return journey. Perhaps the vendor had moved on; many such merchants were transient, traveling from place to place to sustain their living. And she had before entertained the idea that he was ill – perhaps he had even succumbed to his ailment and she had already lost the opportunity to express her gratitude.

Would he think such gratitude odd – after all, what the small sculpture meant to her was perhaps out of proportion to what it was intended for, a mere token, a decoration, a trinket. Not knowing such a thing bothered her more than she liked to admit. And the feeling itself was strange and new. She had never carried such a desire to show another her feelings; it was confusing.

She knew inherently that her yearning to be closer to other people was natural; she longed for someone who could know her as she was and accept her without some other obligation. She missed Kizu and Suhuba every day, and remembered them in her prayers, but she was now, after long centuries of life, unable to completely recall what they had looked like, the sound of their voices. And those relationships had been born out of necessity rather than want, they were her protectors, not her friends or her equals. She both sought and feared such an arrangement – to know another for the sake of knowing them, and she believed it an impossible outcome given the state of humanity and her unusual condition.

Some of the women she had delivered had treated her as a sort of treasured acquaintance over the years, when she returned to evaluate their health and the health of their children, but that, too, was a forced affair. They were grateful to her, while remaining somewhat suspicious, and a little fearful, because she was a creature of legend and magic, and superstition still ruled so many of them. Kusini knew no equal relationship could be had where there was fear or suspicion, even where there was respect for a task performed, and a kindness done.

And because she remained unmarried and had no children, the prevailing culture saw her as an oddity, some sort of failure, even though she would have been proscribed from marriage and childbearing in almost every instance of tribal life. Indeed, many with her condition did not survive, were not permitted to, were *cleansed* from their tribes. Those that survived did so with secrecy and the protection of others who went against the medicine men, witch doctors, and elders, a few of them helping others to survive outside of village hierarchies.

Now Kusini was sought for her own spells of protection, some of which had worked for these individuals. This had only made the fears and suspicions of the people she encountered worse. Her whiteness and her reputation were used by the *mgangas* to justify their prejudices and superstitions about her albinism, and in some cases had probably worsened the situation for many who carried it. Because her magic reinforced the belief that those with the condition were supernatural, extranormal creatures, the targeting and violence had often increased in areas she had visited, much to her horror. In such areas, she only redoubled her efforts to conceal and protect those afflicted and targeted, ironically using some of the most powerful magics she could conjure.

Although the late afternoon sky was threatening rain as she reached the end of her journey, she delayed securing rooms, instead risking a thorough soaking to detour into the marketplace. It was quieter than she remembered, but a storm was coming, and the market-goers had mostly returned home.

As she turned the final corner next to the spice merchant and wandered deep into the heart of the market, the sun dipped low in the west – alarmingly so.

The stall which had housed a thousand perfect birds was empty – the deep shadows of afternoon made the space that much lonelier. Kusini even more acutely felt her own emptiness, her own loneliness. With a sigh, knowing she would be unable to enjoy the melon after making such grand plans to bestow it as a gift, she abandoned it there in the stall, leaving it as one would a burden too heavy to carry any farther, and set off in search of lodging.

Dusk drew down over the space, and the heavy clouds held on to the deluge they contained long enough for the missing merchant to arrive and claim the gift she had brought for him. It would be years before the mystery of the melon would be solved, but its miraculous appearance was swiftly forgotten in his efforts to seek shelter from the storm. The tiny lizard clinging to the underside of the awning and watching with its shiny eyes went entirely unnoticed. The merchant shivered in the cool, wet wind, and satisfied that the space would be fit for business after the rains, took advantage of the break in the storm to duck back out onto the stones and make his way home.

30

THE *NKOKUA* LASTED LONGER THAN usual, not only making travel impossible over the flooded goat paths that Kusini favored, but under any circumstances, since the farm tracks and cart paths were also flooded that year. She was stranded in the city all four months of the seasonal rains, able to pay for her lodging due to the kindness of a local merchant's wife, who appeared unaffected by Kusini's appearance, and who, due to an unfortunate illness, required a dedicated nursemaid.

When the woman's husband decided that she would recover better in the warm coastal air, they returned to Zanzibar, but still the rains persisted. They left their bungalow to Kusini for her use while she remained in the city, and she was grateful for this abundance of kindness. Kusini knew that the merchant loved his wife, as it was her influence that had swayed him; she could see that the man was suspicious, repulsed even, by her appearance. As much as it saddened her, it was even worse that she had come to expect such treatment.

The deluge subsided to a persistent misting rain, as the *nkokua* rains made way for the mists of the *oloirurujuruj*, the next season of drizzle, and Kusini could see the evolving green of the surrounding hills, but the rural roads remained impassable. On days when there were short breaks in the weather, the markets teemed with humanity, as if all the world needed only to get outside, for any reason, for even the shortest duration.

Kusini, being made of heartier stuff, braved even the mists to wander the marketplace, noting that some merchants had resumed their trades, knowing that to hold out for better weather might mean waiting for starvation. Fruit and produce vendors did a brisk business, as rainy weather brought agricultural bounty. Spice and dry goods merchants suffered, as their inventory was dependent on wares transported from the coast and mountains.

The tiny stall down the twisting cobblestones was also thriving. Birds yet more varied and beautiful appeared each week, and when she dared, on the driest days, Kusini loitered under the awning of a nearby abandoned stall to watch as the man produced them. She had been relieved when she discovered his return, shortly after the heaviest rains. He remained covered as he hunched over his tiniest creations, able to create the semblance of life in half an afternoon. Such a miraculous gift from one who, by all other outward appearances, had to be suffering from whatever ailment was masked by those bandages.

Occasionally, he would lift his head and turn it in her direction, tilting it in a questing manner although he never directly acknowledged her presence. She was fairly certain he did not know she was there. She, still feeling guilty about her failure to find a way to express her gratefulness for his gift of the prior year, neither directly approached the stall nor passed by in front of it. When she left, whether she came merely to comfort herself that he was still there or lingered through an afternoon, she would retrace her steps so as to avoid any further contact.

The sunshine began to re-emerge, and the landscape began to dry, and travel became a possibility, but Kusini discovered a strange reluctance to depart. Surely, there were souls that required her intervention, but she was unable to point her feet away from the city, and away from the mysterious merchant and his birds.

The owner of her own temporary dwelling did not return, and she felt in her deepest heart that his wife had passed. She was saddened, unsure of what use other than grief this gift could bring her, but she took it as a sign that she needed to stay and ensure the home was secure, until it could be reclaimed. Rather she knew that was the excuse she made to keep herself there, knowing that out along the quieter paths and among the isolated villages, there were those who needed her assistance perhaps as much as they needed her counsel and her protection. But this time, she could not bring herself to take up her staff and her cloak and set out wandering.

The tiny blue bird was permanently taken out of its place in her waist pouch and displayed on the kitchen windowsill, near sprigs of lavender and the succulent leaves of aloe and echeveria, where it could greet the morning sunshine, where she could see it always. Something in her was tired of wandering, tired of searching, and she was selfish for the first time in her long life. What she could acknowledge was that she was waiting for something; she just could not name it.

The merchant's bungalow was delightful in any weather, built with graceful arches and large windows under generous overhangs that kept out the water on the mistiest of days. Kusini made use of the largest downspouts and collected rainwater for the kitchen garden. She used the hemp ladder to the roof and found an abandoned flat space with empty planters that she used to grow the few vegetables she would need for her stews, along with some sequestered herbs for healing. She could not relinquish her habit of making unguents and disinfectants, as she wanted always to be prepared, and she was afraid to leave her hands idle.

The merchant had also traveled extensively and amassed a library of books. On the hottest afternoons when she did not wander abroad in the city marketplace, she retired to a shady corner of the terrace to read, or, for those tomes which were written in languages foreign and unknowable to her, to scrutinize pictures of maps or drawings of places exotic and strange. She loved seeing these oddities, somehow aware that she was visiting places she might well never get to see. She found a very old fabric-bound journal that appeared to recount the travels of someone across many varied lands, and though she did not understand the words, she spent many hours perusing the person's drawings of these places, which were very detailed. She found herself fascinated with one, of a forest of strange trees covered in white, and a beast with the teeth and claws of a lion but a body and head more typical of the wild dogs and hyenas of the plains of her own homeland. Its eyes were much more focused and predatory than the shifty canine gaze of the hyena; this animal was the king of this snowy kingdom.

She knew the drawing captivated her because it was the place of trees and snow that she saw in her dreams. The beast was familiar as well, was it the one who breathed so heavily in her own fractured slumbering visions? There was something else at the edge of her memory that she could not quite grasp, and she felt the *Mjusi* would know something of this, not that it ever offered clarity, only confusion. And it, like her wandering spirit, was strangely absent in these days of calm.

Another drawing, obviously from a locale very unlike the snowy forest, showed a scaly lizard with knowing eyes and the tongue of a snake. Its scales appeared thick, and its broad stance was more squat and upright than the reptiles she was familiar with, indeed the sketch suggested the animal had some significant size, if it was to scale with the palm trees she recognized in the background. She was struck by this image much like the other; there was something strangely recognizable here, and it had no connection to the obvious parallel the creature shared with her shifty familiar.

And dream she did, sometimes more vividly than before, since her days were filled with thinking, and not the relentless exhaustion of caring for the persecuted and abandoned. Sleep was often slow to come and associated with frequent awakenings from dreams she could not understand. As she had aged, and her power had matured, she had become able to banish her visions to her sleeping brain to contain them enough to preserve her sanity. While this had accorded her some semblance of conscious peace, when she awoke, she was never certain that her dreams were not visions of other happenings that were in fact reality. Were some of these things actually occurring somewhere out there in the world?

One afternoon, she drifted to sleep in her chair as she flipped through the drawings for the hundredth time and screamed herself awake as an excruciating pain traveled up her left arm. She flailed uselessly with the limb, which refused to relent. Although she was aware and conscious, the pain was relentless. It felt as though the arm were rent in two, the flesh torn, the agony white-hot and real. She was dizzy and nauseous, even though her own eyes showed her that the arm was completely intact, resting across her torso where she clutched it in anguish.

She closed her eyes, and her brain flooded with rage and desperation, and she was suddenly in another place, warm and green, the shadows throwing patterns down onto her form, and her breathing was coming in loud shrieks that she tried to stifle – danger was nearby. There was a confusing tumble of thoughts about how to achieve relief, escape, and hasten to freedom. Her mind, desperate to escape the pain, returned to thoughts of her travels across the plains of her childhood, and the arid, dusty acacias laboring under the searing sun.

The vision grew, and she knew it was not a dream. Her form was not her own, the breathing overloud and ragged, and the source of pain was the limb of a shaggy beast, the fur white and gray like no animal she recognized, her hand gone, replaced by a heavy paw that ended in claws sharp as blades, piercing the soil of this shadowy forest and mangled in some mechanical contraption with manmade teeth as evil as those of any predator. The pain came in waves that threatened her very sanity, and her heart thudded with a strength and fury that disturbed her.

She used all her power to push the vision away, frightened by its strength and the intrusion to her waking mind, and she found a kernel of something else among the desperate thoughts of escape, cold and instinctual, a murderous, calculating rage that contemplated the taste of human flesh. In this strange, forced dual existence, she found her own thread of consciousness, separate from the other, and focused on the trap that had ensnared the beast.

Kusini concentrated on her own form, separate from the shared pain and agony of the vision, and pulled her hands together, sending the energy outward into the world, whispering, *"Free me."* As her thumbs touched, she felt as much as heard the pinging recoil of metal, and she was free, of both the trap and the illusion, the pain subsiding more slowly than the vision, the desire to hunt and kill the last to leave her mind, and she found herself alone once more, on a terrace now shrouded in darkness, hearing the whispering rustling of some small animal, perhaps a lizard, retreating over the garden wall.

31

UNABLE TO OVERCOME THE RESTLESSNESS that arose from the disturbing vision, she tried to distract her mind with meaningless tasks, trimming herbs in the garden and mincing root vegetables in preparation for stew. But she had no stew meat, and so the job was finished before she was ready to be done, knowing she had to wait until morning for a visit to the butcher, hoping that goat meat would be more readily available now that the roads were passable.

Frustrated, she pulled on her hijab and veil, and hastily smudged kohl around her eyes. Ignoring all prudence, she set out into the night, reasoning that she had no need to be as wary here of persecution, and satisfied of the anonymity that her clothing could provide. Her wandering spirit was returning, a need to move abroad no matter the hour, so she followed her feet and they led her down the wandering streets and into the quiet of the heart of the bazaar.

Along the main thoroughfare, the night market was in full swing, but she traced steps she had taken thousands of times, down side streets and past now silent empty alcoves, to where she knew thousands of birds still roosted, ever awake, flightless, and silent in the artist's stall. Adolescent boys and young men slept across the entrance of these many darkened spaces, makeshift nighttime guards bought for a meal or even a few coins that would help their own families survive. They slumbered on as she passed, not particularly vigilant, both because there were few real threats to protect against other than the occasional theft, and because most of them had daytime labors as well for which they sought much-needed rest.

Warm light blazed forth from the stall she sought, the place to which she was inexplicably drawn, cast from the glow of numerous lanterns of intricate design, making elaborate shadows over the birds and their maker. Although she was certain her sandals were silent on the stones that paved the path, the artist lifted his head as she approached. No slumbering sentry here, he guarded his own wares, and she absurdly wondered whether he slept here himself.

The sound of his voice in the quiet of the evening startled her, as much because of its hearty timbre as for the fact that he knew she was there, having slowed to a halt several awnings away. "You should not be abroad at this time; it is not safe for one such as you."

"One such as I?" she replied, her voice a papery whisper from the rareness of its use. She could ill afford to expose herself to any danger, but her feet carried her forward, into the light that shone onto the street from his shop opening. The night breeze was cool and pleasant here, carrying through the open air from one space to another, but his face remained obscured by his hood as he bent over the tiny figure he painted with a brush as fine as an eyelash. She wondered how he could see, even with the illumination provided by his many lamps, and she shivered in the chill, perhaps influenced by the illusion that she was watched by many small pairs of avian eyes.

Then she realized that it was not an illusion, there were many more birds here than had been displayed in the afternoon market hours; tucked among the lifelike sculptures were swallows and kiels of a rainbow of hues, settled among the mimics he had created, they had sought shelter. She was both intrigued and delighted, such small birds spooked easily, but here they were, calm and sedate in his presence, indeed, she noticed a few that hopped around his bandaged feet, partaking from a crust of bread that he had likely left for them.

He paid them no mind, and continued to finish the detail he placed on his tiny sculpture as she drew near.

"You are no Arab wife, unless I am gravely mistaken. A woman with a husband is sequestered after dusk," he observed quietly. "There are others…but you are not of these, either. You have carried the smell of sickness before, but no longer. Your patient has gone?"

Kusini was shocked at these revelations, but should not have been surprised. Such a talented artist captured many details about many things, using every sense at his disposal. She stopped her question as soon as she started it, as much because her thoughts answered it as because he gestured to her to remain quiet.

"Your distress is felt by them," he explained softly, waving his hands calmly around himself, and she noticed that some of the birds were shuffling about before resettling to a state of repose among the sculptures. She tried to quiet her questioning mind, and the birds resumed their resting watchfulness.

"Come closer," he commanded, making it seem more of a suggestion than it probably was. "If you wait a bit here in the light until I have finished, I will escort you back to your dwelling."

"I need no such escort," she protested softly, nevertheless drawing nearer the entrance.

He abandoned the low stool he was perched upon, setting it in the doorway and gesturing her to sit upon it, not even paying attention to whether she did or not, remarking just as calmly, "Don't be foolish. It is likely a lone woman abroad is watched by many eyes, seen or unseen, and unchaperoned you invite unwelcome advances, or worse. The kohl around your eyes is a flimsy disguise at best."

"I can defend myself," she added unnecessarily, taking a seat on the stool as he turned away and reached to place the completed sculpture on a high shelf, the live birds shifting to accommodate their brother impostor. They moved and settled together, unperturbed by his closeness, but he curled his finger and one tiny blue bird, likely the model for her own sculpture, climbed happily onto the bandaged joint and perched with a tiny chirp of happiness. He turned in a semicircle to deposit the bird onto her wrist where her hand had come to rest in her lap. She felt suddenly trapped, unwilling to move in the event she should disturb the tiny guest, and in turn, the other denizens of the shop.

The bird tilted its head, fixing her with a bright eye, and stepped prettily along her forearm before seeming to make a decision. It settled quietly in the crook of her arm, nestled against the fabric of her abaya, and placed its head beneath one bright iridescent wing. With the minutest shiver of its feathers, it became still. Kusini could not help but reach out with a fingertip and stroke the downy feathers, for the briefest moment feeling the thrill of its staccato heartbeat as it slept.

She guessed, correctly, that this was some sort of test, and she was surprised that the bird could sleep next to the booming drum of her own nervous heart. But she recognized her own discomfort and intervened, forcing herself to take several long, relaxed breaths, calming her distress at the newness of the experience.

The artist nodded his satisfaction and turned back to gather his brushes together. He took his time cleaning and arranging them in a small pouch, ensured that his pots of pigment were secured, and put out the lanterns one by one, pinching the small flames until they were blanketed in a darkness that felt companionable rather than ominous. He seemed as comfortable in the gloom as he had in the light, and she sensed when he drew near, but did not move, not wanting to disturb her feathered charge or any of the other birds. His own touch, when it came, was light and quick, and she barely registered that he had lifted the bird from her arm and deposited it elsewhere, all without any apparent upset of its rest.

Then his attention was all on her, and the next touch was more purposeful, as he took her arm and helped her to her feet, his bandaged hands surprisingly warm and strong for one she suspected of illness. Again, she noted with surprise and an unfamiliar emotion, pleasure, that he was unaffected by her power to repel those who touched her without consent. She felt him move the stool away from her feet and lead her through the doorway, avoiding obstacles. Once they were both back on the path, he rearranged their limbs so that she held his arm in such a way that she could easily let go and free herself. It was a meaningful gesture, his way of reassuring her of his chivalry, giving her an easy escape if she chose it.

Kusini had to admit that his presence was strangely reassuring, and she found that she did feel safe with him. It was a foreign emotion, unknown to her since those long-ago lost days with Suhuba, since her prolonged lonely and admittedly self-imposed social exile had begun centuries before. Some of it may have been the unfamiliar sensation of being next to a man whose stature exceeded her own, an unusually rare occurrence. Most men did not approach her height, but he overmatched her by a rare few centimeters, and he was closer to her than she normally willingly permitted. Their long garments brushed together as they moved.

He started away from the stall, but she resisted, pausing to turn back toward it, slightly concerned at leaving it unguarded. He must have sensed the reason for her reluctance to leave, and murmured, "The birds deter the curious; most of the local cultures have suspicions about large gatherings of birds and they leave the place alone. Birds are thought to be the accompanists of the dead. Anyone determined enough to steal in their presence usually needs whatever they would take more than I; they are welcome to it." And with this bit of wisdom, he guided her away along the stones and out to the main thoroughfare.

32

KUSINI FINISHED HER STEW AND proudly placed some into a gourd, waiting until dusk to set out for the marketplace, blending in with other women who carried food to their expectant families. When she reached the familiar turn down the path, a tiny friend appeared, curious and welcoming, in a flurry of blue feathers he settled on her shoulder.

The artist was working, as she expected, lamplight already spilling out onto the stones. She slowed and approached carefully and quietly, so as not to disturb the birds that had already arrived. His face moved under its bandages, in what appeared to be a smile, when he saw that she had remembered bread for their many companions.

He was not painting on this night; rather he was carving what appeared to be a series of large pegs. He set aside his work and gratefully accepted the food she had brought, eating much less than she thought he needed before returning to his project. He set the gourd aside, but returned to it occasionally, eventually finishing the meal. She, in turn, remained quiet on the stool he had abandoned for her, breaking bread into tiny hunks to ensure that all were well-fed.

He surprised her on subsequent evenings, telling her the names of each kind of bird, most of which he had also bestowed with personal names. In turn, she surprised him, and the birds, by remembering a number of their calls which Kizu had taught her centuries before. The birds began to arrive in larger numbers as the heat of the day passed and night came on, sheltering from larger birds and other predators by hiding within the shop. The light and the presence of people were added protection. Sometimes, when she arrived with bread and food, she would call out for them with their own songs, and they would come even sooner, in greater and greater numbers than before.

To her immense pleasure, the carved pegs were the legs for a second stool, built just for her, a gesture of hospitality that was unmatched by any other in her long and complicated life. "You needed a proper welcome to this place. And a name," he explained, shrugging his shoulders in a gesture inclusive of the watchful birds. "Yours is still unknown to us," he observed.

"I am Kusini," she whispered conspiratorially, in the same hushed tone she always adopted here, in this worshipful aviary that with each visit felt more and more like a place where she belonged.

"South?" His mouth formed the question, although he kept his attention on the sculpture he was working on.

"More truly, *upepo wa Kusini*, the south wind. It was the name chosen for me by my parents before I was even born," she clarified, abbreviating the explanation she had received from Suhuba in another life.

"Ah," he nodded, as if this was better understood. "Warm, strong, and beautiful. A well-chosen title."

She flushed with pleasure, and realized she had no name for him. "But what about you? What do I call you?"

"I am Ambakisye," he told her, softly emphasizing the compound transition at the end.

Her eyes widened, and she smiled, hoping she was guessing the translation correctly. "'God is merciful?' From the *Ndali*, right?" She secretly was unsure it was a proper name for one who was suffering from the disfigurement he appeared to be hiding from the world.

"It is my name. Both in a descriptive and a literal way," he remarked mysteriously.

"You are of that tribal origin?" Kusini inquired, suddenly shy about asking the details of his life.

"My mother was *Ndali*," he nodded slowly. "I was the tenth child she bore, and the only one who survived more than a few months. She waited an entire year before she bothered to give me a name, and it turned out to be even more appropriate than it seemed." With that, he withdrew to his project, falling silent once more.

Kusini was comfortable in silence, and thus surprised herself when she broke this one, especially to speak. "Has god been merciful?" she asked, unsure whether she was asking him or herself. She observed, "You are not eating tonight. Are you ill?"

"What makes you ask?" his tone was deliberately evasive, she felt, and sensed that perhaps she had offended him. Her discomfort increased, but she could not help but answer.

"Your bandages, your coverings," she gestured helplessly at him, but he appeared not to see it. If he heard her distress, he did not give any indication of it, but responded quietly, almost too quietly for her to hear. "Perhaps it is what I would have people believe. Eyes can deceive."

Uncharacteristically, Kusini felt the need to explain herself. "I only asked because perhaps I can help – I have been a…caregiver of sorts…" She trailed off, feeling foolish, then added, "I do have some healing skill, even if only to alleviate suffering." She was careful to keep any pity from her voice as she spoke; whatever his ailment, his temperament had never seemed to invite it. And she was, as always, far too afraid that she would give away too much, hoping the deeper truth was absent from her tone, that to her chagrin, she had also been the source of suffering on far too frequent an occasion.

He suddenly set aside the sculpture he had been creating, making space for the unfinished form on his workbench. Uncharacteristically, he left his brushes and other supplies in disarray. Full dark had not come on, but he rose and put out the few lamps he had lit against the dusk and beckoned to her. "Come, I will cook for you for a change – you could use a bit of fattening, and perhaps yet, an explanation," he observed, laughing. His laugh was a rich, welcoming sound that reassured her that his mockery was in jest and not meant to injure her in any way.

33

THEY STEPPED TOGETHER OVER THE stones, and she held herself apart, still concerned that she had said something wrong, but when they reached the main road, he tucked her arm in his as he had so many nights before, this time leading her away from her home and deeper into the heart of the city. They passed the mosque, and crumbling tenements, skirting the shafts of light that spilled onto the street, before he turned in at a massive metal gate with an iron-banded wooden Judas door set into the wall just to the left of it. Through the bars of the gate she could see a private outer courtyard.

He produced a key from his cloak and opened the door, which admitted them to a large garden that led around the side of a looming shadow that she quickly discerned was a spacious stucco villa. The courtyard she had glimpsed through the gate was a narrow ornamental area, probably meant as a place to receive visitors on horseback in earlier times, but closed off from the throughway now for security and privacy. The sounds of the street were quickly left behind. The garden was lush and flowering, and she could smell fragrant exotic blooms, many of which were likely transplants from the coast, or even other lands. She could smell jasmine and hibiscus, and from the depths of the garden she thought she heard a nightingale's call.

The path through the garden split, and he led her down a short passageway to a broad door, stepping over the threshold and helping her over it behind him. He ducked down and slipped her sandals gently from her feet, then led her carefully over the smooth floor to a scented pool set in the center of the room. He helped her step into the cool water, a relief to her tired, dusty feet, and then she heard him move away from her.

He was gone for several minutes, and she stood alone there in the dark, wondering if she had made a mistake and walked into a trap. She had heard of those who put up a pretense of friendship in order to ensnare those of her kind. In the countryside, these were the apprentices of the machete-men, who did the dirty work of dismembering and delivering grisly talismans to the *mgangas* for their potions. But she doubted he had fooled her; for weeks on end he had spent evenings at the shop with her, and escorted her home to safety – he'd had better opportunities to harm her, and it was unlikely he would do anything to jeopardize his own home.

For this was a home. She could feel it in the stillness and quiet of the structure, the care of the gardens, the many mixed scents of spice and flower coming from deeper inside, herbs from a kitchen nearby.

When at last the room began to brighten, she realized that it was because he was lighting the oil lamps along the walls, and that his absence had been prolonged because he had been doing this throughout the house, readying it to welcome her. He lit the lamps farthest from her in the long salon, letting her eyes adjust in the gloom before lighting those nearest the door. It was a lovely space; all the walls painted with the colors of sky and plants, and everywhere in the complex mural were flowers and birds of all hues of the spectrum. The pool at her feet was a complex mosaic of colored stones collected over a lifetime, arranged in the perfect semblance of a hummingbird in flight.

Ambakisye offered her his arm and helped her step onto a thick woven rug which absorbed the water from her feet, then reached to help her remove her abaya. He paused for a moment, perhaps to allow for her assent to this; his desire to avoid presumption was endearing. He led her through a domed doorway into the short hallway beyond, where he hung the garment. He turned away from her to lead the way into the next room, and she gasped aloud at its beauty. It was a high-ceilinged kitchen with a massive wooden hearth, swept clean and smooth from frequent use. She could nearly have walked into that space upright. The floors were smooth tiles, she had seen their like before, in a rented room in Dar Es Salaam; she had been told they came from Spain, a land on another continent, which to her might as well have been another planet. There were shuttered openings in the roof that were propped open; through these she could see a few early stars. But there were nearly a hundred niches in the wall opposite the hearth, each one of which held its own lucifer, like a clustering of light, casting the room in a soft natural glow that mimicked early morning sunshine, but was ultimately the softest, kindest illumination possible for the coral and yellow murals that dominated the wall of windows that ran the length of the space. There was an interior garden along that wall, with succulents and herbs growing in hanging baskets from the ceiling and even up onto the arch of the soaring roof, with flowering plants spilling inside through the windows. The entire room was a deliberate showcase for the care and love that had been expended to create this unusual oasis, which she knew had taken years of faithful devotion.

When her eyes adjusted further to the light, she saw other spaces, up above, carved into the downslopes of the ceiling, and more live birds and treasures lived or were kept in each and every one. She had never seen the like of it, a purposeful display of all the things gathered and collected by one who treasured what he loved. It was a silent, vibrant story of a life. She wandered the perimeter of the room, murmuring aloud to herself, as each new pleasure revealed itself. He waited, out of the way, leaning against the doorway they had just traversed, apparently watching her, silently witnessing her wonder. His head was tilted slightly, as if he listened closely to her sounds of amazement.

She looked over her shoulder, suddenly aware that she was still unable to see his eyes, realizing by his patient reaction that she was the first person he had ever brought to this place. But still he stood in a hooded long djellaba over his pants. He had removed his outer cloak, and though he had shed his sandals with hers, his feet remained wrapped, as did his hands, which gestured toward the table, where bunches of herbs had been neatly organized, tied in bundles to dry. She noticed a pair of small trimming shears, and he sat down near these, patient for her to understand.

The table itself was a massive slab cut from a single old tree, its patterns told the story of its millennial existence. She could tell the benches that flanked the table had been fashioned by his hands, and because he took his place on the one nearest her, she saw the invitation to know more. He offered the shears and bowed his head as if apprehensive.

Kusini's heart pounded so loudly she feared he could hear it from where he sat, and she took a deep breath before she approached. Slowly, she pushed back his hood to reveal a tightly bandaged skull. His eyes were closed, as patiently he awaited her further actions, so she began to tentatively unwind the muslin strips, uncomfortably the reverse of placing grave cerements.

It was the only thought that came to her, but she pushed it away, determined to look upon whatever terrible ravages had been bestowed by his disease. She was almost sure that the beauty of the man she had come to know would hold any horrors she might find or feel at bay once his lesions were uncovered. She had looked upon many inflicted uglinesses, bestowed in war or enslavement, rape, dismemberment, and mutilation, and she braced herself for what she could not predict might be missing – each leper was afflicted differently.

The lamplight first revealed the ordered platinum curls at the crown of his head, and as the bandages fell away from his face she discovered a princely visage, alabaster perfection, with a proud nose, full lips, high regal cheekbones, and a strong jaw. The eyelashes she had only glimpsed before were long and lush, golden in the flickering light.

Then the gauze came away from his neck and shoulders, revealing unblemished skin and the strong taut muscles of a still vital, youthful man. She had to stop then, aware of her own womanly response, needing to preserve his modesty, and she cast her eyes downward as she pulled his djellaba closely around his shoulders to cover him once more.

"Is something wrong?" he asked, reaching out for her. Something in his voice made her look up. He had opened his eyes and they, too, were a pale, jewel-like color. They wandered back and forth, as if relentlessly questioning, and she realized that their point of focus was indeterminate, and he was, constructively, blind.

34

"BUT HOW-?" SHE STARTED TO protest, unsure, really, what to say next. Was she to tell him that she had assumed the worst, that beneath his bandages was the slow rot of flesh that marked a leper? Was she to ask him how he knew certain things she had assumed he would have to be sighted to know? As she had no idea where to begin, she let her unfinished question hang between them, where it unfortunately demanded an answer.

He reached his hand out to her, just as he would if he could see her clearly, and when she failed to grasp it, he stood. He stepped over to her and repeated the gesture, but rather than hold it as he was inviting her to do, she took it gently and began to tug loose the wrappings that covered his hands, reverently uncovering nimble, long, tapered fingers. With the bandages hanging from his wrist, she held his hand, palm up, in hers, placing her other hand atop it, absorbing its warmth, marveling at its beauty.

But he was not to be deterred, and he curled his fingers through hers and led her the few steps back to the table, gesturing that she should sit next to him. Meekly, she did so, still at a loss for words at this unexpected outcome. They were similar, hiding in plain sight, for perhaps some of the same reasons. He remained still beside her, but regrettably released her hand before she was ready to let go.

After several moments, he stood up.

"If you will excuse me for a moment?" His question was merely a nicety, because he took leave of her and the room. Minutes later, he reappeared, wearing a soft blue tunic and green pants with silken slippers in an Arabian style, and the transformation was complete. If she had thought him a leper before, here he was, gloriously beautiful, well-made, and unlike any man she had ever seen. He moved with the confidence and grace Kusini had always felt she lacked; he had a presence. And then he smiled at her, and she found it difficult to concentrate, because that smile was like sunshine, and impossibly, made him even more handsome and appealing.

"I owe you an explanation, as promised, I think," he said softly. "But first, let me cook you some supper. I am grateful you agreed to join me."

Again, he stepped out of the room for a moment, returning with a second pair of slippers with fanciful, curled toes. These were yellow, with gold thread adornments and little bells, and he ducked down, murmuring, "I apologize for my poor manners. I should have offered you these before. Your feet must be cold on these tiles." He slipped them onto her feet and then stood once more, beckoning her into the kitchen.

He cleaned his hands and produced a small chicken that had been soaking in cold brine nearby. This he placed on the wooden countertop and went over it carefully, feeling for any residual feathers or defects in the skin. She followed his lead, washing her hands in the basin and awaiting instruction on how she could help.

He produced a salt cellar and a flask of oil, then turned away from her briefly to light the fire in the hearth. He chose one of the small herb bouquets from the table and cleaned his shears carefully, putting these with his other supplies.

"Could you oil the bird?" he asked her, turning away to the interior garden under the window, where he took his time selecting a variety of vegetables, including dwarf tomatoes, mild peppers, and numerous onions the size of large pearls.

Kusini was at a loss; cooking was never such a formal affair for her. She had spent much of her life living encamped on the high plains, even now she did not make much fuss over her meals. She was unsure what he wanted her to do, and suddenly too shy to ask.

He returned, and sensing her hesitation, stepped up behind her and gently pulled back her long sleeves, folding them up and away from her hands. Deftly, he doused the bird with the contents of a small glass cruet, and taking her hands he guided them to its flesh, showing her how to cover the skin with the slippery, rich-smelling oil. While she completed the task, he snipped the fragrant herbs and helped her spread them and the grainy salt over the chicken. The smell was wonderful, and she inadvertently sighed in pleasure.

He pulled her palms up toward her face, pausing when she flinched, unsure of his intent. He waited until she relaxed and brought her hands in nearer her nose, so she could better appreciate the aroma of the oil and herbs.

"The oil is made by pressing olives. The herb is called rosemary," he explained, having quickly realized that all of this was new to her. "We will use some in our bread as well. I hope you will like it."

His voice, like his touch, was warm, gentle, and reassuring. He was reading the tension in her limbs, but he guided her through the steps to make the flatbread that would accompany their simple meal, and by the time they were ready to season the dough, she had relaxed as he leaned against her and reached around her to assist and teach her how to shape it for baking.

Kusini had no words for the experience; it was relaxing, sensual, and comforting. Her fear of another's touch was lost in the pleasure she felt having him so near, and she felt robbed of something nameless when he disengaged to place the chicken on the spit.

Ambakisye washed his hands in the basin at the same time she did, and did her the kindness of drying hers with the soft cloth he kept for that purpose before attending to his own hands. He gestured for her to sit at the table, and taking his time choosing an apple from a small bowl of fruit by the window, presently he joined her.

Using a small knife, skillfully he cut the apple into thin slices, offering them to her as he went. He took occasional small pieces for himself, but passed most of it to her. She noticed that he frequently closed his eyes and simply experienced their interaction with his other senses. She started to learn about him, feeling free to watch him at her leisure.

His movements were spare, economical, and graceful, these in contrast to her awkward uncertainness. He had a constellation of tiny brown freckles across his nose and cheeks that endeared her further. When his eyes were open, they made him look thoughtful, as if their movements were measuring out his thoughts like a metronome.

He remained quiet for quite some time, content to sit with her, not needing to talk. Kusini was grateful, as she found she had nothing to say. When he spoke, his words surprised her.

"You are *Maasai*, your voice carries a trace of the *Maa* pronunciation that is heard only rarely in the city. I recall it from a traveling hunter that was hired as a guide by white men to accompany them to Kilimanjaro. Like the *Maasai* of your village, you have continued to live off the land, and simply, but you have no village anymore, because of this affliction we share."

Before she could protest, he continued, "You are a woman who travels abroad alone, has no husband, dresses like an Arab wife but perhaps does not realize that such women are locked away from the eyes of the world. Your height does not necessarily betray you, as they can also be tall, but their scents are not those of one who digs in the earth and heals others."

"Your stews are of root vegetables; thus, you have learned to forage and garden as need be, and it explains your spare build. You have no constant place to stay, so you have no reliable way to store and prepare meat, and thus you rarely eat it.

"You have smelled of sickness, and often smell of pungent

herbs, those that are used less for cooking, some of which are poisonous if ingested, many of which are placed in healing unguents. You have done this work for a long time, which probably explains your wandering and your skill with medicinal plants, both of which explain your naiveté with culinary preparations.

"I do not have to see well to notice the dark voids created by your kohl crayons, but your eyes are light, and your skin luminous, so I identified you in your likeness to me, because your condition explains why a woman so young and so beautiful has not been taken to wife, and would explain her desire to disguise herself."

"How can you know if I am beautiful if you cannot see me?" Kusini inquired, thinking his last statement one of empty flattery.

"Your voice is soothing, and your actions are kind; this makes you so whether I see you with my eyes or not. A bird will not easily trust a stranger. Much less will one sleep where it is at the mercy of another creature that could endanger it. My little bird took to your hand when I teased you with my magic trick. He slept on your arm without waking."

"And what of my youth?" she pressed on, curious. "Perhaps I am not young."

"Again, I know what my senses tell me. Birds are frightened by evidence of infirmity. Age and frailty bring instability and unpredictable movements, which are jarring. They are initially avoidant of asymmetry of appearance for the same reasons – these are nature's cues that something is amiss. Your grip is firm, your hand is smooth, and the joints of your fingers are straight. You have no scent of personal sickness; that which I smelled upon you was from a charge. All these clues together tell me of your youth."

Kusini smiled, and considered the innumerable days of her long life. Her unique magic concealed her age, but she was not prepared to reveal such a secret. Not yet, not even to this extraordinary youth.

"Were my sight better, it would only distract me from what is truly important. You have some magic about you, but it is real, unlike the sleight of hand that I deployed with my sculpture. Your body sings with power, it thrums through you. I felt the energy the first time I took your hand, and every time since. I am guessing that if I were a threat to you, that energy would repel me."

35

AND IT CAME TO PASS that Kusini abandoned her wanderings that year, for the first time in centuries she allowed herself a respite, instead cleaning out the little house near the city walls for the last time; a respectful gesture that she suspected would never be appreciated, if ever it were known. It was clear that the merchant was unlikely to return to the inland city to reclaim it. But she was no longer comfortable staying there, perhaps especially because she knew she was not being a responsible steward of it, spending most of her time elsewhere.

Ambakisye patiently assisted her in transplanting her rooftop herbs into small planters. For these he wove small slings made from the deconstructed hemp ladder, knotting the ends opposite holes he made in a long plank. He hung her plants from it, and in this way easily transported her medicinal ingredients across his shoulders, bringing them safely across town to the terraced home where she had been spending increasingly more of her time, which quickly prompted an invitation for her to live there.

It was this gesture, and many others, that were most instructive of who he really was. He expended energy to care about what she cared about. Her happiness was important to him. He wanted to care for her. She understood little about where his motivation for these feelings came from, but she should not have been confused. Because she had never acknowledged her loneliness as anything other than an accepted reality, she was unable to see how her presence in his life was an answer to a prayer.

She was not at all blind to the way in which his presence in hers was a blessing. She had the vague remembrances of life with a companion, but those warm memories were of caregivers, teachers of a young, untutored child. In some ways he taught her about art, and plants, and food, and he did try to care for her, but it was different. The daily struggle to get food, create shelter, and find meaning were now shared tasks completed with little, if any, effort on her part. If she had some guilt for what she was not protecting out in the world; an unspoken selfishness kept her from wandering, for a time.

It was a strange feeling to belong in a specific place, where the end of each market day was a celebration because she knew he was returning, and the only wandering she did was down to the market — far too often finding an excuse to do so, because she realized that she did not have to wait for him, she could go to him. It might have been wonderful, too, but something in Kusini ignored this, was unable, really unwilling, to acknowledge it.

And into her life came another phenomenon, previously one which was strange and uncommon to her, the touch of another human being. This was not the spare, economical touch that was occasionally a part of her exchange with others in her outreach. Nor was it the rough, unkind touch motivated by disdain, hatred, or violence that had been too often part of her history.

This was a celebratory thing, a ritual repeated upon his daily reunions with her. Sometimes it was a lingering, sweet, slow departure after a leisurely breakfast, when he would sit next to her, pressed against her as he shared fruit, floral teas, and simple breads, and there was no need for conversation, because he was communicating with her by proximity, enjoying their togetherness. Sometimes it was the softest caress on the back of her neck as she sat reading, always a pleasant surprise that stirred up many other things,

things she knew he could read, even if he didn't see her avert her eyes, or notice the immediate flush of her skin.

Yet he never pursued more, always remaining chivalrous and kind, disinclined to press any advantage he may have had. He seemed content to have company, but his actions made it abundantly clear that he was discerning, and that it was her presence specifically that he sought.

And how he welcomed her company, whether it came to him or him to it. He was proud to present to her a room overlooking the back garden, a long narrow salon with louvered doors onto a small terrace. He had draped the bed in colorful silk netting that was as beautiful as it was functional, arranging the bed far enough from the terrace doors, which stood open day and night, to avoid the rain, but close enough to enjoy the breeze and the songs of the night birds. Plush woven rugs covered the tile, so her feet would stay warm, and she also realized it was so he would not disturb her in his nightly wanderings.

For there were many nights when she awoke suddenly, realizing he was sitting in the doorway, looking out on the night. But he never purposefully disturbed her rest. And on other nights, she would awaken and lift a lamp from the niche in the hallway, and travel down to the kitchen to look for him there, or in his makeshift studio in the long reception room at the back of the house, that looked as though it had once entertained many people but was now overtaken by his paints, fabrics, and other treasures. It seemed he rarely slept at all, that his mind was too busy to rest.

Some nights when she looked for him, he was gone entirely from the house and grounds, and she could feel his absence keenly. So in tune was she becoming to his signature energy that she could tell he was not about, even if she stepped out along the garden paths. It was as if the residence became dormant in his absence. Even the nightingale's call was more plaintive, as if its muse were missing.

On a few of these latter occasions, she would pull her abaya around her and venture out to the market, and here she would find him, singing or humming (how it put her in mind of Suhuba!) and carving or painting among the birds.

The small blue bird was Yabluu, and he became a sort of scolding messenger, taking on the protection of Kusini in Ambakisye's absence. Eventually, when he went to the market at night, Yabluu would stay behind, chirping in protest if Kusini tried to leave the house. It amused her mightily, but the bird seemed to know his mind.

Although he was never disappointed to see her approach in the depths of the night, he disapproved of her roaming abroad in the small hours, even though he despaired of her ever abandoning the practice. As much as he wanted to keep her safe, neither did he want to put her in a cage. For that was something he knew plenty about.

On one of the nights that he absented himself, she awoke to the sound of raindrops on the terrace. When lightning flashed and arced across the night sky, she could watch the dancing drops as they splashed upward from the tiles. The breeze brought some of the cool spray to her among the silken bedclothes. She stretched out, watching the storm outside the doors, and thinking of the way it must look out on the high plains. She had a momentary pang of guilt, thinking of all that remained unprotected beyond the city walls.

That moment was enough to bring her fully awake, and the beauty of the tempest was no longer enough to keep her attention. She took up the lamp and followed her feet to the salon where he kept his many treasures. She set the lamp in a small niche near the door and explored the space in its glow.

In one corner, she could see that he had begun to collect very brightly colored rags and strips of cloth. Some of the strips were from a bolt of red material that was shot through with yellow thread, but others were of varying hues of color, mostly reds. Their softness was inviting, and the colors certainly drew her eye, as most of the tapestries and rugs he owned were not of these bright colors. It recalled to her the clay of the gorge of her childhood, and the brightest, most vibrant shades of the sunset. She had even seen the moon that color, over the dusty plain of the Serengeti, when the rains ended.

Her curiosity about this new collection of reddish cloth strips was soon satisfied when, on a warm afternoon several days later, a deluge of rain trapped the two of them indoors. They shared a simple meal of fruit and cold chicken, and then, with a sweet but mysterious smile, he gently took her by the arm and guided her to the interior wall, where he invited her to sit against the cool stucco archway. His lips gently brushed her raised brows before he disappeared for a time into the dim depths of the house.

He returned with a basket under his arm that was overflowing with the collective scraps. This he set beside her before stooping down to gently remove the adorned slippers he had given her at her first visit.

He hesitated only briefly, then carefully chose several long soft strips of cloth, mostly by feel. These he looped around all ten of her toes, working so economically that any ticklishness she would have felt was minimized, but lingering long enough to express his affection for her, and his obvious delight in this new task. The long loose ends he draped to each side of her, looping the ones in the middle up over her shoulders. The central-most strip he tied in a long loop that ran from one great toe to the other and was then gently pulled over her head to rest behind her neck, like a strange yoke.

She felt ridiculous draped in all those strips of cloth, and tried to give him a stern look, which he disregarded, or more realistically could not fully appreciate in the dim ambient light of that grey afternoon, given his diminished visual acuity. Kusini still could not tell whether he actually visually perceived more or less than she thought he did, still did not know him well enough. Of one thing she was certain, his perception of the world around him was keen. He used all his senses with uncanny acuity, augmenting whatever limitations existed to his eyesight. It was deceptive; just as in their early relationship, he still seemed to 'see' her — her expressions, her posture, visual cues… it seemed strangely magical to her. Her own sight had not been affected by her albinism, which to her knowledge was unheard of. She attributed this as relative to her other gifts, since one of the stigmata of the condition was visual impairment of variable severity.

So he ignored the distress she telegraphed, and started to choose shorter strips of cloth, weaving them tightly into the strips that flowed over and around her. As he finished the row, he seated it tightly against her toes. After quietly completing a few such rows, he handed a new strip to her. She was surprised, but he encouraged her with a wordless gesture, so she gamely tried to mimic what she had watched him do. She had learned almost immediately that he had a talent for making certain tasks appear easier than they were; after completing a few rows she was secretly glad he was almost blind. His rows were tight and orderly – hers were disastrous; the weaving did not lie in flat rows or show any evidence of order. As if he sensed her distress, he did the next few rows and once again gestured for her to continue.

This time, he inclined his head toward the basket, indicating she should choose the next strip. Kusini could see that the strips were varying shades of reddish-orange to yellow hues, and this made her concerned about the way each might look.

"There is no wrong choice," he said, after letting her agonize a brief time. "Just take the first one that catches your eye – it will be the right one – you'll see."

His gentle encouragement did little to distract her feelings of frustration with this forced project, and she surprised herself by saying, "There must be quicker ways of restraining me." In turn, Ambakisye surprised her by stifling a laugh – she wasn't in any way trying to be funny – but then seemed to consider her statement carefully. He shrugged. "It is likely. But none of them would be this much fun."

She obliged him by weaving a few more rows, actually grateful to him for empowering her choice of color, and when he took over, she could see that it really was going to work out. They wove like this in companionable silence for some time before she began to wonder if it bothered him that she talked so little. Yet he did not say much, either. Most of their communication was nonverbal, comfortably so. But Kusini loved the rich timbre of his voice, loved the teasing tone he sometimes took with her. She knew if she talked, he might talk as well. Besides, very little progress was being made with the weaving – at the rate they had set, whatever-this-was would never be finished. She sighed.

"Say it," he commanded, but there was a smile in his tone.

"Maybe you should take over," she suggested. "It would be faster. It would look better."

"I'm not in a hurry," he replied. "It will look as it is meant to. I want your help with it. It is nice not to be alone," he added.

"Why *do* you live alone?" She asked then, unable to stop herself. "You could fit your whole family in this house," she observed.

"I live alone because it is a respite," he answered, then clarified, "or perhaps a refuge. Besides, my family is all gone."

"I'm sorry," Kusini said.

"I am not," he whispered, his fingers paused briefly in their work. "I predict that you have lived alone out of what I am sure you perceived as a necessity – perhaps it was one. Safer, certainly, given the tribal superstitions that confront you in the countryside.
"But I was always protected. At least from *that...*" he trailed off seemingly thinking of something, but then began again. "My mother died when I was not quite a man – she had been sick for a long time, it seemed, but I question that now. My earliest memories were of her tears. She missed her village, and her family, but that was all that she ever told me.
"We lived with an Arab merchant. This was his house, and I thought he would send me away after she died, but he didn't.
"Instead he locked me in her room. Apparently, his friends found me an exotic prize. I was kept in that room, fed, bathed, and groomed.

"I had the best tutors in music, art, and philosophy. The nightingale in the garden was kept in a cage in the reception salon beyond the carriageway. I was only one who noticed when he stopped singing.

"The Arab entertained many visitors from faraway lands, and traveled abroad himself. He kept a large staff – mostly to entertain and serve guests.

"It wasn't long after my mother's death that I began to have visitors come to me in the night. I was too afraid to disappoint, sure that it was the price one paid to be kept in such a home.

"When he came to me, it was always the same; I didn't have to perform as I was expected to for the wives of his guests. I was expected to submit. He wore the key to my door on a velvet ribbon around his neck. It always felt cold against my skin."

Ambakisye paused and shivered, having a visceral reaction to the memory. Kusini extricated herself from their weaving, noticing that twilight had come. She reached out to him, hoping he did not interpret this as her intent to stay his words, and when he took her hands in his and shook his head in gentle understanding of the distress his words had caused her, she stilled, and remained quiet. She could see that there was something here that he needed to say; it was time for it to come out.

"This went on for some years. One afternoon, I was awakened by one of the house servants, his favorite – she was the unfortunate one most often chosen to share his bed.

"She had that key in her hand and the ribbon was broken. She saw my fear. She shook her head to let me know she was not there expecting me to perform. Then she said, 'Your father is dead.'"

Ambakisye brought his face up to Kusini's. "It seems he had died during the…well, with her. She gave me the key and left the room. She called for men to remove the Arab's body and sent the staff away. Then she herself took leave of this place. No one else came.

"The house was mine, but I only knew it as a prison. And the Arab had never told me he was my father. It took me four days to leave my room.

"I didn't come out to bathe or to eat. The first thing I did was set the bird free. I wish I could tell you that I can't understand why he stayed in the garden, but I can. I know why he stays. At least he found his voice, and maybe that means he knows he is free."

The house sat dark and silent around them, and neither moved to light the lamps.

After what seemed an eternity, Kusini flexed her wrists slightly, tugging gently on his hands. He accepted the invitation, crawling forward and allowing her to pull his head onto her lap. She caressed his curls, and did not stop this gentle attention even when his silent sobs were spent.

Long after he fell asleep there, she heard the nightingale's song begin. She rested her head against the wall and closed her own eyes in sadness, feeling silent tears track down her face.

36

HIS STORY EXPLAINED SO MUCH that Kusini felt guilty for having asked the question at all, worried that it had caused him to revisit his suffering. But he seemed to be better for it, not worse, and she could imagine, with all that she had seen and heard in her travels, all she had borne witness to, that there was healing in letting it out. She recognized his shared confidence as the gift it was, and the subject slipped into the past, where she felt it rightly belonged, for his sake more than anything.

Here was the reason that there were no doors in the house. She eventually discovered them later, in an unused horse stall in the detached outbuildings beyond the garden, when peering through one of the garden windows where he had allowed, and probably cultivated, a very beautiful but particularly thorny wild rose to outgrow all bounds. The plant was taking over the wall of the building and had grown up and over the garden wall at the back of the property, escaping what few efforts appeared to have been made to prune it. Kusini thought that the choice of this particular vine, with its utter and complete resistance to containment, had been purposeful.

Here was the reason he had put on the costume of illness and decay. He was hiding his exotic beauty from others, avoiding revisiting any situation in which he could be coveted as a lover – or indeed viewed as an object of desire or scorn.

Here, the reason he slept so poorly in the night. It was still a time of apprehension and waiting. Waiting for forced lovers that were no longer coming, but the soul carried the imprint that they could come at any time, and what she couldn't know was that in his dreams he still revisited that terrible robbed adolescence. Still woke up in skin that felt tainted, in a state for which there would be no further sleep during the night. Why she came upon him in doorways, on the kitchen bench, under a tree, fast asleep.

And here, finally, the reason he had been so concerned for her own safety. He had discovered as an adult that his own mother's life had been that of a captive, to a husband who had likely taken her absent consent from her own people, and when she bore such a lovely, radiant child, had made certain that there was no escape for them. He could not know the extent of Kusini's particular talents, that it was she who posed a danger to any who got too close.

At present, their togetherness was a necessity to Ambakisye, but if he thought he was protecting her he was mistaken. And she was still unable to accept that he saw her as more than a refuge, and more than kindred, because Kusini was as yet unequipped to understand that there was more than one way for her to be seen by another. With all her gifts, she was possessed of an enormous ignorance in this matter.

It was this, and the end of another rainy season, that drove her to tell him that she must leave him, and his house, and the sprawling grounds she had come to love. Wandering was what she knew; more importantly, the healing was what she had to offer the world, and her heart was unquiet for some time. She could feel the very suffering of others, visited their plights as visions in her dreams – some that she knew were real, others she was less certain about. She had begun wandering in circles in the garden to keep her feet occupied and her heart quiet, but still the calls of distress from beyond that she could not ignore pulled her away in spirit, if not in reality.

The *Mjusi* sent her dreams of deaths, stolen children, sometimes just feelings of pain or dread. Once she woke from sleep gasping for air, having had a dream that she was wrapped up in linen, in a shroud, and was starved for breath, stolen away in the night. She could hear the screams of too many souls, too many children. Some were voices she had really heard, but some were the screams of lost souls that accompanied the Serpent and its Master.

And when she awoke from that dream, of smothering, of the struggle for breath, Ambakisye had been there, sitting in her doorway, watching the rain, watching her. She merely sat shivering for a time, head down, unable to speak. And he did come to her, came right up onto the bed with her, and took her in his arms, saying softly, "I wanted to wake you, but when I tried, I got a terrible shock. It was as if – as if you were keeping me away." He said this last very sadly, and she felt sorry for him. But she also felt the need to explain to him the truth in what he had already guessed.

"You are perhaps the first person that my magic has not in some way repelled. At least when I am conscious, and aware," she told him, admitting that there was magic, as he had sensed it. "I cannot control what happens when I am dreaming, or having visions, or whatever comes over me at those times, and I have even hurt those who have tried to intervene.

"I have been selfish, for the first time in my life, I have put my wants first, and have set aside all caution about the warnings that the world sends me. Warnings of distress and pending disaster."

She took hold of him gently, and allowed him to settle next to her on the bed, burrowing into the warmth of his arms, and returning his embrace. His body language conveyed his initial surprise and pleasure before he relaxed next to her, waiting for her to say more.

After what seemed hours, she began to speak, and once she did, she did not keep any of her secrets from him. To him, who had made himself vulnerable to her, she returned that gift, relieved and appalled that she was doing so. She told him the old stories of the evil mischief-maker, the *Mjusi*, and its cohort, *Nyoka*, the serpent-man who reveled in the suffering of the innocent, who had tortured her into committing atrocious acts and had shown her the true destructive power she carried within. How she had paid for those acts, and would continue to pay with servitude, kindness, succor, and any other help she could give, knowing that it wasn't enough, that it would never be enough, that not even her self-imposed martyrdom was just payment for unclean hands.

And when Ambakisye tried to settle her, to calm her, she wasn't fully sure that he believed what he had heard, couldn't know if he was merely patronizing, and she hated the thought of being pitied or suspected hysterical. Still, he held her, and tried genuinely to comfort her, but his hands on her body were suddenly too familiar for her to withstand all that she felt for him. She was afraid that if she couldn't leave him at that moment, she would lose her own self-determination, and her guilt was a terrible place to start such a relationship.

So she extricated herself from that warm and wonderful embrace before he could kiss her, before there was no return for them, and left the bed, wandering to the doorway. Her words were truth, not unkind in their purpose, but the truth can cut, and wound, in its rawest expression.

"You hide here, because the pain was brought here. When it left, you remained, still imprisoned by these walls, no longer having to face the reality of what you are to the world. There are so many like us, to the north and west, away from the cities and their jaded views and tepid acceptance of what is different, who are hunted, maimed, raped, and killed. Every day, lured to their deaths by those with aspirations of power and magic. Lured by those who claim to heal, stalked and rent asunder by strangers for money. Sometimes the promises of money and power are so great that those closest to them will turn them over to the *mgangas*, husband abandoning wife, mother sacrificing child, convinced by the medicine men that those like us have no souls, have no worth except in sacrifice. Their limbs stolen for potions, the innocence of young girls stolen because of a false promise that such a violation will cure impotence and disease…" Kusini paused when she saw him flinch away, heard his gasp of distress. "I bear witness, I try to prevent these things, to use my gift to empower, to educate, to heal. And still I am feared, cast out because what I am only reinforces everything that they don't want to be associated with. The myth is that we are magical, but in reality, we want to be innocuous, normal, unremarkable beyond the stigma that our whiteness creates, as anonymous as everyone else. The medicine men point to me as proof of their lies, and my presence, while it may alleviate some of the suffering, probably fuels ever more destruction.

"I will pay with my life, with all the power I command, until I can do no more. I must return to the wilderness, and go where my heart directs me, and I do not deserve the rest and peace that I may find in this oasis."

He was still for a long time, and unable to hide his very real hurt, he took his leave from her. She sank down on the terrace tiles in the rain, the remains of their exchange still scattered around her like ghosts that haunted her and would not leave her. She listened to him moving about in his studio at the other end of the house. She sighed in resignation, and did the easiest thing next to do – she started straightening the bed linens and embroidered pillows and hangings, and tidying the space, leaving it as he always did, order and beauty side by side.

37

SHE WANDERED IN THE GARDEN for a while, and uncharacteristically, the rains abruptly ended, and Yabluu alighted on her shoulder briefly before launching himself back toward the house, and the distress he must have felt coming from his keeper. She began to twist the deep purple roses from the vine, gathering many, ignoring the thorny injuries to her hands, thinking them a right punishment for causing him pain. But she still did not fully understand his hurt. He, like her, had lived peacefully and contentedly alone.

So distracted was she that she did not pull her arms free of the thorny climbing vines as soon as she sensed the change in the air, and the dreaded *Nyoka* wound through them so rapidly, slithering around her wrists in an endless seeming loop, binding her hands to the garden wall, completely separating them, so as to nearly neutralize her power. Its dull dark eyes watched nothing, as its forked tongue darted toward her, seeming, as it so often did, to taste her very distress.

She struggled mightily against the snake but only managed to tear more of her own skin on the thorns, which seemed to give the serpent no trouble at all.

Then, realizing she was helpless, she thought to call for

Ambakisye, but could not find the voice to do so, unsure what the *Mjusi* might unleash upon him, hoping she could hide what she felt. And just like that, the Monster was willed to being, no mere lizard at play on the garden wall, but flesh and blood, or the illusion of same, fully formed as a man, he appeared some feet away, near the garden gate, fully enjoying and amused at her predicament.

"Next-born, witchborn, child of sun," the odd voice was in her head. She had no difficulty identifying the creature, although this was the first time she had seen it incarnate of fully human flesh. Its features were striking; most arresting was the dark, wavy hair that seemed alive somehow. Its eyes depthless shiny discs in a handsome face that brought to mind neither African nor Arabian, but still somehow was oddly akin to both. She remembered those eyes from her childhood. Its language was still that indecipherable tongue that nonetheless was understood. "Quite the predicament we find you in."

Without seeming to move at all it walked behind her, and pressed itself close to her, so she stopped struggling, not wanting to give either of them any satisfaction. But some of her memories of attempts at violation were still too near her conscious mind, and it read this easily, and placed too-familiar hands on her body in compromising places. She closed her eyes and held her breath against it, because she could taste its foulness in the air, the stink of decay and the dead things that it had probably eaten. These thoughts came to her mind as if it could put them there, and her flesh was a living thing, crawling in disgust, trying to escape that awful intrusion, coming so close after Ambakisye's attempt to seduce her.

It knew she was defenseless, and leaned its weight into her, pressing her into the thorns, satisfied with her gasps of pain and revulsion at its continued touch. "We know you want *him*," it sneered. "That will only lead to ruin. There is no redemption in that path; he is headed to his death like all the others and you still have our work awaiting you in this world. His fate is determined, and your interference with his life could be costly to him."

"You leave us alone," Kusini grunted out through gritted teeth, which only prompted the serpent to constrict further, enjoying her distress at the pain and numbness in her hands. She was rapidly losing feeling in her fingers. She concentrated on that pain, focused on it, and used it, pushing the limits of what she was feeling throughout her body, transferring it to the hands of her tormentor. With satisfying cracking noises, its fingers deformed and broke, or at least the fingers of whatever being it currently possessed, and this occurred as if they were crushed by some great weight. Suddenly the screams of the tormented rang in her ears, perhaps heralding the pain felt as it was injured, the *Mjusi* was no more, and when it departed, the *Nyoka* went also, the weight of the dead snake across her wrists the only fleshly remnant of the encounter.

Kusini was surprised, until she looked more closely at what had allowed her to rein in her power – her own blood smeared the scales of the serpent from the piercing thorns. Still, blood magic had never served her so well, which told her that her feelings for Ambakisye and this place had powered her ability to transfer distress into force. She was wary of blood magic, because its outcomes were less predictable, and in her experience, this was the kind of power that was abused by the *mgangas*. The kind of power that she suspected the *Mjusi* wanted her to use. Because she generally had no clear awareness of how her power would serve or fail her, she took some satisfaction in knowing that she had also surprised the *Mjusi* out of its host, and back out of time. But her satisfaction was short lived, when she caught a whisper of its laughter on the breeze, and realized that it was satisfied that she had used this dark and powerful augmenter, no matter how inadvertently.

She feared retaliation could be directed at what she loved, which strengthened her resolve to leave the city. She returned to the house, delivering the flowers, and washed her hands carefully, clearing them of blood, before seeking Ambakisye in the depths of the dwelling. He was sitting in his studio, carving quietly, when she came in.

"Did I do something wrong?" he asked, so plaintively that she understood better what his concern might be. He did not want to cause her distress, and she knew that he was concerned that his advances were unwelcome.

"Not at all," she began, then amended her answer to make it more definitive. "Not ever. 'Kisye – "she began, noting how his head moved when she involuntarily used this shortened version of his name, "It is that my work needs to be done. I think of it as my particular responsibility to help those who cannot help themselves. Outside of these walls, outside the walls of this city, is where those who hunt us for power are strongest. There are those like us who must live in hiding, never having a moment's peace, never able to make a living, learn a trade, care for themselves. I have pledged my life to try and do what I can to make things better for them, if and when it is possible."

"And what about you, what about your life?" he asked quietly, knowing he was unable to tell her that she had changed his days, his possibilities, his life. He could not know that she was even less equipped to tell him the same thing; that her own life was never to be the same as it had once been.   She had never felt so anchored to another person and place as she now found herself, but it did not change the deep sense of responsibility she carried to mitigate the ugliness she knew was out there, the evil that she knew touched it all. The evil that implicated her in its worst plans.

"My travels are such a part of my life, that is, they allow me to find greater meaning in my gifts," she said, acknowledging her magic. She had been careful to use it sparingly here, in an attempt to avoid the interest of the *Mjusi*, which she had long suspected knew everything anyway, and which her garden encounter had confirmed.

He nodded, as if he fully understood, but of course she knew there was no way he could. Perhaps someday he might, and that thought made her feel slightly less alone. As there was little else to say, she took her leave, not wanting to make any promises she was unsure she could keep.

Ambakisye waited alone and continued his carvings, wanting to follow her but respecting her decision, unable to categorize this new kind of pain. It was assuaged when, upon emerging into the central salon, he saw the dozens of wild roses floating in the hummingbird pool. This gesture and her bestowal of a nickname were his assurances that she would indeed return.

38

IF KUSINI HAD NOT BEEN entirely clear about how much Ambakisye had changed her life because she was unable to see it without the perspective of distance, her wanderings abroad in the world brought her startling clarity. Now, every family situation brought thoughts of him, and how she had been given a place of belonging. When she stopped to eat, every lonely bite was taken with sadness, knowing that the vibrant meals she had shared with him had tasted better, had been gifts she had denied herself.

She continued to learn, as Suhuba had taught her, paying attention to her own feelings, a most unusual task. Now it was also a distracting one. She could imagine his voice, and longed to hear it at the loneliest times. She could recall his touch on her skin, or the way he brushed his lips against her forehead, or her shoulder. His hand on her back, his fingers curled through hers.

She was able to focus on her predestined role as healer, and was given many opportunities to help others, suspecting, as she always had, that there was some unique energy signal she expended that attracted her to those in need. She knew that she had a unique talent for finding them as well, and had never questioned this.

After two months making her rounds in the countryside, she was ready to return to Dodoma, but she felt guilty about cutting her circuit short, so she forced herself further west and north, traveling up near the great lake, near the *Maa* village of her birth. Her legs led her back through the gorge, right to the shelter carved in the rock that had been her early childhood home many hundreds of years before. She smiled to herself when she realized that she had once been small enough to fit inside, but no longer.

As was often the case, her legs carried her to the origins of the old spring, where she had so long ago healed from her worst hurts. The quiet and peace of the place was preserved, like a sacred sanctuary. She had waited centuries hoping to catch a glimpse of the chameleon once more, but it was not to be. She was beginning to believe it a vision of a reality that she had created from her own need to find some inner calm. Whatever well of power was here, it was strong, and felt secure. As was common when in this place, she felt out of the world, but less in the disjointed way that came with the artificial reality of the *Mjusi*, and more in a connected calm; she felt as though her power would hold no sway here, but also felt as though all that she was or would ever be was part of something greater and better than herself. She was overpowered by the energy of the gorge, an oasis, and it gave her a deep sense of relief even as it mystified.

She was returning across the crater from the west when she sensed a disturbance, something that made her hair stand on end. She could hear nothing, so she kept onward, feeling the dip in the air temperature, the gathering clouds as the afternoon went on, carrying a sense that she was watched. It felt as though her lizard nemesis were nearby, and she wanted nothing less than to have to deal with its mischief.

She detoured to the water to fill her gourd and discovered the source of the disquiet. A juvenile giraffe had been savaged near the spring that fed a tiny stream, and the creature appeared to have nearly bled out. She was on the ground, her hind limbs tangled, and she was near death, her voiceless pleas transmitted by her wild eyes. She was spattered with gore, and it appeared that whatever predator had attacked her, it had abandoned her before the kill, really before doing much more than leaving her suffering at the water's edge.

Kusini looked into those eyes and knew that she could end the animal's misery, but something in her heart felt too weak to do it. She could not understand the failure in her resolve; she did not want the animal to suffer, neither did she want to carry its death, no matter how merciful, on her heart. She was tired of death, tired of endings. She considered her options and settled for offering the animal some much needed water.

The baby giraffe drank gratefully, and Kusini told herself that perhaps she would survive, surprised at the vigor with which she took the water. Then she noticed something else – the pale color of the animal's coat. Her pattern of pale spots on white fur was familiar from the lessons of Suhuba in those days when he was finding examples of albinism in nature. The giraffe was kindred, and after the gift of water, she lay her head down quietly, exhausted.

Kusini reached out and stroked the soft nose gently, and whispered, "Peaceful rest," and its eyes slipped closed, the long lashes resting gently against the pale fur. Perhaps, Kusini hoped, that was mercy enough.

Knowing she could not stay and see more without facing her guilt for being unable to curtail the animal's suffering, she set off eastward, not stopping to rest until morning, when her feet had carried her out of the crater and far away.

39

KUSINI STUBBORNLY REFUSED TO THINK of Dodoma, and followed the longer circuit, a pilgrimage that she knew could take as long as a year to complete. She prolonged it as much as possible by stopping to check on her young families and some of the invalids that she continued to monitor. The length of her journey had kept her away for the entirety of the dry season, through rains that trapped her to the west, where she took refuge with some of those she felt part of her network, and through another long dry season of work, until she knew that she must return to the city for recovery from all the strife she had faced.

And when it was time to rest, to break from the often morbid and tiring work that she found herself immersed in, she determined that it would be wisest not to travel so far south. She determined that making Arusha her home during the rains would be a prudent change, telling herself that once they ended, she would be closer to her childhood home, to the remote areas where she was so often called to intervene, where most of the suffering occurred.

Such were the lies that she told herself, and they served another purpose – she could avoid complicating both her life and 'Kisye's with something that was probably ill-advised. Clinging to this ragged bit of belief, she secured a single-room flat in an outbuilding on a spice merchant's property. The merchant's wife was the landlady, as her husband traveled widely, and if the woman was perturbed by Kusini's appearance, she made no fuss, seeming grateful that the space was in use.

Kusini swept the floors and opened all the windows to allow the place to air out in the last few dry days she expected to see. She unpacked her bedroll and those few items she kept at hand. Last of these was the tiny blue bird, its colors surprisingly unfaded by travel and time. She had not removed it from her pouch in many moons, but the sight of it made her happy. Its intricate and lifelike detail continued to enchant her, even now, when she knew so much more about the talent behind it.

The following morning, it was the first thing her eyes found when they opened, and she smiled. It provided her purpose for that morning, to indulge her curiosity by browsing in the market square in town, an aimless task that could eat hours of her day as she took in the various wares of the ever-changing nomadic merchants.

Her burdens of the last several months, and all the witnessed sufferings were lifted from her during the rains, when travel was impossible in some areas, and she was forced to still her wandering. She set out into a bright dry day whose slight coolness hinted at the rainy season that could begin at any time.
Inadvertently, she hummed an old tune of Suhuba's as she made her way through the market, and was delighted and confused when a small bird lit on her shoulder in a flurry of blue feathers, and then hopped in frenzied succession from there to her hand, and across to her other arm. It chirped happily at her, and reminded her of both Yabluu and her own tiny sculpture. On closer inspection, however, she could see that this little bird's wing had been injured slightly, either in an altercation with another bird, or in a mid-flight collision, which occasionally could occur. This small irregularity suggested it was not the same bird, and she sighed happily with the memory as it hovered momentarily and then flew away down the avenue.
She purchased greens from a local farmer, and took a different path

out of the market, hoping to see some new things. She turned the final corner of the square, and there, under a multicolored makeshift awning, sat her beloved 'Kisye, carving patiently, as though he had been there waiting for her all this time. She stopped mid-stride, wondering if hope was giving her a vision, wanting to be sure she was really seeing him, and utterly unprepared for such an outcome.

As always, he knew she was there, and the curve of his mouth betrayed it, his wry smile enough to give himself away, though he did not look up from his carving. On cue, the strange blue bird landed daintily at the end of his workbench and chirped happily.

"Apparently, love has messengers," Kusini observed quietly. "But how -?"

"I knew you loved me when you gave me a nickname," he said quietly. "I knew how *much* you loved me when I saw the roses, since they probably left wounds that took a long time to heal. I knew when you were gone more than a year that it was really true love, and that you were going to deny yourself, because that *is* what you do," he paused here, finally looking at her, gesturing pointedly at her once again spare figure, "whether it is with food, or other things you might really need.

"You told me of the suffering of people in the north and west, and given your background, I guessed you were most probably referring to the lands of the *Maasai mara*, which meant that when you decided to rest, you would find a place closer to your outreach where you could avoid me.

"But knowing all that, I just had to find the most likely place for you to stop off for a while, and so I picked three villages I hoped were good candidates, since they would serve your purpose *without* being the city that I lived in. I got lucky since Arusha was the first place I tried. It just felt right, and I remembered what you taught me about small magics, love being one of them," he said gently, putting his eyes back on his carving briefly before turning his moving gaze more directly toward her. "It was only a matter of time."

"How could you be so sure?" she asked, with a smile, anticipating the answer.

"Simple. You can't resist a busy marketplace," he told her, in that teasing tone she had come to love.

"And an arrogant artist," she teased back. She approached the stall, still awed by the detail of his work. Like magic, he produced the second small stool that he had carved for her in Dodoma, and she laughed, perching next to him, then frowned at the small bird.

"What happened to his wing?" she asked.

"Not sure," he replied. "But it's *her* wing. Yabluu died last fall; he was old. I think this bird may have been a member of his family. She has always had a problem with her wing."

The new bird showed the same enthusiasm and familiarity with Kusini, happily dancing onto her forearm. "And what do you call her?"

"Yabluu," he replied mischievously.

"Endlessly imaginative," she observed.

<h1 style="text-align:center">40</h1>

LIFE IN ARUSHA CERTAINLY SUITED Kusini better, because it was smaller, and admittedly closer to her homeland plains. Artistically, it was favorable for 'Kisye as well, because he was closer to nature, and able to take advantage of the few days' walk along the cattle road toward Moshi and wander in the foothills. He loved the coffee plantations and could climb among the plants for hours. He befriended one of the coffee stewards, and spent hours learning about the process of preparing the cherries and roasting the beans. Some of the stewards made tea from the ripe cherries, and this 'Kisye preferred to brewed coffee, which was so bitter he could not understand why anyone would drink it for pleasure without significant amounts of sugar. He made it once for Kusini, who was surprised that his palate was discerning enough to tell the difference; she could stomach neither coffee nor this odd tea.

He was painting much more, and covered large canvases with skillful renderings of the countryside, some with the *Kilimanjaro* in the background. These were astonishing in their majesty and detail, and she could not entirely understand his reproduction of details he couldn't really see. Kusini asked him about this one morning over tea and an incredible fig bread that he had made for her, and he merely shrugged. After patiently waiting for her to finish her breakfast, he tucked his arm into hers and directed her to lead him out of the city. He slowly walked with her for several hours along the road to Moshi, stood with her in the middle of a grass plateau, and turned her to face the mountain obliquely. His descriptions of the contours of the peak, its shadows, and glacial faces was nothing short of miraculous. She could see that he was some sort of savant, that his functional blindness had left him with a gift for discerning *chiaroscuro*, and it was this ability to differentiate light and shadow that gave him his uncanny talent for simulacra.

"What city shall I guess you will be returning to next year?" he asked mischievously, and she marveled at his willingness to let her go, and the understanding and love that supported it.
"Arusha is a good compromise," she whispered. "I won't make you move all your paintbrushes again."

41

THIS TIME, WHEN SHE RETURNED, there was a quiet anticipation about him that was so strong she could feel it. He was happy to see her, and he showed this by rejoicing anew in her company, and fussing about the apparent lack of food in the countryside and her ignorance of it. He talked of his days in the market, and showed her new carvings and paintings, and virtually forced admittedly delicious food on her while Yabluu happily flitted about their rooms in celebration.

When she had been back only three days, he pulled out their weaving cloth once more, and she sighed, not entirely happy to see that he was still determined that they should finish it.

While she washed up and drank the tea he had prepared for her, he did a few more rows. As usual, they looked perfect, and as usual, when he turned it over to her, it took her twice as long to do a single row, which to her eye was not at all improved from her early attempts at it.

"I have an idea how we could complete this thing once and for all," she suggested with a smile.

"No magic," he admonished, in a mock-stern tone that was entirely unconvincing.

"Then I hope you are prepared for it to remain unfinished," she grumbled in a soft voice, hoping he heard.

"Finishing it is important," he told her. "All my hopes and dreams are tied up in it, so do your part with love, okay?" he teased. There was a smile in his voice when he said it, but she could hear the earnestness, too. It made her feel more than a little guilty, and she suspected he would use that guilt to get it done as well. At this point, any motivation at all was warranted; it had been almost two years since they had first started it, on that stormy afternoon in the house in Dodoma.

"It's taking forever," she lamented, fully aware that two years to her was less than the blink of an eye. The fact that she acutely felt every moment of the project as if it were a human lifetime was instructive of her frustration.

"I am willing to wait that long, if that is what it takes," he replied calmly. "At least we are doing it together."

Then he surprised her by sitting with her on the floor and helping her complete several rows. She had to admit, her work did make the thing interesting, if one took a *very* generous view of things. And for the first time, she could see that the end of the project really was in sight. There was less than a meter of the long strips to weave through, perhaps less than 100 rows, especially if she did the weaving, as her work was less orderly and not as snug. She almost smiled at the progress they had made, and she had to admit it was beautiful. She ran a hand over it, allowing herself to admire it.

When she looked up once more, his face was only inches from hers, and before she could even think, he leaned forward and touched his lips to hers, gently, softly, reverently, but there was nothing remotely chaste about it. She could feel the heat pass between them, and at the end he gently caught her lower lip between his for the briefest of moments, so that it pulled toward him as he moved away. It was the first time he had even tried to kiss her on the mouth, and the intimacy of the gesture spoke volumes.

Those wandering eyes searched her face, and he whispered, "It really is time to get this done." That said, he lifted his frame gracefully off the floor and went out onto the terrace to paint, leaving her to sit there in shock, seemingly unable to function. Still feeling that kiss on her mouth and in other places that she had assumed would never fully be awakened, she was blissfully raw with desire.

42

STUBBORNLY, WANTING TO BELIEVE THAT she was doing it because there was nothing else for her to do, she continued to help him with the weaving cloth, working on it at first every evening when the light was too poor to read, alternating their techniques.

But more often than not, when she could no longer tend to her healing herbs in the garden of an afternoon (begrudgingly admitting that his skill with plants was very great, and he had cultivated her plants with the same care he showed his own vegetables and herbs), she found herself drawn back to the weaving. The cloth now held pride of place on his workbench, as he preferred to work outside during the dry season, under a triangular awning that she had helped him stretch over the terrace to protect him from the sun's rays. It draped down off the sides of the bench, a masterpiece of reds and yellows woven randomly together, nearly complete, calling her somehow.

But perhaps, too, there was another reason to finish. Since that scorching kiss, he had held himself aloof, as if withholding that fire should motivate her. She would never acknowledge that it did so, which was of no real consequence, since he probably read her as well in this as he seemed to in everything else. She caught herself occasionally putting her fingers to her lips, subconsciously, recalling the feel of his mouth over hers, and just what his voice betrayed.

Eventually, on drier nights when he opened his stall in the night market, and she was alone, unable to sleep, she was drawn to do a few rows all on her own, and she began to wonder if his kiss had worked some magic on *her*. She was creating something, for no real reason other than to do so, and she started to understand some of the lovely frustration he seemed to feel when his work was not going the way he wanted it to, or a single sculpture was eluding him.

One morning, in the wee hours, 'Kisye arrived home to find Kusini fast asleep, the short ends of the final weaving strip still in her hands, her head down on her chest where she sat. He didn't have the heart to wake her, so he stretched out beside her and got some much-needed rest.

When she awoke, stiff and sore, 'Kisye was already up and about, singing to himself as he carved happily at his workbench. When he noticed she was stirring, he came to bring her some strong cinnamon tea, which he deposited next to her on the rug. He gave her some moments to herself, returning to his carving, respectfully quiet for a time, before he observed, "Now, you are an artist. You finished it, because it became something you loved enough to return to, again and again, even though it wasn't going as you planned, or even as you'd hoped it to."

She finished her tea and gazed at the completed work at her feet. She smiled at the compliment, and then, as only Kusini could, immediately complained. "Yes. All that work, and now what?"

"I think we should make a gift of it," he immediately suggested.

"A gift?" Her tone gave away her utter confusion.

"Yes." He put down his carving. "A wedding gift, I think." He tilted his head and awaited her response, but she gave none.

"Who is getting married?" she inquired earnestly. He had not mentioned any weddings, but she knew that he met many people in the market, and sometimes, certain works he did were commissioned. Perhaps someone had inquired about a wedding gift, and he thought the cloth a worthy present for bride and groom.

Ambakisye sighed, and shook his head. He stood, and pulling the cloth around his shoulders, came to her, offered his hand, and pulled her up into his arms, wrapping her within it as well. The dawning realization came to her quickly. "Why didn't you say something?" she was honestly confused.

"I had to wait until we finished it. It was the right thing to do. Until even *you* came to love it, in your own way."

"What if we had never finished it?!" Kusini exclaimed, incredulous, pushing him away.

"I'm not sure," 'Kisye teased. "It is said that once the cloth is finished, if you still like the person, you should marry." This he managed with almost a straight face.

Kusini narrowed her eyes, skepticism in the very angle of her head. "I think you just made that up," she accused.

'Kisye sighed. "*Sini-ma*, you must admit it is a wise observation."

When her expression did not change, and she remained silent, he said, earnestly, softly, "I believe in the time that has passed we have had an opportunity to get to know each other. That may be the most important reason why it made sense to finish it first."

She was still quiet, and finally looked away from him. There were too many reasons not to do this. And finally, for her, there were even more reasons to go through with it.

'Kisye rushed to fill the silence. "I knew what *I* wanted before I looped that first piece over your toes. The project simply gave me an excuse to spend time with you."

"It took two years," she groused.

"If you're not ready, we can weave another one," he suggested smartly, ducking when he saw the flash of color as she tossed the cloth back at him, and laughing as she advanced on him, uncannily eluding her attempts to grab him.

He finally allowed himself to be caught, feeling the sharpest surge of energy he had yet experienced in her touch, almost painful, but he grabbed her up in his arms anyway and spun her until she had to laugh. Then he backed her up to the cool wall and placed a hand on each side of her, his eyes seemingly searching her face.

To her great surprise, he kneeled at her feet and bowed his head, murmuring, "I don't deserve you, so I will understand if it is not what you want."

"Get up!" She pulled at him, and he could hear that she was almost laughing.

"I can just stay here, worshipping at your feet," he suggested, bowing to put his mouth on the bony arch of her foot.

"I will say yes, if it means no more tapestry weaving," she sighed, as 'Kisye reached up and put his hand on her chin, opening his fingers wide and stroking downward, his hand tracing her body, traveling from breastbone to belly to hip.

Her breath hitched in response, and he accepted the unspoken invitation to stand. Cradling her face in his hands, finally, finally, he pressed those soft full lips on hers and gave her the kiss she had traveled through time for.

43

AFTER SOME SLOW, LAZY KISSES, 'Kisye reluctantly let her go, returning to his workbench to work on his carvings. He spent the rest of the day with a secret smile on his face. Kusini went out to the market in the afternoon, returning with several ripe melons and a small chicken that she transported in a cloth sling he had fashioned for her use.

When she set down her burdens in the kitchen and wandered through the rooms to find him, she gasped with pleasure to see the woven door hanging proudly displayed across the entrance to the alcove where she slept. Realization hit her then, and she sank down onto her knees in grateful happiness. She saw the tapestry for what it represented, and its beauty struck her, because she was seeing it with new eyes. It was so lovely, and the colors so striking. It brought the space together, tying the colorful pots on his workbench to the many carvings, candles, and other small treasures that they had begun to collect.

She called out to him, but there was no answer from the rooms or the terrace, suggesting he was out wandering, or perhaps had decided to open his stall for a few hours in the evening market. After a while, she got to her feet and packed the chicken in salt water to preserve it, deciding that the wisest course was to stay their meal until he returned. He ate her cooking, but she knew tolerance was the better term; he had far and away the better talent at making meals. His food tasted much better, and she preferred his company when preparing and eating it.

Still tired from her labors of the previous night, she pulled off her abaya and climbed into the alcove to rest. A small bar of late afternoon sunlight entered the small space through an open transom at the top of the wall, and she admired the colors of their weaving. She reached out to place a hand on the textured surface, and the smile that had persisted at the corners of her own mouth for most of the day came back. She was unused to this kind of happiness.

Without realizing how fatigued she was, she fell asleep there, a restful, dreamless sleep unusual for her. When she awoke, it was full dark, and the flat was quiet. She sensed that 'Kisye was home, but no lamps were lit. The pale light from the transom told her the moon was near full, and she got up, pushing the tapestry aside. The floor was cool under her feet, which carried her into the kitchen. A single small lucifer gave the space a soft glow, and she could see that 'Kisye had opened one of the melons. It appeared he had shared a bit of it with Yabluu, who slept peacefully next to a wooden bird on a small perch near the window. It made Kusini smile. He hadn't cooked, had not wanted to disturb her rest.

She wandered out onto the terrace to look at the moon. Heavy and bright, it appeared to hang close enough in the sky that she could reach out and touch it. She bowed her head and thanked *Olapa* for blessings, and asked for a happy marriage, as these things were the province of *Ngai's* wife, the moon goddess.

All was quiet, and she should have returned to her bed, but she could not resist looking in on a slumbering 'Kisye. As usual, he had surrendered poorly to his rest, working on something up until the moment he had succumbed to exhaustion. He was, at least, fully atop the bed, his long limbs stretched from top to bottom, one hand dangling off the side, still holding the small paintbrush he had been using.

Rather than leave him, she sat down on a small bench by the

wall and watched him for some time. Something kept her from rest, but she was unable to determine the cause of her restlessness. Sometime later, she started from a dream and noticed that the sky appeared to be brightening. She turned her head slightly away from 'Kisye's form to listen for the morning birdsong, but there was none.

The movement did bring a small, furtive sound to her ear that seemed to come from the far side of the bed. She rose slowly, and thought she caught a small movement there in the deeper shadows. She took a step closer, and was convinced something moved, but was still unable to see anything. She jumped when a short squawk from Yabluu rang out – it sounded as though she was in a tree across the thoroughfare that ran past the front of the dwelling, but it was definitely her tiny, distinct voice.

Kusini called out to the little blue bird in reassurance, expecting her to fly into the room, but soon the cries of many birds reached her, all distressed, warning calls. It was the sound they made when predators were near.

The darkest shadow near the bed suddenly moved, and she recognized the slithering, writhing movement of a serpent just before seeing its glittering black eye spot as it rose its head. She recognized the slate grey color of the mamba and froze where she stood, because it swayed with a curious rhythm only inches from 'Kisye's dangling wrist.

The birds were screaming down from the trees, and she realized that this was not real, the sounds were inside her, as form after form coalesced from the shadows, sinister and deadly, twisting over the floor, stretching up their heads with the glittering, flat eyes, swaying in a hypnotic rhythm as they surrounded the bed, all poised to strike her beloved, and she saw them as she had on that long-ago day, before her torture had begun. She realized that loving him was as terrible a mistake as she could have made, because that love would now cost him his life. Following that thought was another, that she could right the wrong she had done him, but she didn't yet know how. Any spell she used to stay or destroy their flesh could affect

'Kisye equally, and she was loath to lose him to her own magic, which she knew would be an immeasurable tragedy.

But when his eyes opened, and he did not appear afraid for himself, she realized that his eyesight was too poor in the dim light for him to discern the danger.

"*Still*," she whispered, not wanting him to lift his head. She touched her hands together and felt the power flow over her hands like water. Like water it seemed to reach the bed and the floor, and not only did 'Kisye still, the snakes did, too. Kusini felt her energy flow around them all, could almost feel the energy that drove them pushing against her own. But her spell had frightened 'Kisye, who was now unable to move, and his eyes rolled wildly in her direction, so she said, "*Sleep, Ambakisye.*" The pull of his distress lessened sharply as he drifted back down into slumber, the power of his invoked name compelling him to obedience.

The snakes were still watchful, and her slight distraction had allowed them a moment of freedom; the ones closest to him poised to strike, one at his hand, and one nearer his foot. Kusini had only a moment to decide, so she reached out quickly, grasping 'Kisye's ankle, but she was only a fraction of a second faster than the snake, which sank its fangs into her flesh instead of his, quite painfully.

"*Kutosha!*" she whispered fiercely, squeezing her bitten hand into a fist which dripped her blood onto the floor. When the first drop hit, the serpents turned to ash, and the second bite, to 'Kisye's hand, was thwarted.

"*Next-born…*" a disembodied, sibilant hiss came from behind her, and she saw the ashes scurrying across the floor, swirling and coalescing into a shadowy form that resembled the *Nyoka* as man-serpent, but its flesh could not hold in this place of her magic, and the particles dispersed, and all was silent. Too silent. 'Kisye was not moving, and she climbed onto the bed feeling a cold terror. He did not appear to be breathing, nor was he responding to her touch, but she quickly realized he was still bespelled.

"*Awaken*," she begged, locking her thumbs together, and nearly sobbed in relief when he began to move, slowly recovering from the false slumber she had created to keep him still. By naming him, she had isolated him within the protection of sleep, and her touch had somehow shielded him from her more powerful spell. It had spared him, and she had dispatched the *Mjusi's* most powerful messenger with blood and love, preventing it from re-animating the flesh it had borrowed.

'Kisye shook, whether from fear or awe she did not know, and he could not tell her. It was clear he remembered initially awakening to her presence in the room, and he remembered her first spell, because it had held him fast. She reached her arms around him and held him close, and after a few moments, he relaxed against her, until he realized that she was bleeding.

"I was bitten," she waved away his concern, but he did not give up.

"A snake?" he asked, when he saw the wound.

"Gone," she assured him, shaking her head sadly.

He considered this, and then gently took her hand and led her to the kitchen where he filled a basin with water and soaked her hand. The bleeding had stopped and there was little evidence of any effect other than the two small punctures. "How?" he asked her, searching for answers.

"I have been bitten many times before, and I must have some immunity," she explained, not knowing whether that was the reason she was unaffected or not, and not wanting to admit to him that it was part of her reasoning, how she'd known when she reacted what had needed to be done.

"The bite was intended for me," he guessed, in that uncanny acuity that he displayed so disarmingly at times.

"It would have been fatal for you," she replied, not disagreeing but not wanting to tell him it was so.

"Was it *him*?" 'Kisye demanded, and the anger in his voice surprised her. "The *Mjusi?*"

Kusini shook her head. "Be careful. Names carry power," she

advised. "It was not. The serpent, one of its powerful servants."

"Why here?" 'Kisye demanded, still furious at the intrusion to their home.

"The evil follows me," she explained. "It is not always predictable, but this attack is not surprising. Whatever its plan for me, it attempts to eliminate all who are close to me. This was a message to me. It would kill you because you are a threat."

"I?" 'Kisye tilted his head and surprised her further by smiling in satisfaction. "It is right. I am a threat. And I will fight it to my last breath if that is what it will take to protect you. I will be ready."

"'Kisye —" Kusini began, and found she did not know what to say to this. She did not want to discourage his bravery, but shook her head, not beginning to imagine what horrors could be visited upon him if he were caught in the crossfire of unpredictable magics.

Still cradling her injured hand in one of his own, he reached out with the other to gently touch her face, and she felt the energy of his emotion transfer between them. "What power do you have that can stop an elemental force?" she whispered, not expecting an answer.

He shook his head in turn, because he knew she blinded herself to the obvious. "Love," he responded, now much more calmly, but there was no waver or doubt in his tone. "I have love."

44

THEIR WEDDING WAS A QUIET, deeply personal affair, which consisted of the two of them declaring their love for one another near the flowering wall of roses at the back of the garden in Dodoma, with only Yabluu and the slumbering nightingale as witnesses.

"And may *Enkai* bless us," 'Kisye declared to the heavens, while Kusini mentally changed the name to *Ngai* in her thoughts, smiling at how slight differences could make one worry that one's superstitions might not hold. Just to be safe, she said a small prayer to *Olapa* as well.

He undressed her slowly, beginning in the back salon, after lifting her across the step into the house. It was as if he believed her a present to be unwrapped, removing the layers to discover the gift inside, and she felt cherished.

He led her to the bed he had prepared for her when she first came to live with him, and she was touched when she saw that he had transformed the room with roses and many other flowers from the garden beyond the terrace doors, exotic blooms side by side with simple fragrant herb bundles, and she murmured at his thoughtfulness. It was a loving gesture, and the space was beautiful, his wedding gift to her, she knew, and in her characteristic way she felt guilt at not being able to express herself in kind for him.

But what he wanted was another expression of love, one he had denied himself, had once even assumed was not to be, but this vulnerability that he felt with her was appropriate to his feelings, and he was unsurprised at the ardency of his desire for her. She, despite her many years, and all she had seen, was suddenly shy and admittedly nervous, but he was ever gentle and patient, though she could feel his passion.

Although they were alone, he pulled the colorful silk hangings close around the bed before removing her simple linen shift, and his own clothing. He lay back on the pillows and reached for her, settling her on top of him, facing away, arranging her limbs with his own, gently allowing her head to rest in the hollow of his shoulder.

He placed her own hands on her body, against her skin, and covered them with his own. He moved them slowly, urging her to touch herself, teaching her the caresses, showing her where he wanted to explore, while placing gentle kisses on her neck and shoulder. When she arched in pleasure, she could feel him smiling against her skin, and she moved her hands atop his, so that his fingers explored in place of hers, finally gripping his forearms tightly as he gave her ever more pleasure.

As she relaxed against him, he felt her energy surge through him, powerful, raising gooseflesh on his skin, almost but not quite painful, matching the excitement he brought her. And he kept on touching and kissing until, in her delight, she gave voice in moans, an invitation.

He gently turned her onto her belly, and carefully balancing over her, placed himself against her, pausing so she could feel him, and pressing forward made them one, feeling her power flow over him and around him, heightening everything he felt. He was as patient as he could be, but he was quickly consumed and overwhelmed by his desire, and when she sang out in her bliss, it was the song that the poets write tributes to.

45

WHEN NEXT KUSINI LEFT FOR the frontier, she did so as the wife of Ambakisye, a woman with a home, and a hearth, set to wander as her instincts instructed her, but forevermore with a place to return to that was defined, anchored, her own. Their connection grew stronger, and in 'Kisye she found as much friend as lover, and she had not imagined how much more they would grow together in intimacy and closeness. There were no secrets, and she did not hide the spells she used to surround their home with protections from the *Mjusi* and its interlopers, but she was warier than ever about leaving him behind.

She marveled at his fearlessness, and after he reassured her once more that he could defend himself, she surrendered to her journey as she had so many times before. The rainy season had ended, but its hold was still on the land; streams were swollen and the floor of the *Ngorongoro* crater was green with vegetation that had yet to wither in the hot sun. Kusini set up camp at the end of her descent and went in search of water. She filled two gourds at the streambed, careful not to disturb the animals that came there, and returned to the spot where she had stowed her bedroll and few belongings, at first unaware that she had attracted a visitor.

After a few moments, as she was settling down to make a cooking fire, she felt a firm nudge, like a push on her shoulder, and turned in surprise to see a juvenile giraffe poking its head through the vegetation. It was the source of the nudge, and it blinked at her slowly before bobbing its head up and down in a sort of greeting.

Kusini stepped through the red grass that fringed her campsite, expecting the animal to flee, but it stood its ground. Looking more carefully at its pale markings, Kusini recognized the juvenile she had assisted at the watering hole. To be certain, she stepped carefully along the animal's flank, placing her hand on the rearward haunch, and sure enough, there was a substantial knot of scar tissue.

The little giraffe did not appear to have grown much, if at all, but Kusini knew it was hard to tell the difference – before, she had been on the ground, broken and suffering, and now she stood tall – at least a few hands taller than Kusini herself when standing up straight. But in the time that had passed, she should have matured.

Kusini did not have time to consider this fully, because she noticed movement out of the corner of her eye – an adult bull giraffe was approaching quickly, and with determination. Kusini wanted to stay out of his way, as a well-placed kick would cause her significant injury that would take a long time to heal. But the youngster stepped out in front of her, bowing slightly to the old one, and this seemed to calm him. He turned his attention to the trees and began to gingerly take leaves from the tops of them with a nimble purple tongue. Kusini surmised that the juvenile was his daughter, and perhaps she needed protection because her growth was stunted somehow.

The calf refused to leave Kusini alone, so Kusini stroked her nose and spoke gently to her, whispering nonsense, and finally the animal went off in search of food. Kusini returned to her cooking, set up her bedroll, and slept a few hours before nightfall.

When she awoke, it was full dark, with weak moonlight filtering through high, pale clouds. She packed her few things and set out across the crater, soon noticing that the young giraffe followed behind her. She smiled, certain that it would soon abandon this behavior when Kusini wandered too far afield of its family, but it kept on walking next to her for most of the night, and into the next day.

Kusini was concerned, but soon noticed that the giraffe did not seem lost; she would detour to water when needed and stopped often to strip the leaves of the acacia. But when Kusini left her behind, she always caught up, sometimes galloping for several yards beside her on open stretches of plain.

"You need a name," Kusini remarked to the calf during the second night it shared her travels. "I think *Bahati* is appropriate, don't you, lucky girl?"

The giraffe stopped chewing on a mouthful of leaves as if she were contemplating this, and then resumed chewing with a small bob of her head, which made Kusini laugh, since it recalled the way a child might consider something and deem it acceptable. "Bahati it is, then."

If Kusini fretted about the animal following her on her entire circuit, it seemed Bahati had other plans, wandering off in the direction of Oldupai a few days later. Kusini waved her off and continued heading west as planned, on a circuit that would eventually lead her back to Arusha, and home.

Her life fell into a daily rhythm, each day bringing her closer to her return to 'Kisye, with whom she found renewed delight when her travels were ended for the year. They spent the rains companionably indoors, she making clothes and tending the garden, while he sculpted or painted at all hours. They kept the terrace doors open in spite of the wildness of the weather, and lived with a view of the mountain's peak when it wasn't raining. The front of the house in Arusha was kept shuttered because it faced the street, and prying eyes, and sometime during the second year they lived there, 'Kisye rearranged their belongings while she traveled, turning the lower floor into a large studio for him to store his wares and work around the clock without disturbing Kusini. This afforded them even greater privacy and intimacy in their living quarters, and when she returned the following year, he had secured the entrance to the yard with a gate, which would inexplicably come open in the wind, invariably requiring one of them to go out to secure it, just as the rain would pour out of the sky. It resisted all efforts at repair, and it was the sound that would come to haunt Kusini in her dreams in the years that followed; it was the sound that heralded the darkness to come.

46

WHEN KUSINI COULD HEAR THE familiar sounds of the merchants returning from the bazaar one summer evening, and 'Kisye still hadn't returned for his supper, she became restless. She had been on edge all afternoon, her senses tweaked, but she could not name her dread.

So she departed from her usual precaution of avoiding travel abroad here in darkness, and set out for the center of the hot, dusty city. She was hoping – praying – that she would encounter 'Kisye along the familiar route.

She kept the hood of her deep cowl up over her head, knowing that in the dusky dark her paleness could not easily be concealed – Arusha was more provincial than Dodoma, its citizens more apt to superstition. She ducked around small groups struggling to their homes as she raced over the dusty cobblestones. She turned down the short cul-de-sac where 'Kisye set up his wares in a busy corner of the market, an angled niche between a textile merchant and a spice vendor. It was quiet, neither of the neighboring proprietors remained as late as her husband; they were gone before the call to prayers sounded from the mosques.

Her feet slowed as she approached the blind turn that would

lead to the stall and she listened for him. When he worked, whether alone or with customers, he often hummed cheerfully. It was dark back here; no lantern blazed forth.

Kusini assumed he was not there. She could not detect his signature energy, but she felt something. And it smelled wrong, different from her previous visits. Strangely, she could pick out the sharp scent of lantern oil, so strong that she suspected someone had spilled it. But that scent was layered over a second, darker one, something that her now racing mind was trying to recognize, wanting nothing more than to turn back because she knew it well.

"*Light*," she whispered, holding her thumbs together and raising her hand to call her magic to illuminate the space.

What she saw in that moment she would wish to unsee for the rest of her days. Suddenly, a woman was wailing somewhere in the market, a woman with Kusini's own voice.

Her beloved 'Kisye lay broken on the stones, seemingly drowned in a sea of gore – his own blood. It was everywhere, splashed in great arcing gouts over the walls, his precious sculptures scattered, his workbench broken and overturned.

One eye was open, unfocused and unseeing, the other swollen and crusted with blood. His lip was split, his clothes were torn, and whatever violence had been expended, one of his sandals lay alone on the stones of the path, some distance from him, where it must have come to rest following the force of its ejection from his foot.

She sank to her knees next to his motionless form, unmindful of the blood that immediately soaked her abaya and found her skin. It was cooling and coagulating, and it had stained scarlet his perfect curls. She placed a shaking hand atop his head, knowing the end had come and gone.

Ignoring the state he was in, she stretched out over him, soaking him further with her tears as she tried to cover him, hold him, as if she could console him and he would get up and come back home with her.

Something was very wrong with his form, and her hands slid

strangely over his shoulder. Then she knew – they had hacked off his arm.

Her grief was redoubled by the realization. They had come for him and he had been alone. Had he called for her? Perhaps so; her entire purpose in her long life had been to prevent such tragedies where she was able, but she had utterly failed her own Love. She examined his market stall with renewed sadness and dismay.

'Kisye was a large, strong man. They had come for him and he had fought them. They had held him, hurt him, maimed him, and still he had resisted. The bloody patterns on the stones and the walls of the enclosure told a story; he had been bleeding out from the fatal wound and still he fought. He had been in agony – the victim's suffering was thought to increase the power of the sacrificed limb – and still he fought. Somewhere, perhaps still nearby, there were men yet covered in his blood, with their stolen harvest, ready for a buyer who was surely readying the ritual to make the potion, unwilling to dirty his own hands. And still.

She put her own bloody hands over her open mouth and howled to the heavens in a murderous rage she could ill afford. She did not want to leave him exposed, neither could she transport him through the streets as he was – they were both still – always – targets.

She stood up slowly, unsteadily, and swallowed hard to control her nausea. She refused to let her body rebel in such a way. "He is our husband," she admonished herself, and was surprised at the volume of her voice in the small space.

The sounds of Arusha crept back into her consciousness, and she calculated that she could wrap 'Kisye in a shroud to get him home, but she had nothing at hand that she could use to cover him.

"*See it not*," she whispered, crossing her thumbs and placing a spell over him, she felt her power blanket the space, and she took her leave.

Kusini was aware that she could be watched and followed, too, so she took her time returning home. She wandered in seemingly random circles, forcing herself to take a circuitous route back to the dwelling, as 'Kisye had often insisted they do. The night was unusually cool, but in step with her grief, and even the stars seemed out of place she felt so lost.

So great was her abiding anguish that she failed to notice the wraithlike figure that followed, haltingly, in her wake.

<h1 style="text-align:center">47</h1>

SHE APPROACHED THE SMALL ALLEYWAY that led to the home with her usual caution, and slipped like a shadow through the gate and up the stone steps to their doorway. She peered briefly from each of the windows, a habit she was unable to shed, but saw nothing of concern in the streets below.

She disdained the lantern, as was her custom, preferring to work by feel, and she knew the place in her heart. It was a game she and 'Kisye had shared, a sweet nighttime ritual that was both intimate and precautionary. It kept stray passers-by from glimpsing them through a window, and always felt like a secret they kept for each other, with gentle touches as they completed their respective evening tasks before reuniting in their bed.

Kusini worked quickly, stripping linens from their bed to wrap 'Kisye in so she could move him from that awful place where he had suffered unimaginable insult. The soft, slapping sound of the gate against the stones caused her to stand upright, listening as if with her whole body to that familiar, but now ominous, sound.

The gate hinge was loose, and if the latch were not secured properly, it would cause the gate to swing and strike the stones; it had happened many times before. Had she failed to latch it completely in her haste and her grief? She felt not. She would have heard the gate swinging and scraping before she reached the door at the top of the steps, and there was really no breeze to rattle it now. No, the sound was new.

Before she could decide whether she had been followed or if it was simply an oversight, she heard a strange shuffling sound, and a scraping noise from the courtyard below. It was almost a random sound, as if someone unfamiliar with the house were casting about in the darkness below. She thought she heard a muffled moan, but could not be certain.

Her fright and panic were unusual, she knew, as it was unlikely that her magic could be successfully challenged here, in her home. But the trauma of seeing 'Kisye broken on the stones was making her understandably fragile, and even the best of spells was no precaution against certain evils, like the Morningstar. Even another witch doctor could overcome her with its assistance, and perhaps it was one of these who had commissioned the robbery of her husband's arm.

She heard nothing for some time after that, and began to assume that she'd been hearing things, her frayed senses causing her imagination to play tricks on her, or that perhaps it was only a disturbance caused by some small nocturnal animal. She turned back to her intended tasks, readying herself to set out again into the night, when she heard another sound.

It was the scraping of a footstep on the stairs outside, followed by a strange slapping, and then the scrape once again, and the sounds were purposeful now, coming ever nearer as whomever it was advanced upward to the doorway. Instinctively, Kusini drew deeper into the rooms, backing against the furthest wall from the doorway, feeling a small ledge at the small of her back. It reminded her that 'Kisye's work chest was to her left, with his many small carving tools, one of which had a wickedly sharp blade like a filleting knife. Without taking her eyes from the door, she slid open the drawers one by one until she found the small tool by feel, curling her fingers around the smooth cool handle carefully and quietly.

When the shuffling, agonized approach ended, and she could

hear that last step up to the landing, all became quiet. There was no further sound from the doorway, as if the being outside had paused to listen, or reflect. After what seemed an eternity, the door was rattled, tentatively at first, and then more purposefully. Kusini had not bothered to latch it, knowing that she would be leaving again soon after she had arrived.

Finally, the handle was turned, once, twice, unsuccessfully, as the attempts of a child who is working out how to open a door for the first time. Kusini cocked her head and narrowed her eyes, puzzled.

Repeatedly, the door was attempted without success, and her curiosity drew her off the back wall of the dwelling, and she stepped through the central alcove into the room that faced the street. Whoever was at the door was unable to open it, for whatever reason, even though it was unsecured. They continued to attempt to open it, unsuccessfully, and then began to bump against it, probably in some frustration, but there was little force. Kusini heard again that soft moan, this time she could sense the despair in it. Yet her feet would not move any closer to the door, she was frozen in place, waiting for an outcome she could not foresee.

The voice, when it came, was a piteous, strangled thing. It spoke her name with a plaintive, searching cry, "*'Sini-ma*, Kusini…"

Whoever was at the door knew her name, which was shocking enough, but only one person used that term of endearment, and her legs felt like water, as if the bones inside could no longer hold her. Still, she went to the door, indeed pressed herself right up against it, and leaned her face against the rough, painted wood, closing her eyes, as afraid to open it as not.

The sounds on the other side of the door increased suddenly, as if sensing her presence, but still the door was not opened, the handle was turned slightly, but with insufficient force to get inside.

"*'Sini-ma, tafadhali*, Kusini, *tafadhali*," the voice pleaded once more. "*Kile kinachotokea kwangu?*" it asked, wanting to know what was happening.

The whole exchange was so piteous that Kusini's heart surged, though she still did not understand what was happening herself, and when next the handle moved, she helped it through its full turn, and the door opened, and as she had both feared and hoped, her beloved, broken 'Kisye stood on the step.

48

KUSINI SANK TO HER KNEES. Seeing him standing at the door was even more disturbing than seeing him lying destroyed on the stone floor of his market stall. His right eye was still encrusted with gore, swollen shut, and his other eye was unfocused and cloudy, with bright hemorrhage around the iris. The darkness of his appearance was deceptive; it was the blood which had dried, leaving him with the appearance of a shade. Her eyes were drawn to the missing limb, which he seemed unaware of for now, but she could see the reason he had been unable to breach the door – his right hand hung down uselessly, likely broken in the struggle. One foot was bare and one shod, as she had found him, and that explained the strange slapping shuffle of his step on the stairs.

'Kisye responded in kind, sinking to his knees across the threshold from her, a grotesque mirroring of her pose. His full lips were split open, and he leaned toward her, rocking desperately, again repeating that pitiful cry, wanting her to explain what was happening. *"Kile kinachotokea kwangu?!* What is happening to me, Kusini, please?!"* His lament seemed to reach the heavens, and her heart was utterly shattered at the fear and anguish in it.

She reached out, forgetting any concern that his cries could wake others nearby, only wanting to help him, and pulled his broken body into her arms, unmindful of the gore, and rocked with him until his sobs of fear subsided somewhat, but his minute struggles continued. Meanwhile, in her confusion, she wondered, hoping against hope, whether she had missed some sign of life in her initial grief, and she leaned her body into his, her own sobs mingling with his, when she realized he had no heartbeat, and was drawing no breath with which to make his cries. It was not the first time in her long life that she was confronted with something which she was unable to comprehend, but it was certainly the worst.

And when it was ultimately impossible to reassure him, for she had no words to draw on, she crossed her thumbs and resolutely said, "*Sleep.*" Only then was he drawn down into stillness, and she was thankful that her magic worked for him – she had not been certain it would.

Knowing that her own sleep would not be soon in coming, she arranged his broken limbs inside the doorway, secured the door, and wept anew.

<h1 style="text-align:center">49</h1>

MORNING'S LIGHT WAS EVEN LESS kind to her husband's battered form, and with a deep sadness for all the memories she was leaving behind, Kusini prepared to travel back out of the world around them and return to wandering abroad, this time out of necessity, realizing that it would be unwise to stay in town. She had to return them to the countryside, where they could hopefully escape detection and where she would have time to make sense of what was happening.

She packed up as much food as she could carry, and looked with regret upon 'Kisye's makeshift terrace garden, knowing it would wither in the heat and much of his delicious produce would be lost to seed. She closed up the shutters, and packed his carving tools and paintbrushes, unsure if they would ever see use again. She knew that his other wares in the marketplace would be lost to them.

'Kisye himself was quiet, having regressed into a sort of stupor that she could not explain. He had given up asking questions, for which she was grateful, because she had no answers for him. Other than her spell-induced sleep, he had since remained wakeful, and watchful in a strange and disturbing way. His eyes followed her every movement with a kind of feral interest that was increasingly uncomfortable to her, and so out of character for him that it distressed her even more.

Most disturbing of all was the job of concealing him enough to travel. She took her time cleaning the blood away from his face and rinsed most of it from his hair, which she knew would carry the crimson staining for some time to come. The pallid color of his already pale skin was disturbing, and he was marred by the bruising of his beating. The raw, rough edges of the stump of his arm repelled her and reminded her constantly of her failure to keep him safe, but her attempts to clean and dress the wound did not seem to hurt him, for which she was grateful. Ultimately, she knew there would be enough flesh to cover the bone, but the wound would need to remain open for a bit to prevent infection, which was her own absurd concession to whatever denial she held to; the dead could not sustain disease.

His skin remained somewhat cooler than was normal, and there were still no signs of life, no return of a heartbeat. In a painful mockery of their early courtship, she was finally obliged to wrap him head to foot in bandage cloth made from strips harvested from their bedsheets in order to travel, as his appearance would surely draw unwanted attention. She didn't want anyone to lay eyes on her once-beautiful husband in fear or disgust, but in her innermost heart she knew that she also was relieved not to have to look upon him herself. His limbs still did not function in graceful concert as they always had, and his broken foot flopped uselessly with each step he took, but he remained able to walk. She had risked returning to the market in the pre-dawn hours to retrieve his other sandal so that he could be shod for the journey.

They left that night. Travel was slow, and she was pleased to see that little Yabluu followed along, albeit reluctantly. The blue bird would land on Kusini's shoulder, whichever was farthest from 'Kisye, and peer quietly around Kusini's head, but she refused to approach him, and he seemed not to notice his little friend's distress. As the trip progressed, Yabluu disappeared for longer stretches, and if she approached them at all, she remained in a nearby tree, safely out of reach, suggesting she felt some danger.

Kusini had to admit, she felt it too. By the third day of their trip, he had refused the fruits and root stews she had offered, obviously unsure whether he needed food at all. But there was something in his manner that made her feel he *was* hungry.

Furthermore, his jerking movements had all but disappeared, but rather than returning to his former athletic gracefulness, his actions were almost stealthy, slow and purposeful, in a way that reminded her uncomfortably of the big cats on the high plains of her childhood. His eyes no longer exhibited their former involuntary movements, and she was left with little doubt that he could see, and see well.

And those eyes had changed. At first glance, she had thought it because the bruises of his trauma were clearing, but instead, she soon realized it was that his eyes were no longer the jewel-like amber color they had always been, rather they were the glittering red of some wild animal.

Still, he did not rest, but she needed to, so when they stopped for the day in the shelter of a stand of acacia, she was unsure how to get the sleep she required because she did not feel safe. It was as if he was seeing her in a whole new way, and her flesh was crawling with apprehension.

But even she had no magic to resist her own exhaustion, and feeling a significant amount of guilt, she bespelled the space around them. Once done, she kept her thumbs crossed for her own protection, feeling not a small amount of guilt, and went to sleep.

At some point she was jolted awake to find him pulling her arms apart, knowing the secret of her spells. Her distress was not transmitted to him by touch, it seemed; while he had been less affected by this tactile defense previously, he appeared to be experiencing no discomfort from it at all in this new state. Now she was truly afraid, and 'Kisye seemed to sense this. With an interest that she didn't like, his eyes met hers. He half crawled over her where she lay, then sniffed the air, frankly predatory.

As he looked down at her, something in the depths of his eyes was not unlike the *Nyoka*, and they glittered with a frightening satisfaction. Then he smiled, but there was nothing of Ambakisye in that smile, and she shuddered.

Since her personal magic did not seem to be deterring him, she decided that one of Suhuba's old lessons might, and she reached for her spear, using it as leverage by getting it between them and using it to throw him from her. Surprise was on her side, and she was able to escape the trees, but she resisted the urge to run, also a valuable lesson from her father. Predators love the chase almost as much as the capture, and surely that was what her husband had become, to her great despair.

She waited, squinting in the sunlight until she remembered to pull her hood up, so she could better see his approach, but he remained watchful and still on the ground where she had landed him. She waited some while, but he didn't move, so she ventured closer. She did not sense a trap, but remained cautious, and when she reached the boundary of the shade, she stopped.

He lay panting on the ground, in obvious distress that was well out of proportion to the force she had used. She took another step into the shadows, and saw that he was cowering from her, but not in fear. Something of her husband had returned, whether from her retaliation or what, she could not say. He held up a hand in warning, and in a piteous tone, said, "No, leave me."

She could see something warring in the depths of those eyes, whatever feral hunger was now driving him was struggling with the higher mind that had built a life with her. She wanted nothing more than to comfort him, but before she could reach him, he pushed away from her and rolled to his feet with some semblance of his former grace, and sprinted away across the plain, his hurts of a few days prior seemingly gone.

She dropped the spear and gave chase, but it was useless. Her long limbs and considerable pace could not match his, and she suspected that some of his own speed was now unnaturally augmented.

She called and called to him, wandering aimlessly in the direction he had taken, but the only answer was the whispering breeze as it stirred the grasses, and the disturbed calls of many birds, but Yabluu's voice was not among them.

Not wanting to give up but still in need of rest, she nearly collapsed in exhausted heartbreak many hours later, the sun an orange ball descending in the west. Knowing there were many predators about, now one for which she had no defenses, she climbed into the nearest tall tree, a precaution she had not taken since her long-ago childhood, and cried herself to sleep.

50

LIGHTNING LIT THE EASTERN HORIZON, crackling around her in the heat, and the rolling thunder brought Kusini fully awake. She watched as the white arcs dashed toward the ground and lit the landscape in stark relief, but no real rain fell. Far off in the distance, she saw fires burning on the dry plains, and prayed to *Ngai* for mercy she wasn't sure she deserved.

As the sky lightened and morning drew near, she could see that the fires had burned themselves out, and she could hear birdsong from the trees around her. There was still no sign of Yabluu, but her beloved 'Kisye had returned, and he sat at the base of the tree, disheveled and despondent. As she climbed down, he peered up at her and she could see only bewilderment and confusion in his eyes. The bandages she had placed so lovingly hung from his neck and arms in bloody tatters, and his mouth and chest were smeared with blood.

When she reached the ground, she looked him over carefully, concerned about the blood because she wondered if some of it was his. He was in a terrible state, with deep scratches on his forearms and one particularly nasty gouge on the left side of his neck, another on his thigh. The redness was gone from his eyes, along with that feral, hungry expression, and he no longer scented the air or exhibited any predatory behavior.

He didn't speak, but when she reached out to him he leaned into her abaya and clung like a frightened child. He appeared exhausted, and the open wound at the end of his maimed arm looked terrible. She held very still, allowing him to hold onto her, and eventually he allowed her to move away; apparently he was satisfied she would remain nearby.

She collected their belongings, and he shadowed her closely, keeping her in sight and within reach. She felt terrible for him, and was unsure how to really comfort him, or if there was even a way to help someone understand this outcome.

Finally, she coaxed him to sit still so she could address his injuries. The wounds to his neck and arms appeared to have been made by a feline predator; the neck injury in particular suggested the shape and size of Suhuba's facial scars. But the edges of the slash marks were straight and did not appear to have caused much, if any bleeding. The scratches on his forearms were certainly much more superficial, but these, too, did not appear to have bled.

There was blood around his mouth, and she got a horrible feeling that perhaps the animal that had caused this damage had come out the worse in its battle with her husband. Perhaps these were not defensive wounds at all, but wounds he had sustained as a hunter.

She looked him over again carefully, and he watched her patiently and mutely. She asked, "Did you find something to eat?" She already knew the answer, but still he did not talk to her, merely showed her his teeth in a slow grimace, which were now stained with the blood of whatever he had eaten. Again, this was not a threatening gesture, rather was akin to a childlike demonstration of what had been done, and he shook his head and turned his eyes away as if ashamed.

She stroked his curls gently to comfort him, to let him feel her love and concern. "You were hungry. I am sorry I didn't know how to help you. It must have been very frightening for you."

His eyes confirmed this, and he made a sound like a soft moan; he had acted out of instinct and now was both repulsed and more than a little guilty about what he had done. He, unlike her, had never had to live off the land, had never been subject to Mother Africa's oldest adage: eat or be eaten. He still carried the vestiges of a protected life within city walls, and it could not have been an easy transition.

She cleaned him up, coaxing him to drink water that she wasn't entirely certain he needed, and replaced the bandages that had been destroyed in his madness. When she was finished, she tried to compel him to rest, but her small magics worked poorly on him now, and the best he could achieve was a kind of mumbling, fitful trance that lasted no more than several minutes. She knew they needed to move on, so she stood motionless on the cattle road until her feet led her onward into the quiet morning, and he silently followed behind her

On the second night to follow, as she approached Lake Manyara and the soda flats to the south, she realized they were being shadowed. She only caught glimpses of fluttering movement on the dark plains behind her, but there was no sense of accompanying danger, and she suspected that their small companion was Yabluu. The moon was near full, lighting the moving grasses as a hot wind swept across the plateaus.

Kusini kept moving, using the relative brightness of the moon to navigate into the no-man's land between Manyara and Eyasi, to a hidden valley that opened out onto a large floodplain once fed by the Wembere River. This flat plain was surrounded by rolling hills and large trees that obscured it from the cattle roads to the north, and she knew the area was served year-round by a spring that flowed throughout the dry season, fed by underground aquifers between the two lakes, the only potable water between the soda flats and salt plains of Eyasi.

It was here that she set up camp and waited, delaying building any fire, but gathering water and storing their belongings. It was here that she had intended to bring 'Kisye all along, an accessible area just off the road, with a nearby water source, but also simple to obscure from other people and animals. Not even the tribesmen of the northern plains knew that there was clean water to be had within a day's walk of the largest clearing – she had discovered it during her years of wandering by following animals who haphazardly found their way into the valley from the south.

Their path from the city had been a very indirect looping trek, and they were only a bit more than a day's walk from Arusha, nearly due west of it, with Lake Manyara in between. She recognized the small form that came floating down the wash through the valley and out into the clearing, landing on her shoulder for only a moment before shooting up into the shelter of the trees. Little Yabluu, their constant companion, had caught up to them.

"*'Sini-ma,*" 'Kisye suddenly begged, and his voice was soft and bewildered, but coherent. She waited for him to say more, but he didn't; he simply sank down onto his knees and waited.

She left him there, knowing she had a decision to make. To delay it, and whatever there was to face next, she began to gather brush and downed wood, waiting until dawn's light crept to the edge of the eastern sky and then starting a fire.

Still he did not move or speak, but she could feel him watching her, and she set up camp as though all were normal, though she felt nothing ever would be again. When she realized her hands were shaking, she walked up the rise to mouth of the valley and listened carefully. She called her spear to her outstretched fingers with a silent command and stripped to the waist to free her arms before wading quietly into the grass. The day was dawning hot, and she kept quiet, searching the red grass tufts and the base of trees until she found what she was searching for some distance closer to the spring. Grebes had nested there, and she tracked them in the direction of the water, downing one that was distracted by its own feeding. Its dull plumage had made it more difficult to see, but it meant that the bird was not part of a mating pair, which gave her some comfort that she wasn't orphaning one of the chicks that were about to hatch.

Kusini returned to the campsite to find that 'Kisye had started to tremble, and she could see he was fighting off that same instinctual ferocity that he'd had a few days earlier. Shrewdly he watched her clean the bird, but crept nearer and nearer to her as she did so, until she was forced to relinquish it to his trembling hands. He looked at her, his eyes red once more, but still they held a silent plea. When she didn't move, he waved weakly at her, not wanting her to remain while he ate, so she turned her back and went back to the spring to gather water, trying not to hear the sounds he made as he took the meat apart.

He was much more composed when she returned, but they both recognized this was the beginning of a cycle they would have to repeat in order to keep the beast inside at bay. She was encouraged to see that Yabluu was inching ever closer to him, at that moment perched on a branch within his reach, should he choose to stand, and Kusini held on to that gesture made by the little blue bird, remembering all that 'Kisye had taught her about their behavior. She clung to it as a sign of hope that she did not really feel.

51

'KISYE ADJUSTED SLOWLY TO THE loss of his arm; its appearance repulsed him, but Kusini tended it, keeping it clean as scar tissue formed over it, at first looking like a pulpy mess, but eventually this scabbed over, and finally new skin grew over the end of what remained. This version was neater to look at, but was no less repulsive to him – indeed, it angered and saddened him even more.

He felt helpless all the time; even as he began to alter his habits and adjust to this new reality, he never felt whole. And during this transition, Kusini asked for more and more of his assistance with the construction of their dwelling, using the strength he had in his remaining arm to help her construct a round hut in the center of the clearing, using stout tree limbs as supports. Taking her time, she was able to fashion a roof of thick branches and thatch made from interwoven strands of *nyekundu*. Although 'Kisye could help her balance on his shoulders, lifting her easily with the augmented strength he possessed following his change, he was unable to do many things that had been simple tasks before.

Meanwhile, she hunted nearby to keep him fed with blooded meat, but was averse to leaving him long enough to secure larger game on the northern plains. She noticed when he went without meat for even a day, the feral eyes and predatory nature that she had seen so soon after his change returned, and loss of control came with it. She tried to teach him the finer points of hunting, but it was contrary to his nature, and the critical skill of making the kill did not come naturally to him. He was a reluctant hunter, and she knew that it was unwise to allow him to deteriorate to the point where his instincts overcame his inborn characteristic gentleness.

It was providential when she came upon a Kikuyu goatherder passing across the plains to the north of the cattle road. His flock numbered in the hundreds, and she smiled in relief, immediately seeing the answer to a prayer. She used suggestion and magic to convince him to turn over several of his goats and impaired his memory of the entire encounter. As she sent him away in ignorance, his remaining animals followed, bleating softly. *"Prosper,"* she whispered, paying him in kind if not in coin. She wished him well and watched him disappear across the plains to the east.

The small herd of goats became a self-sustaining source of milk and meat, and allowed them to settle into a routine that did not require hunting. It was a routine which did not burden Kusini, a routine which did not ask of 'Kisye that he become something he was not.

She followed his struggles to regain some independence, watched him vacillate between anger and despair, and soon realized that he did not fully grasp the extent to which he had been harmed. She tried, tragically, to explain it to him, in the days when he was finally gaining some control, but it was too soon, and he was unable to accept what she was telling him. There was something in the depths of his eyes that told her he already knew, that too many things were changed other than his lost arm.

His eyesight was immeasurably improved; his visual acuity should have been a blessing after a lifetime of near blindness, but the appearance of the world around him was unexpected. It asked little of his imagination, and he had lost any desire to create.

He realized that he could try to carve by trial and error, securing promising pieces of wood between his legs and using the small hand tools that Kusini had salvaged from the house in Arusha, but the forms that resulted were distorted and odd, and something was still lost inside him. Regaining his creativity would ultimately be his most difficult hurdle, but Kusini recognized that it would likely require him to make peace with what he had become.

He made gains in other areas and was successful in building a fence to pen in the goats by securing posts and then balancing the crossbeams in such a way that he could lift one end into place at a time and anchor these beams with the strength in his remaining arm. Kusini watched him improve by increments. With each small success, his confidence grew.

She gave up her wandering, knowing that she had inadvertently created a situation that exposed them both. She had to admit he was still too dangerous to leave alone. It had taken nearly a decade for him to develop a semblance of normalcy with the arm, and adjust to his diet, and still his irrepressibility, his cheerful disposition, did not return. There were days when she feared it never would.

He did better when he had projects to work on, as regaining skills within this new reality gave him challenges that provided necessary distraction. So she asked him to cook for her, and this restored the blessing of his delicious meals, much to their mutual delight. Although he required only raw meat as the staple of his diet, he continued to enjoy cooking for her and watching her eat. Such exercises of creativity seemed to be helping him to heal emotionally.

But she could see that he still felt powerless, and he could not go very long without eating just to maintain a tenuous control over other appetites, and she could tell this repulsed him. Still he would not face the gravity of his more fundamental change, and many more years passed. She missed the closeness they had shared, and the laughter and intimacy that had blessed them so briefly. She was bereft of his touch and his quiet passion, for as a living man he had spoiled her with the sweetness and intensity of it. Now she bore the absence of his touch like a silent martyr, understanding that he was bearing his own losses with the uneasiest of grace.

Finally, she began to believe that he was rediscovering more of himself. He would even occasionally smile, Yabluu was riding on his shoulder in the afternoons, and she noticed that he would touch her, tentatively, lovingly, as he had in the earliest days of their courtship. It gave her hope, until, in an attempt to seduce her, when he realized his body was not responding as it had in life, and his anguish flooded back in. It was this that forced him to face the unthinkable, in the most cruel and unimaginable way, given the progress he had made. She tried to comfort him, but there was no way to placate the pain of the event. It was too great a loss, and the situation stripped away the last of his denial. It was a setback of incalculable dimension.

He refused to eat, despite her pleas, and plunged again into madness. She endured his attacks, managing to subdue him with blood magic and forcing the meat into him at the most desperate of times, hearing the *Mjusi's* laughter in her head. For weeks, this cycle continued, until, in a moment of clarity, he asked her, "Why don't you just kill me?"

"Because you are my husband, and I promised to stand beside you in this journey. I waited centuries to find you, and I do not want to face the centuries ahead without you," she sobbed, finally breaking down in despair.

"Your husband is gone," he spit the words back at her, not bothering to control his hateful tone. "I cannot change this, cannot protect you from the monster that I have become. Why do you do this?" he demanded.

"Because it was *you*, long ago, that taught me that having love was the power that would protect against the worst magic," she explained. "I believed it then, and I believe it now. I will hold on to what you told me until there is nothing left of us. But I am still here, and you are still here, and I need your wisdom to be true."

She wasn't sure if or how these words could make a difference, but at least 'Kisye stopped trying to give up, stopped fighting her efforts to keep him going. He learned the best way to time his eating so as to minimize any desperate uncontrolled urges, and this made the most of his hours of emotional freedom to do other tasks he enjoyed. He may not have been living for himself, but perhaps was doing it for Kusini's sake. While this was an improvement, she knew it would not be enough to sustain him, and if something did not change, it would all be for naught.

52

GIVEN ENOUGH TIME, EXPECTATIONS CAN change, and this was as true for 'Kisye as for anything else. He eventually settled into his new reality, but his wife knew he was still incompletely healed. He appeared to embrace their simple life in the countryside, for a time trading his paints and sculpting for physical labors, building rain barrels for her, and treehouses that he adapted to hang from the most precarious of branches, which prevented snakes from reaching the birds.

He took up his own machete, sharpening it to a razor's edge, and using it to keep the boundaries of the clearing defined. He mowed a path down to the spring to make it easier for her to carry water during the dry months. It was from the spring that he returned one day with a rare smile on his face, leaning into one of the windows of the hut and calling out for Kusini.

She saw his expression and returned it with a quizzical one of her own.

"Come outside, you have to see what I found by the water." He couldn't hide his delight.

Kusini emerged from the hut and discovered him stroking Bahati's nose gently, the little giraffe nuzzling him enthusiastically until she saw Kusini, and then she reluctantly abandoned her attentions to 'Kisye to cross the yard and greet her. Yabluu chirped sharply from the cupola of the thatch roof, stingy and jealous of 'Kisye's attentions.

"Hello, Bahati," Kusini laughed. "How did you find us?" Seeing the expression on 'Kisye's face, she explained that she and the giraffe were old friends. While she told him the story of how Bahati got her name, he listened in fascination. "I don't know why I never told you that story."

Bahati turned back to Kisye, and Kusini's hand briefly slid down her ribs as the giraffe moved away, and that was when she noticed something odd. She followed the animal across the yard, and while Bahati was distracted by 'Kisye scratching her nose, she confirmed it. Bahati had no heartbeat. Kusini placed her head against the little giraffe's chest to listen, but there was no sound at all.

'Kisye noticed this and mimicked her, a question forming in his eyes. He reached the same conclusion that she did; both he and the giraffe had been similarly affected by her magic, although she herself had no idea why or how it had come to be.

If the mystery bothered Kusini, it answered the questions that she'd had about Bahati. Of course, she would not grow any bigger, and it explained her recovery from the awful injuries that Kusini had witnessed when she had found her near the watering hole.

For 'Kisye, it was the catalyst to his ultimate recovery. Bahati - beautiful, inquisitive, and intrusively affectionate – became the balm that soothed his anger and erased his disgust for what he had become. That day in Kusini's mind marked the beginning of his emotional healing, and more and more of his cheerful disposition returned, until she was confident that she had him back.

He constructed a small outbuilding across from the hut, enclosed on three sides to keep most of the elements out, and equipped it with a makeshift workbench. He returned to his carving, Yabluu constantly at his shoulder, singing in satisfaction that Bahati could not fit within the small space. He carved a bit each day, and his work became ever more detailed and realistic, displaying accurately the talent that he rediscovered.

Greater numbers of birds came, some to occupy the various houses he had constructed, and others roosting in his workshop as they had in his market stall. He kept the red grass in the clearing cut low to discourage predators, and was ever vigilant of them. Kusini was touched at his efforts to protect them all.

Bahati made herself as much necessity as nuisance, nudging the goats out to find the red grass shoots on the hill, and chasing them back down to the clearing when the sun sank into the west, ignoring their bleating protests. She did not seem a bit concerned about Yabluu's persistent efforts to distract her from 'Kisye's affections. Of interest, she did not seem to require any special diet, continuing to strip leaves from the trees, or, when she thought she could get away with it, stealing clumps of the plants that Kusini grew inside the hut. It was not unusual for Kusini to look up from mending or preparing breads and find the giraffe with her head in one of the windows.

Kusini could not get her to stop, and gave up trying to discourage the animal's behavior when she realized that 'Kisye was feeding her through the windows when Kusini wasn't looking. It was impossible to get angry at Bahati or her husband. Their connection fed something bigger that each seemed to need.

Eventually, 'Kisye returned to her with passionate intent, picking up the rhythms of their physical intimacy in new ways, clear in his desire to please her, learning that what he had thought of paramount importance was not necessarily what she needed from a lover. They found their way forward and became closer than they had ever been, their bond immeasurably strengthened in the crucible of adversity.

So it came to be that when Kusini's dreams and visions returned to plague her, and the screams of the innocent were brought to her in whispers on the south wind, she felt she could return to the countryside and continue her work with others who suffered, knowing 'Kisye would not be alone. She created a barrier of love and magic that she believed would keep what she loved within, and evil out. She thought it was safe.

53

MORE BIRTHS, MORE DEATHS, MORE rescues, and more work than ever waited Kusini in her travels.   She dedicated herself to it as she had before.   There were far more children born with her condition than before, more surviving to adulthood due to her efforts to protect them and educate their families.   There was, in some parts, a further dampening of superstitions that were becoming diluted by outside beliefs that came with the colonists and merchants who brought more and more of the outside world into their lives.

Kusini was greeted by watchers along farm tracks and cart trails at many points of her journey, led onward to hiding places and small, remote villages that sometimes consisted of a single-family line that had hidden evidence of differences best kept secret from outsiders, and always, something awaited her blessing or intervention.   Outside a coffee plantation near Karatu, she was approached by an elderly woman on the post road one summer night.

The woman introduced herself as Zalika, and bowed low before Kusini could stop her with protests that she should pay such an elder homage, not the other way around.   But Zalika knew of the Sorceress, and said she had awaited her arrival on that road for many nights, hiding from other travelers, such as European traders and other unsympathetic parties.

Kusini was surprised when the woman said her daughter had spoken of the Sorceress from a pregnant dream. Zalika admitted that her family line had some who were born with a special sight, and her daughter had always seemed to be one who dreamed things that later happened. She had told her mother that she was to bear a girl-child, and must be attended at the birth by the Sorceress who wandered the plains. She had not told her mother that she had seen the whiteness of the baby, and she did not tell her mother that in her dreams she was absent in the child's life. She had dispatched Zalika to wait and watch on the road; she knew the Sorceress would come to them.

Zalika's husband had died of illness as a young man, and she had held on to the plantation where they had worked side by side as children, before he chose her as his bride. Her children and their families now worked the land, and they had managed to keep the plantation prosperous despite the desires of outside interests to buy them out. Kusini admired the woman, and gladly followed her back to her home.

They arrived at dawn, and Kusini had been surprised and pleased at its privacy and beauty. Zalika's daughter was close to labor but very weak, unable to eat. Her baby was robust, moving well, but the young mother was ill, and Kusini worried that she would not survive the birth. When the baby arrived, bright as a beacon, white as Kusini, all but the young mother were surprised. But the strong matriarch scolded them all, insisting the child was her heir, and naming her for her brightness, after the morning sunshine, calling her Mwana'jua.

Kusini gave the baby to Zalika, because her daughter was fading, and nothing Kusini tried seemed to restore any lasting strength. When all that was left was prayer, the young woman took Kusini's hand, and said, "The goatherder brought plague to you and yours."

She was fading fast, but clung to Kusini's hand, feverish, seemingly delirious. As she slipped closer to death, she whispered, "I saw his eyes. They were not ours, and looked like coins."

This last gave Kusini a chill. She had returned home from her travels only a few weeks prior, and having found that all was well, had thus resumed her wandering, going where she was needed. Was it merely the raving of a dying girl, or something more prophetic?

Kusini fell asleep at the bedside, slept fitfully, and dreamt of the serpent-man who had tortured her as a girl. She awoke to a red sunrise and a surge of disquiet that she could not suppress. Zalika and the child were well, but the young woman had died during the night.

Kusini slipped out of the dwelling and pulled her garments around her, avoiding the road, and breaking her habit of traveling at night. *"See me not,"* she whispered to the wind, and set off across the plain toward Eyasi, and home.

By the time she reached the wash that led down to the little hut in the clearing, she was running, her abaya flying behind her like a red banner. The distress she felt was enormous, and its source appeared to be her home. She was momentarily relieved to find the barrier intact, but beyond it was a strange and dangerous quiet, and the air reeked of death and decay, which only fed her terror.

She took the small bend between the two hills that hid the clearing from the north, and found Bahati, her eyes rolling in silent terror, afraid to climb the hill. She bolted at the site of Kusini, and charged the barrier at full speed but could not breach the magic that contained her there. Kusini tried to catch her, tried to comfort her, but saw that she had been attacked, bitten repeatedly, and ultimately Bahati kicked out in such a way that Kusini was compelled to release her. The giraffe continued to crash into the unseen boundary, so Kusini whispered, *"Away,"* and Bahati was released from the clearing, disappearing up the hill on the run.

At the mouth of the wash, the stench hit her like a wall, and she saw the carcasses of dozens of goats, apparently having succumbed to some illness, as there were no signs of predation here. Nothing moved, nothing appeared to survive save the flies and maggots that fed on the decomposing bodies. There were no carrion birds, but these had been kept out by the spell.

The wedding cloth that she and 'Kisye had so lovingly made was askew, torn aside with some force, twisting in the doorway with the breeze. Before she could reach the hut, she saw that 'Kisye's workshop was in disarray, and she had a momentary flashback, as its appearance reminded her of the evening when she had discovered his body on the stones. Sculptures were strewn about, but her eye caught a break in the pattern, a single blue bird remained on the shelf, the lone bit of order in the chaos.

Kusini stepped closer and confirmed what she saw. Smart little Yabluu, hiding in plain sight, safe in the eye of the storm. The bird fluffed herself briefly when she saw Kusini, and all but fell from the shelf, unable to take flight because her previously unaffected wing had been broken. She did not bother to right herself, perhaps had no more energy to do so, and remained awkwardly off her feet. She raised her small head and tilted it to look at Kusini, who gathered her up. No sooner done but Yabluu buried her beak painfully in Kusini's hand, forcing her to drop the bird on the ground; Yabluu was responding to a greater threat.

Kusini stilled, sensing movement behind her, and she turned around when a low growl reached her ears. It was a bestial sound, wild, more frightening than the cough of the lions on the plain, but more akin to a man's throaty laugh. It came from her husband, who had cornered her in his workspace. She completed her turn but had no place to back up. She was trapped against his workbench, and there was nothing of her 'Kisye in the being that contemplated her coldly from a few feet away. He was hunched over, wild in every aspect of his bearing, because the dead and diseased goats had not been available for sustenance. Her barrier had held him here, starving, ravenous, and blinded with this madness.

His eyes glittered with feral intelligence, and not much else. He was drooling, and had gnawed his lips to tatters. He had a mark on his forehead that she tried to make sense of, and finally she realized in horror that it was a perfect imprint of one of Bahati's hooves. Such a blow would have killed a normal man.

He did not respond when she spoke his name, merely shook his head as though her voice brought him pain, and let out another gravelly moan, showing her his teeth. Kusini raised both hands out in front of herself, locking her thumbs in place, and began to step sideways, clearing the end of the workbench, and ultimately moving into the open space between the hut and the outbuilding. 'Kisye tracked her like prey, which she wanted, but she could see he would not wait the few seconds she needed to get her words out, and when he charged, she spoke. *"Flesh to flesh-"* she grunted, as his weight hit her at speed, carrying them both to the sunbaked earth. Yet she caught her breath and managed to finish the spell, barely holding him off as he snapped and snarled, trying to bite her, his fingernails already hooked into her skin, knowing if it didn't work she could lose this fight, *"- and flesh shall rest."*

She felt the surge of her power, and the force of it, as she sent it out and then struggled to draw it back to control any unintended consequences. The concussive force bounced her skull painfully against the ground, and she was disoriented for several seconds before she recovered, rolling to her feet. 'Kisye lay where he had fallen, thankfully unconscious and unmoving. She had no idea how much time she had, so she ran to the goats, covering her face with the folds of her garment to abate the smell of rot as she pulled the leads from two of them, their clouded eyes glaring blindly up at the sky.

She used the ropes to bind him physically with no time to spare, as he began struggling violently when she was securing the last of the knots, praying to *Ngai* they would hold. She sprinted down the path toward the spring, startling a young kudu who had stopped to drink. She called her spear to hand and leaped high in the air to anticipate its escape, and she and the animal fell back to earth together. She thanked little sister for this gift of life and dragged the meat back to the clearing.

54

SHE BURNED THE GOAT CARCASSES, and went in search of Yabluu, but the little bird had hidden herself, and would not be seen again for weeks. She fed 'Kisye chunks of blooded kudu meat until he stopped struggling against the ropes and trying to bite her fingers, then fed him more, and stroked his filthy curls to soothe him. She dragged him up against the wall of the hut and propped him there. She sat down beside him and leaned into him, trying to calm him with her nearness.

Night fell, and he sat quietly with her under the cold light of the stars. She jumped with surprise when he spoke. His voice was hoarse, and gravelly, and the words were mangled by the damage he had done to his lips. "The *Mjusi* came for me two weeks after you left. It was dressed like a goatherder, and it brought goats, offering to sell them. It didn't appear to be a tribesman but spoke our common language. Its goats were diseased. They died, and infected the others," he told her. "I couldn't eat the diseased flesh, and the madness was on me too soon to make other plans. I wasn't able to breach your spell, and I am grateful for that now. I cannot imagine what might have happened otherwise."

She said nothing, merely reached to remove his restraints, feeling guilty.

"Not yet, *mpenzi*," he told her softly. "Give it until morning. I need more meat, and I am exhausted. I haven't learned enough control. Just stay with me."

If what he said was true, he had been in that state for nearly ten days, deteriorating slowly and terrorizing Bahati and Yabluu. "How did you recognize it?" she asked quietly, unsure she wanted to know more, but needing to hear it.

"The eyes. It did not, perhaps cannot, disguise them," he told her, and then fell silent.

A short while later, when she thought he would say no more, he added, "I think the snakes were here as well, but that might have been a hallucination."

"No," Kusini shook her head, remembering her own dream. "It is more likely than not. The serpent is attracted to chaos and distress."

She got to her feet and went inside the hut to get what she would need to clean him up. It took her two days to get their home back in order, and another week to help him repair the damage to his workshop.

The goat ashes stank of ill magic, so she churned them with red clay mud and her own blood. Then she cast cowrie shells, white stones from the streambed, and the bones of a grebe that 'Kisye had eaten over them, purifying whatever evil had plagued the beasts, and restoring order to their home.

55

'KISYE RECOVERED PHYSICALLY MUCH MORE quickly than he recovered spiritually, and Kusini had to face a new reality. She could protect the home, and him, from outsiders by cloaking it, but the barrier she had created had disastrous results.

'Kisye was not a prisoner, nor did she think that any perception of the same would be of any help in allowing him to recover what he could of normalcy. She remembered his words of long ago, about love. Love had to trust what it could not know, so never again would she physically cage him in time or space. As she prayed to *Ngai* and *Olapa*, she had to have faith that the evidence of good in their world could balance the ill intent of the *Mjusi*. She realized its visit had been a blessing, of sorts. One that allowed her to grow even closer to her husband.

Never again would she restrain or restrict him in any way. To prove this, she knew talking was not necessary, and would matter less than deeds. So she took him with her on her next sojourn to the north, visiting the *Bantu* villages just east of the great lake, enjoying the travel that much more for having him with her. They returned leading several young goats, and burdened with large ripe melons that Kusini had bargained for. She shared them with the goats during the hot dusty days of travel back to the hidden hut on the plateau.

'Kisye remarked that he missed the taste of melon, formerly one of his favorite things to eat, and told her the story of the mysterious melon in the marketplace. He was surprised when Kusini laughed with delight. She said, "I don't know what it is about you, but my prayers always seem to be answered."

He was confused by this, until she explained that his melon had been her belated thank you for the very first sculpture he had given her. The rains had not lifted enough for commerce to resume in the market, and he had apparently recovered her gift moments after she had departed in a sort of despair at her thwarted attempt at gratitude.

"I can admit now that I wanted terribly just to see you again, and when I went to deliver the melon, I thought I might never get another chance, not just to thank you, but…" Kusini paused, unsure how to finish her thought, even all these years later. But he placed a gentle hand on the small of her back briefly, before reaching to offer her another piece of the melon; it was his way of telling her he understood. He watched her eat it with all the obvious pleasure it gave him to see her enjoy her food.

They made it back to their new home and this new reality unscathed, and went to work at survival; she was determined to hold on to the miraculous gift of their love no matter what form that reality might take. And he was determined to preserve it, and protect her at all costs, from all evils, all threats, even and especially the one he created.

now

56

KUSINI TURNED AWAY FROM THE turnips she was preparing to look for her kitchen scissors. She was unable to find the shears at hand, so she left the roots soaking in the sink and was about to go look for them among 'Kisye's art supplies, since he had a habit of "requisitioning" whatever he needed when a moment of inspiration struck. She had just finished drying her hands when a distant sound caught her attention, familiar but just far enough away that she was unable to fully confirm what she was hearing.

She still felt a bit fuzzy, having awakened that morning from a disturbing dream of being attacked. She had suffered some sort of a shock. It had stopped her heart – so real, as if she *heard* it happen. There had been no pain, but she had observed that while visions sometimes brought her physical pain, the hurts she suffered in dreams were oddly painless. Afterward, she had been lying in a field of flowers, as if she had witnessed her own death, and was now envisioning a funeral. The flowers were large and yellow, standing taller than she, which made the whole thing somewhat absurd. She had been unable to go back to sleep, but wasn't sure that the whole thing had not been some fitful nightmare unrelated to the visions that plagued her ever more often in these later days. There had been a cross, and a man in black, a holy man, but the details dissolved when she awoke, and she felt the sequence of events had been confused, as broken as her sleep.

She abandoned the hut, her chickens scattering at her feet in the lazy morning sunshine. It was already stifling, the humidity from the recent rains heavy in the balmy air. She walked out to the stand of acacia at the bottom of the hill and tilted her head to listen again; this time she picked up the unmistakable hum of a vehicle still some distance away.

Yabluu lit on her shoulder briefly with an excited chirp. "Yes, little bird, I hear it too." Kusini held out her finger, but Yabluu flitted up and away, soaring off toward the road. After a short while, Kusini expected to see a telltale dust cloud heralding the approach of the car, but the humidity was likely weighing down the clay enough that even the big all-terrain tires could scarcely stir up the surface.

Pulling her hood up over her head, she climbed the hill, still feeling much like the bride she had been so long ago, with all the same anticipation and delight at her husband's return. From the top of the rise, she could follow the red road from its approach in the distance to where it curved around the base of the plateau, making a backward question mark where it widened into the clearing in front of the hut.

Even though she could hear the motor, the truck remained out of sight for some while longer, and she waited for the grinding of the transmission as 'Kisye downshifted to make the turn at the rocky base of the plateau; the auditory signal that he was about to come into view. And so, he did, in his usual dramatic fashion, skidding around the turn, throwing mud off the back tires as they slid through the curve. After her long centuries, Kusini still strongly favored walking to any motorcar; she never consented to ride with him, so cavalier was he in his approach to the road, and she adamantly turned away any attempt he made to teach her to operate the vehicle.

While she doubted either of them would have trouble surviving a crash, they could still suffer, and 'Kisye's special needs might not be met, a catastrophe that she cared not to revisit. Nevertheless, she smiled when she saw him. His linen shirt was buttoned to his throat, and down to his wrist, as she insisted in the name of sun protection for his still delicate skin. In lieu of a hat he wore a loose turbaned blue headdress, a la *Lawrence of Arabia.* A few years before, on a rare trip to Dar Es Salaam, he had taken her to the cinema to see an encore presentation of the film. It had been subtitled in Swahili and Arabic, both of which she had ignored. She preferred to attempt to practice listening to it in English, a language of which she now had some rudimentary understanding. The cinematography was gorgeous, and she had to admit she had enjoyed it. She had her own reasons for being suspicious of many modern technologies.

Since then, 'Kisye had not bothered with hats, preferring the dramatic head covering of the Bedouin. To this, he had added modern black sunglasses (he had once told her the brand, something famous, but she could never remember – 'Kisye was fascinated with all things Western).

The International Scout he drove was recognizable for its boxy shape, but its color was indeterminate, probably having been many different things over the course of its half century of existence, in the endless cycle of paint-rust-repaint-blister-repeat that was the result of many rainy seasons and scorching equatorial days. These days, the predominant color was the rusty red of the ubiquitous clay soil, plus the gray of its primed undercoat beneath its latest layer of white; near the corners and inside the doors, one could see it had originally been a sandy olive green. Its canvas top had long since disintegrated, but she knew 'Kisye preferred the open top anyway.

He roared up the approach road to the hut and screeched to a halt at the base of the hill, flashing his dazzling smile at her. He gestured for her to come down and hop into the cab with him, but she shook her head and wagged a finger at him. He threw his head back and laughed his rich, booming laugh before starting up again, caroming around the curve and skidding sideways into the dooryard. The chickens scattered indignantly; the goats recognized the sound and wisely stayed in the far yard, wary of both vehicle and driver.

No sooner had the vehicle come to rest than little Yabluu, seemingly from nowhere, alighted gently on the roll bar and sang noisily, her little voice seeming to reprimand 'Kisye for his recklessness before she flitted onto his shoulder and quieted down. He offered his open palm as he climbed out of the truck, and she hopped onto it happily. He leaned his face close to her and blew softly to ruffle her feathers; she loved this ticklish affection. Once the ritual was complete, she soared up to her vantage point just under the lip of the cupola.

By the time he had unloaded the truck and pulled it around facing outward, Kusini had reached the bottom of the hill. He lifted the 25-gallon water reservoir with ease, setting it down next to the rain barrels, and moved his spare gas canisters away from the house. He caught the loop at the top of his rucksack on the middle finger of his remaining hand and half-turned to lift her off her feet with that arm, smiling at her satisfying shriek of laughter.

He kissed her and spun in slow lazy circles until she was dizzy; whether from his kisses or the motion, she couldn't tell. She simply clung to his strong shoulders until he set her down at the doorway and dropped the pack in a small puff of dust. She reached for his turban, but he shook his head gently. "I'm filthy, *'Sini-ma.*"

'Kisye stepped over to the wash-water barrel and removed the scarf and head covering, dropping them at his feet before undoing his buttons. He undid the one at his wrist with his teeth and stripped the shirt off, discarding it with his turban. He removed his sunglasses and hooked them into the loop of his rucksack before dunking his head and shoulders in the water and washing. He rubbed the dirt from the road from his neck and face vigorously, and came up blowing water into the shimmering air. He looked at Kusini lovingly, and then squinted those golden eyes mischievously before hitting the surface of the water with his open hand, soaking the front of her tunic, amused at her gasp of indignance.

Before she could scold him, he closed the distance between them and kissed her even more thoroughly, pushing her against the cool, shaded adobe wall of the hut. "Oh, you're soaked," he lamented falsely, pinning her against the rough exterior and pulling her leg up over his hip, inviting her up into his embrace. She wrapped her legs around his torso, feeling the denim waist of his dungarees through her linen harems. He cradled her weight in that strong arm by stabilizing her lower back, and she leaned back as his mouth tasted the salt at the base of her neck.

"I wonder why…" she murmured, her voice trailing off abruptly when he nipped her shoulder. He set her gently inside the door before stepping out of his boots, then carried her into the cool depths to properly show her how much he had missed her.

57

AT SUNSET, KUSINI FINISHED HER kitchen chores and went outside to secure the chickens for the night. She made a mental note to top off the water reservoir in the morning before she left for the villages on the high plains to the north and west.

Her chores done, she crossed the yard to the shed, where bright halogen light spilled out onto the ground. 'Kisye was working; he had invested in an industrial gas generator that powered worklights in this, his makeshift studio. One entire half of the shed was dedicated to this purpose, and the spots he had wired into the rafters mimicked daylight.

Kusini smiled when she reached the doorway. Her beloved was hunched over his workbench, carving something intricate under a mounted magnifying glass. He did not appear to notice her, and was humming the tune to *Mungu ibariki Afrika*, the Tanzanian national anthem. It made her smile; 'Kisye was not particularly patriotic, but he liked the tune very much and would sing the song lustily whenever they were in the city and he could catch the beginning of a soccer match on one of the ubiquitous miniature televisions in every market shop.

The goats had been brought in to their pen in the far corner of the shed for the night, but if the light bothered them, they showed no sign of it, having settled down contentedly to sleep. She could smell the sour apple and grain mash that 'Kisye had given them.

His voice startled her; of course, he knew she was there, despite his apparent indifference. "I forgot to tell you, I saw Bahati out on the post road. You may see her in your travels. It looked like she was heading in the direction of *Olduvai*."

Kusini had always been fascinated by cultural differences and language idiosyncrasies, and she was amused that the place that was now referred to as *Loduvai* or *Olduvai* Gorge had always been *Oldupai* to her. It still sounded strange to her ears when the old *Maa* word was erroneously replaced by centuries of changing dialect and usage.

"She is drawn to that place," she responded. "There is a magic to that area, like a strong pull."

'Kisye was quiet, so she added, "A powerful magic."

"Yours?" He inquired, tilting his head and taking his eyes off his work.

"No, not mine," she sighed.

"The *Mjusi*?" he asked it so frankly that she could no longer make eye contact. She glanced away.

"No. This is something else, something fundamental, something . . . elemental. Something essential and – and good," she concluded.

"Does it have anything to do with the skeleton that was found there?" 'Kisye asked, speaking her own suspicions aloud. But probably in the interest of still, even now, trying to protect him from it, she was unable to answer.

"Did she see you?" Kusini awkwardly changed the subject, and 'Kisye kindly pretended not to notice.

"Yep. I pulled into a turnout and she came right to the truck. I think she has forgiven me."

"Well, that's a relief," Kusini almost smiled.

"It only took one hundred years," he marveled with a twinkle in his eye. "She'll be happier to see you, but then, *I* am always happier to see you."

"What are you working on?" she inquired, wanting to be back on a more comfortable subject. She approached the workbench and could see that he had a small piece of balsa wood trapped between his bare feet, and it was well on its way to being something else. He steadied the wood with his feet and carved using a small stylet blade in his right hand. She could see that a form was taking shape. "A lion?" she guessed.

"Yes, for Abram." He placed the small block of wood atop the bench and looked up at her. Abram was one of the young boys who had been attacked by the machete-men in his home village. They had tried to hack off his hands. The boy's father had been implicated in the attack, bribed with the filthy money that was often paid by rich and influential people for the limbs and sometimes the organs of those with albinism. The witch doctors and medicine men did not ask where the supplies for their potions came from; it was sufficient that they were still in power and sought for such things as well as the false wisdoms and prophecies that often accompanied these ill-gotten prizes. Despite all the modern advances of government and democracy, politicians were reluctant to outlaw the witch doctors and their practices, as it was a sort of protected tribal religion, in their estimation.

The truth was that Tanzanians really had a modern religious practice that was a syncretism of inherited Christianity or Islam with the tribal beliefs. Many persons in power still believed in the old ways of the *mgangas*. In fact, the attacks had been escalating over the past several months, and would worsen, Kusini knew, with the arrival of the election year to come. Politicians and influential businessmen frequented the witch doctors, looking for anything that was believed to increase their power, and potions made from the flesh and bones of those with albinism were still highly sought after and created a lucrative black-market trade.

Abram and his brother had been taken into protective custody and were living in a safehouse with other victims. It was still unclear whether he would ever have use of his hands, which Kusini knew would interfere with his ability to learn, his ability to work, his ability to survive on his own.

Worse was the emotional toll. Taken from his family and all that he had known, he suffered from recurring nightmares in which he relived the attacks over and over, making it difficult to overcome his terror. Kusini had cast a spell for peace over the child, but it had only allowed him to sleep; it could not hide him from the dreams, which she suspected was due to a corruption of her spell by the *Mjusi*, who even now could subtly influence the outcome of some of her directed magic, whether she liked it or not. She still had to exercise caution that her intended outcome was not corrupted by unintended consequences. If you cannot sleep, neither can you dream.

"How is he?" Kusini asked quietly, when she realized that 'Kisye would volunteer no more.

Her husband was silent for so long that she wondered if he would answer. He, more than she, with all the suffering she had been witness to these long centuries, understood the aftermath of such a loss, indeed was still dealing with it, would always be dealing with it. What he had lost was arguably much greater, but she knew he struggled with the anger he felt watching children face these horrors. Many of them bled out before they could be saved; they were too delicate to survive the hacking assault of the machete blade.

When he finally answered, he began with a sigh. "I don't really know. I am not sure he knows. He did consent to go to the schoolhouse, but only if I rode in the van with them. He could not stop checking to make sure I had my own machete by my side." He fell silent, concentrating on his carving for a time.

"You make them feel safe; that's promising," Kusini offered sadly, already knowing what he would say.

"'*Sini-ma*, I cannot truly make any of us safe," 'Kisye lamented. "He knows this as well as I. Your magic is the best protection we have."

"Yet I cannot protect us all, I cannot reach us all; my magic will never be enough. The monsters have seen to that."

58

"I THOUGHT YOU WOULD SLEEP longer," 'Kisye remarked wryly when Kusini came up behind him the next morning. He stood at the sink, preparing freshly blooded meat, and he set down his knife and started washing his hand.

Kusini rested her forehead gently between his shoulder blades and gently grasped his arm, feeling something rough under her hand that caused her to flinch, thinking perhaps it was an insect crawling there. He half-turned, looking over his shoulder to try to see what she'd found, but she motioned him to be still. When she moved her hand away she noticed a small, oddly shaped wound on the back of his upper arm. It was a shallow oval on one side, and flatter and deeper on the other side, about the size and lunate shape of a fingernail, but had not been made by a scratch – which was impossible anyway as 'Kisye had no second hand to scratch with.

She looked more closely at the tiny defect, the edges of which were not reddened or reactive in any way. There was a small amount of crusted serum but no eschar; to casual examination it looked as though he may have brushed against something sharp, but there was something so regular about the wound that she studied it further.

She had once assisted a World Health Organization doctor in a skin disease clinic for those with albinism, and remembered his description of a chronic wound on a young man that was really a manifestation of a skin cancer causing local ulceration. The words he had used to describe it to his nurse came to her mind, '*saucerized edges,*' and the edges of this certainly sloped down to the deeper tissue in the center, but this was cleaner, almost surgical. It reached its greatest depth near the flatter edge, and she could see the layers of tissue on that side of the scratch, like the strata of the soil layers along the ridge. She suddenly recalled watching that same doctor perform punch biopsies, and suddenly she felt a cold sensation settle over her heart. The tool he had used, and the technique, was meant to sample all the layers of the skin, and the result had looked strangely similar to this.

Kusini placed a gentle finger alongside it. "How did you get this wound?" she asked, guessing his answer.

"I didn't know I had one," he replied. He finished washing up and turned to face her, leaning against the sink. "It doesn't hurt, *mpenzi.*"

'Kisye no longer felt pain or discomfort in the same ways as he had before…but in this case, she didn't think it was a blessing. Something was bothering her about this, and its apparent deliberateness. He wasn't one to let anyone get too near, but then, he wasn't one to be intimidated by crowds, and moved fairly freely through the city streets when he was in populated areas. He had much less to fear from other people than they from him.

Someone had gotten very close, close enough to steal his skin. She tried to tell herself that it could be just an accident, an unlucky encounter with a sharp surface, and meaningless, but she was unable to shake her suspicion. Kusini was not one to ignore such feelings, but the way he was looking at her told her that he was not going to tolerate her fussing over him.

He gently took her chin in his strong fingers, and tugged at her, pulling her face toward his for an eyes-open kiss. When she didn't respond to this distraction, he released her. "What's wrong?"

She closed her eyes and shook her head. "Nothing," she began, then continued, knowing he would call her on the lie. "I am probably just not ready to leave you again." Which was much closer to the truth, and encompassed her concern about the wound and the fact that she did long for more downtime, more home time, and less responsibility calling her back into the world.

"Then don't. Let me cook for you. Stay. Leave in the morning," he advised, caressing her cheek.

"Those twins could come at any time," Kusini protested, wanting nothing more than another day of his company.

As if reading her thoughts, he said, "I would have been home two days sooner, but the post road was impassable along the river. I think I even took a bit of a risk of getting stuck that last day, but I thought I might miss you altogether."

She sighed. "I shouldn't wait. Even though Amivi is a first-time mother, twins are tricky. And when they come, the danger will be greatest – twins are perceived omens, and they will be coveted."

"Andwale is brave and strong and will defend his family if he needs to – he took to my training without hesitation," 'Kisye argued. "Besides, those twins will come when the great *Mwathani* wills it, whether that is before, during, or after your visit, and Mwana'jua will hide them well on the plantation."

When Kusini remained quiet, considering this, her own desires warring with her conscience, he added, "Besides, I have a scratch on my arm. It might get infected. I need your medical expertise – who else can monitor my recovery?" He looked innocently up to the arch of the roof.

As if to add her own vote, little Yabluu suddenly chirped happily from the windowsill, and that sealed the decision.

"The two of you planned this attack very carefully, then?" Kusini laughed, although to what she was capitulating she did not know, since the decision was in sync with her own wishes.

"You could stay *three* more days if you would let me drive you up there," 'Kisye added, shrugging innocently at her stern expression. "Okay, okay, perhaps not. But I am happy to do it," he said, knowing full well that she would never willingly get into the Scout with him.

59

KUSINI WOKE SCREAMING FROM A dream and this brought 'Kisye on the run.

She waved away his unspoken question, so he climbed back into bed with her, and pulled her against him. She closed her eyes, inhaled his scent, and felt safe. 'Kisye waited for her body to relax, and kept waiting, wanting her to share when she felt ready. He knew she had learned it was worse for him when she faced her distresses alone.

"If something happened to me, I am not sure what would happen to you," she admitted when she finally broke the silence. "I think of you alone and scared about your own part of what I suspect must be a shared ending."

He waited for more, but she remained quiet, and he felt her tears on his shirt, so he took a deep breath, and gave her the honesty that he knew she wanted from him, needed from their relationship generally.

"I always thought I would be gone long before you, and it made life tolerable knowing I would never have to be in this life without you. I know now that isn't the case," he admitted gently, knowing that some of Kusini's only comforts came from her denial. "When that end comes, it will come for both of us."

"Unless you roll the Scout and smash your skull," Kusini lamented, not missing an opportunity to fuss about his driving. Secretly, she wasn't sure that could do it.

To her horror, as if in answer to her unspoken thought, he replied, "Nope. That doesn't work."

She flinched away as though he had burned her, listening as he told her about rolling it taking a corner on the post road. "I over-corrected where the road diverged after a flood. I flew out and the Scout landed on me. I was able to lift it off my torso and head. I took my time getting home to you." Then, seeing the look on her face, he said, "*What*?! I know how you are!"

"Ambakisye!" Kusini flushed with real and rare anger.

"*Mpenzi*, it was years ago – I'm fine." He reached for her, but the air crackled slightly, a small shift not unlike the sound of static electricity, a warning that it was unwise to touch her at that moment.

"Lovely wife, beautiful wife," he sighed, imploring her to relent. "I have known for a long time that your lifeforce stays me from my death. I will be ready to take that journey with you. I have always been ready to take it *for* you, from the time in my living youth that I first loved you. I understand that I am an animate object sustained by your magic."

"You are a human being," she protested.

"I used to be," he corrected her softly. "Now I am something else. I used to hate myself for it."

She was very still and too quiet, so he risked touching her. His voice was barely a whisper as he caressed her face. "I *never* hated you. And with two minor exceptions, I am grateful for every extra moment you have given me."

60

'KISYE HAD FINALLY USED HIS freedom, and his anger and frustration, and channeled it into something else. He frequently provided security for large groups of those with albinism when they traveled, at their safehouses, and at private schools where they were welcomed in large numbers, such as the parochial school in Dodoma. He had traveled with the soccer team, Albino United, on their Tanzanian tour, providing security measures. He had no real need of sleep, indeed could not sleep without Kusini's magic, which he understandably preferred not to be used on him. This meant he could keep constant vigil, especially when the team traveled to places where those with albinism were still frequently imperiled and attacked in large numbers, such as the region of Mwanza.

It was only fairly recently that their cause began to receive some international attention, and a new group had been formed to provide what support and relief it could. *Under the Same Sun* was a relief organization that had been founded to help eradicate prejudice, educate those with and without albinism about the disorder, provide protection and relief measures, and further the cause of those with albinism such that equal treatment could become a possibility, and persecution could end.

Its CEO and founder, Peter Ash, was himself a person with albinism, a businessman from North America. Kusini had met Peter Ash on occasion, as their paths naturally were bound to intersect, what with her travels and his outreach. She found him to be genuinely horrified about the plight of persons with albinism in Tanzania and other places who faced slaughter and prejudice.

Peter was also wholeheartedly committed to furthering their cause as a human rights crisis, and he had passionately presented the case to the United Nations Council as such. He had invested significant amounts of his own personal time and money. Kusini respected him immensely. He could have been resting safely at home half a world away in Canada, but he was frequently here, where he did not have to be, facing the horror and fighting for justice alongside the persecuted. She suspected the witch doctors would have been equally happy to have *his* bones; in some areas, rumor suggested that they may have been even more coveted than her own. It was a dangerous and beautiful task he had willingly undertaken, and he was raising awareness globally.

Although the house in Dodoma had fallen into disrepair, it still had high garden walls and iron gates, the deed still cleanly 'Kisye's own through some of Kusini's special small magics. He made repairs with his own hands, and with some small twinges of regret, replaced the doors on at least the bedrooms, but left the locks on the interior doors disabled. He tamed the overgrown garden, and smiled a secret smile from his sleeping mat on the terrace when the birds returned and sang to him from the trees as they had over a century ago. He donated the property to *Under the Same Sun*, quietly, securing their promise to maintain his anonymity, as it made a perfect safehouse. The irony of its new use healed the last remaining disquiet about his childhood on the property, and gave him feelings of peace and closure that he was surprised to find he had needed.

He toured the countryside villages, teaching local men with albinism self-defense. Those with the best eyesight he recruited, teaching them surveillance techniques, and giving them the confidence to form their own reconnaissance units, providing nighttime protection for local families affected by albinism. These were the contra machete-men, and indeed he taught them to fashion, use, maintain, and sharpen their own weapons. The importance of this kind of self-empowerment was not lost on him, or them, and they were happy to learn how to protect themselves. He inspired them, showing them that even with only one arm, he could protect himself (since his other unique gifts remained secret), and thus, so could they.

The most promising of these pupils, and the youngest, he recruited to his own project, one which he and his wife did not discuss. She could not endorse retribution or retaliation, and he promised her he was not being indiscriminate, but she knew what he was doing was a form of vigilantism. No matter how dreadful things became, there was still a rule of law that had to be upheld to maintain order. 'Kisye had no faith in such a thing. He reasoned that the victims were expected to wait for order to protect them, while the machete-men continued to hunt them, often without recourse from the proper authorities. So, these same machete-men were probably hunted by her husband's makeshift warriors, and they two did not speak on it. Emotionally, she suspected that this was what had ultimately healed him, not knowing that his recovery was a strange combination of all of these things, none of which he could have articulated, even if asked.

In the early days of this practice, which started only after he had found his own control, he would disappear for days at a time, returning exhausted but satisfied. Never did she find evidence of violence on his person, his clothing, or his tools, but she noticed other things. She decided that the less she knew, the better, and she was grateful for his fastidiousness, if not the dangerous errands he undertook. In some areas, the attacks had stopped altogether, although whether this was because the perpetrators had met some end, or was due to the possibility of being caught by this informal militia, she did not know.

For 'Kisye's part, he did not tell her that he rarely took a group to hunt these criminals, only under circumstances where there was evidence that there was a formal gang operating in conspiracy to obtain body parts or rob local gravesites. The men closest to him had spent most of their time contributing the labor required to secure graves with concrete rather than provide any physical show of force. He did the hardest work alone, starving himself to the brink of his madness, letting the feral redness flood his eyes, then using suspicion and fear of the threat of his own monstrosity instruct these men to change their ways. His physical form was enough of a message that he took this work very personally, and he let the beast out on display, waking them in their beds, showing them that he could find them even where they had hidden, in secret dens, in forest camps, in quiet villages.

And the witch doctors, those manipulators and masterminds, those clean-handed mutilators and murderers of children, were reduced to the sorry old men they really were, pissing in their beds in fear, the threat of what he might do to them enough of a deterrent to end many of their practices. They called him *Amazimu* or *Zimwe*, which he felt was an appropriate way that they should think of him, and remain afraid of what he was capable of. While his appearance didn't change their beliefs, many of them were convinced that they should end their grisly supply of talismans, if only to save their own necks.

But 'Kisye was not the angelic artist he had once been. Some he caught were unrepentant, or still in possession of their bloody prizes. He liked it best if they fought, or tried to attack him. In rare instances, when he had let his control slip too far, he probably had some regrettable moments, but these were not the province of his marriage. The hut beside the hill was a haven, and he did not bring these uglinesses into it. The universe of their love was not sacrosanct from these realities, but like the suffering she saw in her travels, they were not explicitly shared.

Each partner tried to understand what the other endured. They came together with eyes wide open; each knowing the other, understanding the world and their tenuous place within it, and their love endured because it was founded on truth, and had once been the simplest, purest thing that either had known. It endured also through a shared cause. That the cause was faced and championed very differently did not change their mutual affection and respect. He was fully aware that his inadvertent survival was a gift of love and he did not want to dishonor it; she recognized that her gift was an accursed reinforcement of every false superstition still spouted about those with albinism. Its effect on his death and rebirth made them both proofs to uphold the madness that gripped the country, for which she carried no end of guilt. For every person with albinism who longed only for anonymity among the masses, Kusini's yearning for the same was a thousand-fold greater.

61

ON THE SECOND MORNING TO follow, Kusini departed the hut and set out for the post road to the villages north and west of their home. She paused a moment in the dooryard and glanced back toward the doorway. 'Kisye slumbered peacefully, having spent the night sculpting before seeking her in the bed just before dawn and awakening her to his gentle lovemaking. As always, she carried the phantom reminders of his touch on her skin, and she smiled.

She climbed the hill and overcame the urge to look back once more, balancing her basket firmly on her shoulder. When she reached the edge of the road, she whispered, *"Protect it,"* touching her thumbs together briefly, feeling a small surge in the existing spell. She took a deep breath and advanced outside of the circle, stepping onto the rocks and clay of the road and committing herself to her journey.

The days were long, and hot. And far too quiet.

She skirted the high plain of the Serengeti and descended into the crater, but all remained silent, as if she had stepped into a false world. The typical insect and animal noises were blunted, and there was no sign of Bahati along the post road, or anywhere near *Oldupai*, where Kusini expected to see her. She was out of the natural world, laboring west toward the sun, in a manipulated reality.

She rested beneath a dry acacia in the height of the afternoon's heat and considered the coalescing form that took shape from the heat shimmer in the distance. She kept her place, quietly considering the *Mjusi* in its approach. It kept the hated form of the *Watende* this time, with the dead head it had harvested those many centuries ago, in the jungle where she had discovered the grisly remains of the man her father had taught her was his village *mganga*.

Despite all she had seen in this very long life, and her refusal to directly acknowledge the fact, it was this form that made her most fearful – there was a dark power in the head of one who had bowed to the evil arts, and sacrificed flesh carried memories. And it came not alone; it brought with it the *Nyoka*, the dreaded mamba coiled up its arm, the most dangerous and vicious of its familiars. The *Mjusi's* movements were not the fluid dance of its lizard host, rather, this was the jerky, disjointed dance of one who has no active governance over its limbs, and it told her something, but she could not fully form the thought, because she knew that all it did was part of a far more elaborate masquerade. A masquerade that she did not, could not, fully understand. She knew that such unnatural movement would strike terror into the hearts of any who witnessed it; but such a display was, by now, entirely wasted on her. The *Mjusi* did love drama for the sake of it.

Despite this, there *was* a cold streak of fear in her heart, realizing as she often did that there was little she did that the Monster failed to see. It often appeared if she had done something it could not understand, or control. Her current errand would be of far too great an interest for it to resist. Thus her relief was great when the creature halted abruptly several feet away and despite its mask-like expression, registered disgust. The serpent scented the dry air and slithered to the ground in one fluid movement, darting quickly toward her feet but maintaining its distance. For the moment.

"Second born, witch-born, child of sun . . . What is that stench?" The cacophony of voices spoke as one, in an unknowable yet familiar tongue. Kusini refused to respond, knowing that to let it speak she

would learn slightly more and impart slightly less. She had learned to resist the temptation to anger when she was able. "Ah," it sniffed the air about her, "You still reek of that corpse you live with."

Kusini could not control her visible reaction at the use of that particular word to refer to her beloved, and that angered her more. This pleased the *Mjusi*, and had the effect of encouraging the minion, which allowed itself to approach, loving the taste of her distress. Which gave her the opportunity she had been seeking. She seized upon it, crossing her thumbs and hissing, *"To me."*

The mamba shot forward, into her hands, and she flicked her wrist to stretch it straight in one fluid motion, and the whiplash popped its neck before she let it go, casting its corpse away into the tall grass. A pity, she thought, such a beautiful creature, miscast as a villain generally, it was a large reason that the fruit trees were protected from bats and other scavengers. The fact that its bite was fatal to orchard workers as well was an unfortunate reality.

"That should balance things out," she observed quietly, finding her feet and brushing the dust from her garments. There had been no indication that the Ghost had escaped its fleshly form, so at present it was stuck in the dying animal until it found an escape, since her touch likely trapped it. If not, it would take some time for it to find another beast to inhabit, and it was out of the way for the moment, so that the *Mjusi* was forced to face her alone, and she did not have to worry about other mischiefs.

She pushed her hood down off her head, fixing the Monster with a determined gaze, and took a step toward it. It satisfied her by taking a step back, out of her reach. Unlike its minions, she could not animate it against its will, and it knew to stay out of her grasp. She smiled a small smile.

"Whatever has become of 'Kisye, he has *life*. I know you have no power to create." Seeing its reaction, she pressed on. "Oh yes, you didn't think I had noticed how you must possess or corrupt living flesh and that you cannot keep it. You cannot allow yourself to be trapped within it or you assume its frailties. Only the great *Ngai* can create anything, and you covet what he brings. Any power you now claim, you got from him – and that is the crux of your evil – you cannot ever fully separate yourself, establish yourself as a power separate from the Creator.”

The creature laughed with such cold derision that it almost gave Kusini some satisfaction that she had angered it. Almost. Because there was a mocking note to that laughter.

“You think your husband’s restoration miraculous? *Ngai* had nothing to do with it. That *creature* is nothing but animated *meat*.” It used the term cruelly, finding satisfaction in her recoil from it.

“They call you Sorceress,” it crooned, pacing. “What you really are is something else entirely: Necromancer. Witch. Purposely brought into this world at *my* bidding.”

When she registered her surprise, it continued. “Your dear mother, Tumpe, legendary in her beauty, but innocent in the ways of men, and naïve to a fault.

“I ensured that the *Watende* prepared her as a bride before she was given to her elderly husband.

“He crafted a spell of my very own specification, telling her that it was a bridal ritual for fertility. She was so willing, so desperate to please her revered warrior husband – but she was smart enough to be secretly afraid that if such an old man was incapable of getting her with child that she would be blamed.

“Add to that, she was truly in *love* with her aging prince and would have done anything for reassurance. Superstition is one of my favorite tenets – I have built an antireligion on its foundation alone.

“She gave herself over to the *mganga* – oh, he wanted to do more to her, with her, but I stayed his lusts, kept him to the spiritual invasion.

“Suhuba had to be your father, you see. I had to know that you could be this spectral being and he had the right building blocks.

“Your mother submitted to the pain and blood of what she believed was a fertility ritual. All it really did was seal her fate – she would bear one girl-child and forfeit her life in the bargain – and that sacrifice fueled your unique development. Her death bestowed the necromancy gift to you and ensured my legacy was delivered.

"You forget, you who bleed, love, and die. Yes, die. Your deaths were never intended by the great *Ngai*, who loved his creation so blindly he thought to give the gift that rightly belonged to us as divine beings to weak and broken creatures. No. It was I who took it away with a word, a suggestion, a curse. I told humans that your deaths were a certainty, and it was weak-minded belief and superstition that gave that lie the power of truth.

"Thus, it was not *Ngai* who created the thing that used to be your beloved husband. You did. Keep feeding it raw meat, and never leave it hungry. I have a feeling it may have a special appetite for pureflesh."

62

KUSINI RETURNED TO HER TRAVELS unmolested and made it to Karatu in time to attend the twins' birth. Andwale had removed Amivi from their village, taking her onto the coffee plantation, as Kusini had instructed them. Mwana'jua had welcomed them without question, as she had so many others, and her security guards extended their protection to all that lived upon her lands.

There was a moment's distress when the second twin decided to enter the world backward, but a bit of manipulation and prayer provided, and soon the young parents had two new healthy members of the family. Mwana'jua watched it all from behind glasses with darkened lenses, and said little to anyone, nothing to Kusini.

Mwana'jua had outlived the rest of her family, had never taken a husband, and over the years she had taken in many orphans abandoned for their mixed race, or their albinism, or their disabilities. She was blind to such things, having inherited the tolerance of her grandmother, Zalika, and showed them love, and made them a home. They often remained on the land when they reached adulthood, loyal protectors of the farm and their adoptive mother.

By Kusini's reckoning, Mwana'jua was herself nearing one hundred years of age, and she continued to work the plantation, rising each day before anyone else. She was wise and severe, and although she had never refused to take in a refugee, she was wary of Kusini, and had never directly spoken to her, other than to observe that she knew the Sorceress had attended her birth but had not apparently aged since. She carried all the superstitions of her tribal forebears, and while she was grateful to have been spared, she believed that Kusini's magic exposed and endangered them as much as it might protect. She put more trust in the protection provided by the human guards here, and Kusini knew that the person who tried to bring harm to this place would face Mwana'jua's wrath, closely followed by a sharp machete blade. At this point in her long, long life, Kusini cared little that Mwana'jua disdained her; the provision of this safehouse was more important. To be perfectly honest, she understood the exposure her notoriety created, and understood why those she sought to protect remained wary in her company.

The day after the delivery, Amivi asked for Kusini's assistance when leaving the bed. She was weak, so Andwale and Kusini each took one of her arms to help her to her feet. Kusini felt something beneath her hand, a hard knot at the back of Amivi's arm, like an insect bite. On inspection, she found a small, lunate defect. It was a scar, with keloid transformation, healed but otherwise the exact replica of what she had discovered on her husband's arm. She shivered, violently, involuntarily, despite the cloying heat of the day.

Andwale disappeared to help outdoors on the farm, the way that many who came here showed their unspoken gratitude for Mwana'jua's kindness. Kusini put her friend's arm over her own, and walked about the small side garden with her, taking in some air while the twins slept. She kept quiet, letting Amivi talk on about her new babies, her excitement contagious, but not quite penetrating the cold that pressed Kusini's heart. Eventually, she convinced Amivi to go back inside, where she insisted on sitting in a chair, while Kusini brought her each infant in turn for their next feeding.

As she often did, while holding one of the babes, she was caught up in her own selfish imagining of what such a gift would mean to her if she and 'Kisye were able to have one, but with a simple sigh and a sad smile, she returned the child to its bed, turning away from the impossible.

She decided to take a walk up the steep hill where most of the plantings were undertaken, to escape the closeness and quiet of the afternoon in the otherwise empty house. Such restlessness had left her with an absolute inability to stay still for very long; when coupled with whatever innate sense drove her to the distresses of others, she was amazed that she had been able to settle down with 'Kisye at all.

Andwale was chopping wood for the fires that were kept hot at all hours to roast the coffee beans, and the midday heat was great enough that he had removed his shirt where he worked in the relative safety of the shady overhang in the rear yard. He did not turn as Kusini passed, concentrating on his task, and she noticed with a start that he, too, had a small healed mark on the back of his arm, in nearly an identical location to that of his wife, and 'Kisye. Her alarm was physical, a wave of unbidden nausea came to her, and she moved away from the house, under the trees at the bottom of the hill.

She walked slowly among the cement and stone monuments that marked a makeshift burial site for those of their community. This was a guarded place, and people knew it as a secret refuge. Many had brought family remains here, where their graves could be secured with slabs of stone and concrete. The stealing of body parts was not restricted to the living; many family graves had been desecrated in order to harvest the remains of those with albinism. She had, over centuries, assisted the living in finding secluded or secret burial sites; in the more recent past, groups of friends would either help create heavy stone monuments or pour cement slabs over the graves to keep out the wicked.

There were even a few places, such as this, where families could bring a loved one, and have an actual celebration of life among those who understood. The plantation was a refuge for both living and dead, and its security force had been trained by her husband. That didn't stop Kusini from a not inconsiderable expenditure of her own magic to protect it, and she hadn't told anyone that she had bound it in her own blood, a fact which she wasn't sure wouldn't make the place even more attractive to the *Mjusi*. As yet, it had not put in an appearance, but that was no guarantee it would not. There was no place that was safe from its reach, of that she was sure.

63

SHE WAS ALWAYS A BIT regretful when leaving the plantation, and it was more difficult than usual this time, as it did her heart some good to watch Amivi and Andwale with the twins. Their happiness lifted her spirits.

But as always, she was also somewhat relieved to go, and remove herself from the uncomfortable dynamic that persisted with Mwana'jua. She never stayed anywhere for long, as she tended to make people nervous, which was an unfortunate part of what she was. She understood this, but it added to her inherent loneliness, and made her long for 'Kisye's company more and more. She was also aware that wherever she was located physically was potentially a target for the Morningstar to perpetrate some devilment. She assumed, but was not certain, that it was less likely to appear somewhere she was not, but even she could not believe this lie she told herself, knowing from her visions that evil was abroad in the world. When there were no signs of it, no immediacy of malice, she knew it went elsewhere. Her universe was a small part of the world, a fact she had only learned fully in the last century or so.

This time, though she needed to take up a route to the north and west, knowing that she had work waiting in some of the more remote *Bantu* villages, and across to Mwanza, her feet turned west, and she looped back towards Arusha.

Walking the streets of the old village, she came to the terraced apartment house where she and 'Kisye had started their marriage. It was very different now, but she believed places held memories, good and bad, and she was ever drawn here when she returned. She attempted visits with three separate families, all with children who had to be watched over and kept safe from the madness of the machete men, but none were home.

She backtracked to the local school, which had a sympathetic and protective headmaster. She inquired as to the families' wellbeing and was told that two of the families had moved back to the countryside and taken shelter with relatives, and that the third had also taken their child out of school and retreated to the safehouse in Dodoma.

"But I don't understand," she protested with feeling, and the beginnings of dread.

He was sympathetic, and explained that there had been strangers about who had been asking specifically about the children in question, and this understandably spooked the parents, but he had no further information. She left a sealed letter in his care, asking him to deliver it to her husband when next 'Kisye came through town. He vowed he would, but she barely heard this. She was already on the cobblestones, turning toward Dodoma, feeling real urgency.

She traveled at night now, knowing that although the anonymity and diversity of larger cities was in some ways helpful to those with albinism, for the same reasons, they attracted more criminal elements, and there was still a black-market trade for her flesh. She reached the city shortly after midnight six days later, and followed the familiar path through the central market and out past the mosques and entertainment district, down the familiar street, which remained fairly quiet still, to the Judas door in the gate of the house she still thought of as 'Kisye's.

She did not bother with the security code at the gate, which would theoretically grant her entry without disturbing the residents within, but whether it would work for her or not was frustratingly variable. This was true of most electronic equipment and technology; it often went haywire if she tried to use it. She guessed that persisting on such a course was not prudent, which was why she had never even attempted use of motorized vehicles. Satellite phones and cell phones often ceased to function if she was nearby, and this probably should have told her something, but what it could be she never fully concluded. She simply avoided.

She waited just outside the gate until the night patrol in the garden came on the hour, and whispered, *"Check the gate."* This brought the sentry to the wrought iron window in the door, but the poor man did not know she was the one who had provided the suggestive motivation. It made her uncomfortable to know that she was capable of such subconscious manipulation.

He gasped to see her there but recovered when the next moment brought recognition. "Sorceress. Please come in." And the locks were deactivated briefly to admit her, securing once more when the gate closed behind her.

"Thank you, Henri," she sighed in relief, exhausted to her core. She pushed the hood of her abaya off, not bothering anymore to ask anyone to use her name. They never would, for one reason or another. They had real superstition, and names did carry power…but the use of the word as if it were some sort of honorific had never suited her. She supposed it was because it was another way to maintain distance from her. She never stopped being sad about this — even 'Kisye was called by name and did not seem to elicit fear within the community the way she did.

She let herself into the house through the kitchen, still stunned by its modern transformation into a utilitarian, no-nonsense space so different from the indoor patio it had once been. The mosaic pool in the salon had been restored, the water circulated to keep it clear, and she smiled at the rows of little sandals that lined the walls. The children came here and used this pool for the same reason it had been used for three hundred years, to cool the weary feet of travelers.

They stomped and splashed around in it, too, but she knew that gave the place life, and she had witnessed her husband join in, thrilled that his house had become such a haven.

She stood still and quiet for a moment before stepping out of her sandals and placing each foot in turn in the cool water. Then, leaving her shoes behind, loving the nostalgic feel of the cool Spanish tiles on her feet, she decided against rousing the housemother and climbed up to her old room, which now held three bunk beds. All the beds were occupied, but this was of no consequence. Kusini sank down on the rug between them and went right to sleep.

64

UNLIKE ADULTS, CHILDREN HAD NO reservations in her presence, and she was awakened to the delighted shrieks of the dormitory inhabitants as they woke up around her. "She's here! She's here!" Their cries of delight brought the adults, who mostly looked worried.

This she ignored, instead sitting among them and absorbing their enthusiasm as they relayed their stories, each talking over the other, trying to out-do one another. They settled in close to her, and she marveled at this. The children at the safehouse gained some comfort from her and she could not fathom it, and of interest, they never seemed to have any difficulty leaning in, touching her, sitting with her, hanging off her garments.

Thus, she felt slightly guilty as each came to her in turn, acknowledging the love she felt for them, trying to mirror their optimism and energy as she surreptitiously examined them. And with each that came to greet her, her horror grew. Not one did not have the mark of the biopsy, and she was dizzy with alarm, trying even harder not to telegraph this fresh distress. She dared not ask them about the marks, wanting to avoid drawing the issue to their attention; children were exceedingly astute, and these were here because they had already been traumatized.

Some had been abandoned by parents who at least had not turned them over to the *mgangas*, but a child does not understand this. Some had been attacked and had survived, others were the children of albino mothers who had been savaged or maimed, brought here with a mother who required refuge. None had been spared this new intrusion. Yet none seemed to notice, and she picked up on the pattern. Starting with 'Kisye, not a single person had raised concern about the mark, and she suspected that even if she did start asking questions, that none would remember. Her heart hurt.

When the children were called to breakfast, she sought out the housemother, who was kind to Kusini, but through her tired smile, Kusini could see her concern about this visit. It was clear that she, also a person with albinism, whom Kusini had helped deliver into this world, was anxious to understand why Kusini was here and then have her on her way.

Kusini inquired about the child brought here from Arusha, assuming that the family was at the safehouse, but the housemother shook her head. "No. They left the girl here and claimed they would return for her. They said it was no longer safe to keep her in Arusha, and they wanted to make arrangements for their safety before they moved her. I expected them back weeks ago."

Kusini asked if it would be possible to meet the child, and she could see that the housemother wanted to refuse but could not bring herself to offend. She stood and silently led the way out of her office. Her blouse had short sleeves, and Kusini saw that she, too, carried the ominous mark. Kusini felt she must lose her mind without some indication of what was happening.

They found the child in the back garden, sitting forlornly beneath an ornamental maple. Kusini placed her age around seven years, and she smiled slightly when she saw the hooded sweatshirt the girl wore. It had an elaborate purple spotted pattern reminiscent of the cheetah, and when they drew closer, Kusini saw that the hood had tiny cat's ears. Kusini was reminded of the cheetah skin she had once worn, for its primitive function of making her look fierce and keeping her warm, while this sweatshirt was all fashion. It was a darling thing, and the detail told her that this was a child who had been dearly loved; she imagined the girl's mother spotting it in a shop and holding it lovingly, knowing the child would love it, or a scenario in which the two were together and the child expressed immense joy at finding the garment, and the indulgent parent celebrating this happiness. This was not the typical abandonment of a child with albinism, never to return. Whoever bought this sweatshirt would cross the globe to return to her.

The heartbreak in the child's eyes was overwhelming; Kusini could drown in them. She sent the housemother away with a pointed look; although the woman did not want to go, she did not have the fortitude to hold Kusini's gaze, much less defy her in her determined state.

"I love your sweatshirt; I wish they made this in my size," she observed as she sat a few feet from the girl. Kusini was surprised that there was a kernel of truth in this; she could see herself wearing such a soft garment at home, with 'Kisye, who had no knowledge of her old cheetah skin. This would certainly amuse him. "I am Kusini."

"I am Ak'ili," the child responded, adding with a touch of real curiosity, "You are the Sorceress. *Ama* and *Baba* used to speak of you when they thought I was asleep."

"Did they? What did they say about me? Can you tell me?" Kusini adopted a tone of conspiratorial friendship, but the tragic coincidence of the child's name rattled something deep inside.

"I know you were there when I was born," the girl told her softly, still not looking up. "Before we left...home, they were discussing whether you could help us. But they ran out of time. The strange man came to the house next door, and I saw him at my school in Arusha."

"Strange man?" Kusini asked, hoping the child would say more.

"He had – "the child began, but stopped herself, unsure how to proceed. These children, unlike others, had learned not to use unkind adjectives.

"It's okay, just say it however you can. It can be hard to describe someone different without saying why they are different. I understand," Kusini encouraged her to continue.

He had funny eyes, not like eyes I have seen before," Ak'ili responded, and Kusini's chest constricted with panic.

"Funny? Were they shiny?" Kusini inquired, hoping she kept her profound concerns from her voice.

"No," the girl's tone suggested that she thought perhaps Kusini was ridiculing her, but she thought for a moment, before concluding, "They were – just different. Not shaped like anyone's eyes I have ever seen."

"Okay," Kusini liked that answer better, although she was not sure what to make of it.

"I think he may be the reason they left me here. It took too long to get here, and *Baba* saw him here, in the city, before they left me behind." At this, she began to cry, silent tears that rolled down her face and dropped onto the front of her sweatshirt. "They promised to be back by now, and I know now that they aren't coming. The only reason they would not come back is if they were dead. That was their promise."

65

KUSINI WAS NOW ON A quest fueled by desperation and an unanswered question. When she left Dodoma, her feet took her back west to the shores of Lake Victoria and up to the *Bantu* villages, following her usual route, looking for those in need. And she found them, in ever greater numbers than before. In hiding, on the move, afraid of something or someone that seemed to be following them.

Other strange events were brought to her attention. One of the political candidates had suggested that a potential solution for the killing of persons with albinism was to provide those who qualified with cellular phones, so they could call for help in times of peril. The program was rolled out as part of a new government campaign. She imagined 'Kisye's outrage. One would likely have to travel to *Dar Es Salaam,* or some other urban center, to obtain the phone, which was an insupportable burden for those most severely persecuted, as they were concentrated rurally. And furthermore, there was still nearly nonexistent cell service in the interior of the country where the attacks were still concentrated.

The politicians needed to outlaw the black magic practices, but so many of them sought power potions from the *mgangas* themselves, and many of their supporters maintained the old superstitions. It had nearly become an issue of personal freedom to choose the old ways.

The solution was a slap in the face, a useless protection rather than legislating appropriately to punish the practices that created the danger. African politics could still be primitive in its proposals. Kusini tried to imagine Jakaya Kikwete and Salum Barwany shouting them down in parliament. It was good to finally have elected representatives with albinism, but even these men were tracked and threatened for their condition alone, and they received frank death threats in many regions where black magic constituted the basis of religious practices, especially during their own campaigns.

Kusini carried all this nonsense with her constantly, and on this trip, she was uncovering ever more evidence of something entirely diabolical at work. It was rarer to find someone who had not been biopsied than otherwise, and she wondered why it was happening now. She questioned whether she had missed it before, but had no reason not to believe that some new evil was being perpetrated on her people.

Finally, exhausted and overwhelmed by dreams so relentless she could no longer continue her travels, she headed back east, hoping to reach the plantation and gather her thoughts before returning home. She had no idea what she was going to do if 'Kisye were not at home, as she desperately needed to tell him of this insidious new threat. She was still unable to discern the cause or even imagine why it was happening on such a large scale, but that alone was terrifying her.

Her dreams worsened as she followed the post road, retracing her steps back to Karatu. Only the child had told her of a man with strange eyes, so that mystery remained. On her journey, she had asked after the other families that had disappeared from Arusha, but none had seen or heard of them.

She dreamed of armies of those like 'Kisye, thousands upon thousands of the undead, but uncivilized, unfed, uncontrolled. She awoke with screams in her throat, her hands crammed against her teeth to keep those screams from escaping.

Then, two days out from Karatu, beside the post road in the dark, she began to have waking visions of being trapped in darkness, unable to free herself from some prison – dark, damp, alone, and suffocating. These flooded over her, and she was horrified at the idea that this was happening to someone somewhere, that these were true visions of confusion and fear being fed to her by the *Mjusi,* visions of one who was tortured. It was a recurrence of a particularly frightful vision that she'd had before in times of stress and uncertainty, but she knew it was not driven solely by her imagination and disquiet.

By the time she reached the plantation, she was certain that she must appear rather wild, after living for months with the fear that age had taken hold of her senses, and she was slowly unraveling mentally after all these years. This was alarming, the last time that had happened, the result had been a loss of control and catastrophic destruction. She held on to thoughts of 'Kisye, thinking that if only she could reach him, it would afford her some peace.

She even thought of bypassing the plantation, forgoing rest, and pushing on to home, but she remained driven by the one unresolved detail that she had not confirmed.

66

WHEN SHE STEPPED THROUGH THE kitchen door of the plantation house, Mwana'jua was waiting there, silent and alone. Kusini could not read her expression behind the dark glasses she wore.

Kusini moved to the center of the room, breathless in her anticipation. She didn't dare speak, merely held out her hand in silent command. The old woman frowned, but stuck out her arm brusquely, barely tolerating Kusini's intrusion, as her sleeve was unbuttoned and pushed up in haste.

When Kusini had confirmed the presence of the small scar, Mwana'jua jerked away from her, fussing angrily with the button at her wrist. Kusini did not understand the reason for Mwana'jua's outrage, but took a step backward anyway, realizing her own suspicions were well-founded. Realization was no comfort.

"You *knew?*" Kusini whispered softly.

"This is from *you*, somehow," Mwana'jua scolded harshly. "It can only be so." And still indignant, she burst out of the kitchen, letting the doorframe recoil with a bang.

Kusini followed, but the old woman had a head start. It took Kusini a moment too long to compose herself, which made it harder to discern the direction she had taken. She reached the bottom of the hill, and was so surprised to see 'Kisye coming toward her that she nearly missed seeing that Mwana'jua was already hacking away at a dormant plot of ground that had encroached on the small side yard, taking out whatever ire she felt on the land. She had avoided the easier path between the trees, and she was beating her machete down on the overgrown plants in a fury.

'Kisye had a bundle of wood to be chopped tucked under his arm, and he touched foreheads with her and made a face. "What's wrong with her?"

Kusini just shook her head sadly and watched as Mwana'jua disappeared into the uncleared growth beyond the vegetable garden. She sighed.

"Why are *you* here?"

It was then that he looked her over carefully, and she knew she must be a sight, given the concern in his expression. At this point she felt that something had to give, as if she were coming out of her skin. She had not really been sleeping or eating, and his eyes reflected real worry for her. He put the wood down and took her by the hand.

"I was hoping to find you here, or at least catch up with you. I just haven't felt right since you left. Strange things are happening, and I had your letter from the schoolmaster a few days ago in Arusha. I came right back here, hoping my timing was about right to meet up with you, but unsure of your duties up north. I couldn't remember whether you had another delivery to attend, or if you were just checking up on tribal families. There has been a lot of fear.

"I didn't feel right returning home, but I was afraid to try to set out to locate you in case we missed each other. I needed to feel that I was between you and Arusha, at least," his voice betrayed something else, but he wasn't ready to tell her what it was yet.

She allowed him to lead her under the trees, where they sat in the shade among the grave monuments, usually a pleasant place where they went to be alone when their respective travels found them together here.

She told him about the entirety of the trip, how she had made the unplanned detour to Dodoma after Arusha, and the reason she was making her way back to find him now. She relayed the story of her relentless visions, the panic that was so unlike her, and the frustrating realization that the entire mystery confounded her. Finally, she shared with him Mwana'jua's emotional and inexplicable reaction when Kusini had merely wanted to confirm that whoever was taking the biopsies had been here, too.

When she finished, he pulled her close and held her tightly, and she leaned into him in relief, thankful that she was not alone with this knowledge any longer. He was not looking at her with as much alarm now either, because he had an explanation for her distraught behavior. "You're exhausted, you have to get something to eat, and rest, and then –" he began, but she pushed away from him suddenly and nearly knocked him over. "What is it?!" He saw the horror on her face as some new realization struck.

She pushed up her own sleeves, impatient, desperate to know, feeling terrible for missing this one last piece of the puzzle. And under the fingers of her left hand she finally located proof of her own targeting, high on the back of her right arm, the defect she had not known was there. The scar felt fully matured; it had been present long enough to heal and heal well, and she had remained ignorant of it, only now thinking to check herself. She shook her head slowly, wanting to will it away, but when she turned away from him so that he could see the tiny divot in her skin, he nodded, confirming it for her.

"What does it mean?" she whispered to him, but she could see he had no answer for her, he shook his head mutely. What he did not say was worse, that whatever had happened, it had been purposeful, thorough, and insidious.

"Kusini, I wanted to let you rest before I told you about the city," he admitted, "but it isn't right to keep it from you a moment longer.

"There are two men asking after you, traveling out from Arusha and Dodoma. Not Africans," he asserted, seeing the silent questions in her eyes. "So, I investigated. I actually saw them from a distance. One looks just like the goatherder that came and killed our goats, all those years ago when…" his voice trailed away, and he made a face before he could continue. "But there are two things that are different. The Morningstar had those awful, shiny eyes, and this one, well, his eyes seem normal. He wears spectacles, and I know that is not necessarily odd, it just doesn't fit. I can't figure it for a disguise.

"My contact and I followed them for a time. They seem to be terrorizing the locals with their questioning, and they have rented Jeeps and guides to take them up-country, up this way. The one with the Monster's face is apparently a Catholic *priest*, sent on order of the Vatican in Rome. It doesn't make sense."

"Is the second man a priest as well?" Kusini was compelled to ask.

"No, but he has strange eyes," 'Kisye replied. "My man from the safehouse described him that way specifically. I just think it is too much to be a coincidence when I compare it to your story." He did not tell her that he planned to get answers about their reasons for searching for his wife, by any means necessary. It would mean telling her now, at her most fragile, that he needed to leave her alone again.

They both upheld an uncomfortable silence, unusual in their relationship, neither one in any hurry to go inside. Although the heat was stifling, neither felt warm. And when they finally left the rear garden, neither was aware of the movements underground.

Below the stones and the slabs of cement, the dead were no longer quiet.

after

*Results of directed DNA study for project **Okori**, initiated by research protocol a15671, tissue samples banked. Results sent to encrypted server file, eyes-only and delivered urgently to Azuma Himura. Receipt acknowledged within 12 hours, no further direction given. Unknown to the executive council of RSI, results were duplicated and delivered by courier to an unspecified recipient within the Vatican.*

Result completed **AGGREGATE result/multiple**
Result reported **30 September 20XX**

Specimen taken/received
Project Okori A specimens/collection window November-March 20XX
Project Okori B specimen collected May 20XX, sequestered into separate cohort by result

Specimen Identification Numbers
Okori A 2XXXXXX468-2XXXXXX731;
Okori B SIN 2XXXXX5342

Specimen **COC CONFIRMED**

Subject Age **VARIOUS; Okori B INDETERMINATE**
Subject Gender **Okori A F/M representatives within cohort;** Okori B DNA Result presence of human Y-chromosome, **MALE** (CONFIRMED)

Subject Race
Okori A, AFRICAN, subset sub-Saharan origin
Okori B, AFRICAN, subset sub-Saharan plus North African origin; **ASIAN**, most likely genomic subset Peninsular Arabian when cross-referenced to RSI genomic library

Method

DNA extracted using proprietary protocol and expansion performed with PCR, subsequent STR, genomic and mitochondrial analysis completed as specified in original request

RESULT
Relevant findings follow

Determinations
D1. Autosomal recessive albinism present in all specimens Okori A; present Okori B

D2. Protocol AZ analysis initiated with negative result Okori B; no responsive protocol modifications required

D3. Okori B specimen exhibits complete loss of DNA methylation akin to and more pervasive than the specimens from the centenarian studies (see Gonzalo, 2010; Horvath, 2013; Heyn et al, 2012). This finding persists irrespective of preparation technique and proteinase degradation has been ruled out. No contaminants found.

Conclusions

C1. Okori A specimens all contain preserved evidence of G1Ω and its associated genetic byproducts, preserved across taxonomy when compared to genetic structure of the concomitant DNA of albino plant and non-*Homo sapiens* animal species; Okori B contains preserved evidence of G1Ω WITHOUT associated genetic byproducts

C2. When compared to the Okori exemplar, none of the Okori A specimens nor the Okori B specimen contained the supernumerary unexplained STR segments that cross-referenced positively to control specimen alpha

C3. Okori exemplar confirmed as cross-species/superhuman chimera beta (the second confirmed, with contaminated specimen

1XXXXXX4 remaining unconfirmed as potential cross-species/superhuman chimera gamma)

C4. Although the Okori exemplar contains G1Ω and has partial genetic expression 46XX human female with autosomal recessive albinism, there is no familial genetic pattern identifiable between the exemplar and the Okori A specimens nor the Okori B specimen to suggest a genealogic connection. Said genealogic connection is distantly present for all members of the Okori A cohort and for Okori B.

***Addenda**

C5. All three identified cross-species/superhuman chimeras have alleles in common, each to the other, which confirms confraternity and suggests the presence of a shared origin organism [redacted]

C6. Conclusion 5 notwithstanding, the Okori exemplar is the only chimeric carrier of G1Ω; the gene is absent in chimeras alpha and gamma [redacted]

**Findings added personally and privately to an amended report on her encrypted server by Azuma Himura, who maintained sole permission to view and compare findings on the chimeric results collectively, and therefore unknown to the Vatican recipient.*

BY THE TIME ALETA FINISHED her hospital rounds and began the long walk across the medical campus to her office, the long shadows of late afternoon were beginning to fade as twilight descended from the tops of the buildings to the trees. A pervasive chill was settling in the winter air, as if the season knew it held reign in the post-holiday torpor that had taken hold of the city. She shivered beneath her lab coat despite her wool turtleneck and tweed slacks, and wondered absentmindedly whether there would be a rare freeze.

She followed the sidewalk past the physical rehabilitation center and on toward the doctors' parking lot, where surprisingly few cars still lingered. Given the season, this was one of the busiest times of year for healthcare facilities. Her gaze wandered idly over the lot, and she paused for a moment, leaning on her crutches. A sleek, dark, late-model Jaguar was parked in the only other handicapped slot beside her own.

She frowned, as she often did when passing this spot, totally unaware of the distasteful expression on her face as she contemplated her silver Volvo in its "assigned" space. When the board had approved funds for the small lot that would allow the specialists to park closer to their clinics in the outbuildings, space was dear, and each slot was allotted to a specific physician. As a gesture to her, she supposed, and to the prevailing laws about the ratio of handicapped to regular spaces in any parking lot, they had placed two blue spaces near a zero-grade ramp onto the sidewalk. When she had staged her own silent protest, refusing (quietly) to use them, she had been summoned to the medical director's office for a meeting. In hushed tones that confirmed the embarrassment she suspected he felt, he gently explained that space in the lot was at a premium, and if she wouldn't mind? That way, there would be enough room for everyone to park. Aleta wasn't sure what made her more furious – their absolute smug certainty that she required this special consideration, but let's call it what it *really* was, pity – or the fact that she had been unable to hide her hurt and disappointment from him, which in some silly way made her feel as though she had failed to be strong enough.

Because any new additions to the staff were greeted with the kind of fanfare that could make Mardi Gras pale in comparison, she suspected that one of her perfectly-abled colleagues had a new toy that needed more protection than it could get in the back row between the only slightly older Audis and BMWs. Besides, everyone knew that the other blue spot was always vacant. Except on the odd occasion when Aleta herself staged a secondary rebellion and parked in it just because she could.

"I guess I should start double-parking across both spaces," she murmured, surprised to hear her own voice aloud in the silence of the encroaching darkness. As if in response, the sodium arc lamps of the lot popped on with an electric hum, startling her. She realized it was getting even colder, so she resumed her journey, quickly forgetting about the new car as she tried to focus on other tasks to be finished before her day could end.

But foremost in her thoughts was Amaoke, now gone more than three weeks. The feast of the Epiphany had come and gone, marking the start of a fourth week, but there was still no news of him. Heightening her concern was a telephone call to her mobile that morning by his landlady.

The woman was clearly concerned, noting that she had not seen Amaoke for nearly a week, and she was just wondering if he was with Aleta. When Aleta had returned the call, the landlady explained that she didn't want to pry, she was merely concerned about his well-being, and admitted it was silly to worry over a grown man who did sometimes travel. Aleta was mildly amused, fully aware that while the woman's sentiment ran much more to the latter in that while she was clearly fond of Amaoke, of course she could not help but inquire. Which, promptly, she did, rambling on, stammering something about just having a feeling that he and Aleta were *close*, the emphasis on the word suggesting that she was seeking some sort of confirmation that a romantic attachment had been made. As if Aleta was simply going to admit that Amaoke was now overnighting elsewhere, with her. Because she didn't want to worry the landlady, and wanted even less to admit that she did not know where he was, she simply said that he was likely to return soon, and that it would not be fair for Aleta to speculate on the reasons for his absence.

She let herself into the building with the keycard that dangled from a lanyard on the lapel of her lab coat, and the motion-activated lights came on in the short hallway that led to the back of the reception area. She paused long enough to tuck the bundle of mail that her staff had left for her under one arm, securing it close to her side before continuing to her office. There had been several nights of late when she had arrived after they had all gone home. She thought that the place was even creepier at the dark of the year, when, as now, the late afternoon brought full dark. Or perhaps lately she was more easily spooked; it seemed she couldn't get used to the shadows in the conference room, although she had probably never given them a second thought before all the recent unusual events in her life.

She turned the last corner into her office; the door was slightly ajar as she'd left it, and the motion sensors did their job, immediately flooding the space with fluorescent light. As soon as the space was lit, her senses screamed that something was amiss. It was that horrid feeling that one was not alone in a place where it was assumed one would be, in a place that had once felt safe, but would not feel so again, ever.

In the second of the twin armchairs that faced the couch, in the seat she would now forever associate with Amaoke, sat a too-handsome man in a very expensive suit. She absurdly recognized it as this season's Armani from a billboard she drove past at least weekly that was located next to the elevated segment of I-10, *en route* to visit her sister, or less frequently, her parents. The suit on the billboard was brown, but this was a sooty charcoal color that reminded her of ash, worn with a shirt black as night, and a pocket square that matched socks of deep red, which she took in all at once, because one leg was casually crossed over the other, as if this *creature* had every right to be right where it was. Its shoes were soft loafers, with a velvety texture, and what looked like hand-stitched cross hatches over the arch, certainly cobbled to order and extremely expensive. She focused on these details, clung to them, really, to try not to see the rest of it. She recognized her tumbling thoughts about the origin of the suit, the billboard, its shoes, as her mind's way of trying to stave off panic and shock and to keep her from the other details that she was finally unable to ignore.

Its eyes flashed unnaturally in the light, inhumanly shiny, and its fingers were too long, with needlelike fingernails, which appeared black, or more likely, a dark red that was reminiscent of dried blood. That color was all too familiar to her from her days as an intern, when injuries and wounds were still a regular part of her medical evolution. In the left hand, it held what appeared to be a business card, which it flipped over and through those fingers with supernatural dexterity. She noted with some distress that the card was her own.

Worst of all was its hair, slightly longer than was fashionable, wavy, and darker even than the clothing. It seemed to draw all the light from around it, and appeared to be in motion, slowly drifting around its face as if free of gravity, as if, somehow, alive. It was utterly disturbing, and she stared at it for what felt like hours, but could only have been seconds.

The mail slid down her side and scattered slowly at her feet, and one of her crutches went clattering after it, but those eyes never left her face. It wore an ironic smile, as if it knew a terrible secret, knew every thought she had ever had. Aleta knew immediately who – what – it was. The Morningstar. And then it spoke.

"You are even more lovely than we imagined," it said. "Our . . . mutual acquaintance has always been less than forthcoming about what he was doing. But this is no matter; I learned the last time that his attachment to pureflesh only interferes with my greater plans for his future. This time I am inclined to intervene before it gets out of hand. A shame. You really are exquisite, and I must admit that I am going to enjoy myself very much." It smiled, and Aleta recoiled, partly due to the fact that the smile was every bit as terrible as she could imagine, never mind that those teeth were white, even, and perfect, which was worse, because she knew it to be an elaborate glamour. She was sure that she would see it as it really was before the worst was over.

Then it stood up, and she smelled sour decay and death, and her vision began to fade, and she had to put her head down to clear the spots from her eyes. She fought against her rising gorge, fought for strength and control, fought to manage her terror and prevail over it this time where she had failed when witnessing Amaoke initiate *his* change. She merely managed to stay upright, and as it took a step toward her, she was convinced that if it touched her she would go insane, that her death on this night was a certainty.

Her irrational brain was hard at work trying to process the intrusion of further evidence of the extranormal, and it grasped at the ludicrous idea that if this were a movie, Amaoke would appear now to save her. But her rational mind was already accepting the terrible reality she faced and would not be further distracted from her fate.

Her legs and one crutch were ultimately too little to keep her upright. As those fragile legs failed her and she felt herself falling, suddenly there was a strong arm encircling her waist, but the face of the tall man at her side was not that of her beloved Amaoke, rather it was the bespectacled twin of the Monster near the armchair, and she had enough time to realize that he wore the collar of a priest before he spoke to her, and she recognized that somehow, he knew her name. He ignored the Morningstar entirely; his focus was on Aleta. She reached out to push him away, but he was too strong, and her hands were unable to find any purchase at the front of his cassock. He held her fast, and she did not fall, noticing before she lost consciousness that the priest had eyes that were fully human – a warm brown color – and kind. She could hear him repeating her name, ever more insistent, but she was unable to stay focused, and her shock pulled her down into its depths, away from the fear.

Acknowledgements

I SPOKE WITH THE VERY kind and understanding Don Sawatzky, Director of Operations at Under the Same Sun (UTSS), for background on persons with albinism and for more information on how to approach my second protagonist. I sent a blind email query through the website, asking to be put in touch with Peter Ash and not entirely expecting a response. What I got, about four weeks later, was a very personal answer to my query, and I think even a cell phone contact for Don. He was available to speak with me almost immediately, and late on a Tuesday afternoon, he spent nearly two hours talking with me about my own life, his background with the organization, and the philosophies they espouse. I felt so comfortable with him that I think I even divulged what it is that LJ is short for, and in turn I became part of what he described as his "collection of alphabet-soup acquaintances" – persons who go by initials rather than names. He was generous with his time and patient with my questions, and passed along nearly seventy scholarly and fictional sources for me to refer to in building my story.

Persons with albinism (PWA) face an especially cruel kind of ostracism in nearly every country they live in, on every continent and subcontinent on the planet, and the genetic phenomena associated with the condition are true hardships, from the ocular sequelae that can leave them severely visually impaired, to the absolute inability of their skin structure to protect them from ultraviolet damage, which means many of them will die from complications of skin cancers before they achieve their sixth decade. In the one glaring exception to the ostracism, PWA in Panama's native Guna population are deified, which is also probably not ideal. It is human nature to want to blend in, fit in, and be able to lead a so-called *normal* existence.

Don was most frank with me on this point: my idea to make my heroine a magical being was frowned upon by those with PWA and their friends and protectors, because it is one of the underpinnings of the superstition that leads to their often-violent persecution. I agreed to consider in what way I could mitigate this, and I spent many sleepless nights with it until I realized that I had set my course, but I had the power to tell this story in my own way. It is the reason that much of the detail, background, and historic events bearing on the bloody history of the killing of PWA in Tanzania (and other places, mostly in Africa) are based on actual events and my all-too-clear editorial feelings about them. I wanted to preserve my story but pay-it-forward for my sins with as much information and education that I could pack within it.

I will note something that is scientifically fascinating about albinism; it is a condition that is seen across all species – plant, animal, and insect – a preserved genetic state that persists in nature. I recall my time in undergraduate Genetics, when we learned that preserved traits are the absolute proof that the existence of those traits is somehow essential to the gene pool of all life on earth, as they remain present across taxonomies. In other words, albinism is essential to what it means to be human, critical to the blueprint of our, and many other, species.

Under the Same Sun (UTSS) is a fully recognized human rights organization with the goal of educating the world about people with albinism, such that those with albinism can contribute fully to a society that will recognize their humanity, provide them equal treatment in education and career opportunities, and live in peaceful coexistence with others, without fear of attack motivated by superstition and fear. They do incredible work around the globe. You can learn more about UTSS and how you can help by visiting www.underthesamesun.com and exploring the many educational resources there.

I must also applaud the work of influential activists who give PWA a public face, such as Mpho Tjope, Josephat Torner, and Ikponwosa Ero. Models such as the particularly outspoken Diandra Forrest and Shaun Ross provide another platform from which to raise awareness, and help to broaden historically narrow standards of attractiveness. They provided my mental framework for Kusini and Ambakisye, and they are truly beautiful from the inside out.

While there are real persons, some living, mentioned in this book, it should be viewed entirely as a work of fiction.

Glossary of Terms

Abaya *= a cloak or robe-like dress, worn most often by women in predominantly North and Eastern Africa and the Arabian Peninsula; also,* **aba.** *Traditionally these are black, but can be found in many colors, sometimes fashioned from a large square of material draped over the body but more often similar to a caftan (traditionally male robe that drapes from the shoulders or head)*

Amazimu *= man-eating monster (also,* **Zimwe***); although 'Kisye was referred to using this term by the witchdoctors he was frightening into reform, the most specific cultural term for what he became would be* **umkovu***, which means the newly dead, reanimated familiar of a witch*

Djellaba *= traditional long, loose-fitting unisex outer robe with full sleeves, originating in Morocco and/or countries along the Southern Mediterranean coast*

Hijab *= a traditional head covering worn in public by some Muslim women; also, the religious code which governs the wearing of the garment itself*

Ildorobo *= a term derived from the Maa (Maasai) expression* **il-tóróbò,** *meaning hunters — the ones without cattle*

Kenge *= the Swahili term for 'chameleon'; the name of the messenger sent by Ngai to bring news of immortality to the people*

Kikuyu *= Swahili for* **Gĩkũyũ,** *the largest ethnic (Bantu) group in Kenya, literally, the word means 'giant sycamore tree'; the tribe refer to themselves as Agĩkũyũ, thus the Kikuyu are the children of the sycamore*

Maasai *= the semi-Nomadic people of southern Kenya and northern Tanzania; the chosen people of Ngai (according to themselves) since they are the keepers of his sacred cattle*

Maasai mara = *large area of land now protected as a game reserve along the Kenya/Tanzania border which is contiguous with the Serengeti; it derives its name* **mara** *from the Maa word for spotted, which describes circles of scrub, savannah, trees, and cloud shadow that mark the region, but also carries the Maasai name in honor of the ancestral people who inhabited it*

Mbaya = *evil, tainted, unclean*

Mbulumbulu = *geographic region on the high Serengeti plain near the southeastern border of what is now the Ngorongoro conservation area, it lies in the Arusha district, near Karatu*

Mganga = *a witch doctor or medicine man;* **nganga** *in Bantu, along with* **inyanga**, *may also mean a qualified physician or traditional healer — they are believed to have religious powers to tell fortunes, and to change, heal, bless, or even kill people*

Mjusi = *the word means 'lizard' in Kiswahili; the mischief-maker who thwarted Ngai's messenger, Kenge, and convinced humans of their mortality, in this book, the primary incarnation of the Morningstar*

Motori = *a mixture of milk and blood tapped from a cow's jugular vein, this ceremonial drink is used to celebrate births, and to toast bravery following rites of passage such as circumcision or admission to the warrior class*

Mpenzi = *the Swahili term of endearment for a lover, essentially a sweetheart*

Munono = *a mixture of meat, blood, and fat that is the principal diet of Maa warriors*

Ndali = *a subgroup of Bantu tribespeople originating in southern Tanzania and northern Malawi*

Ngai (Mwathani) = *the people's God, the name is related to the word* **nyaga** *or whiteness, and he is known as the Possessor of Whiteness, as an indicator of complete purity*

Ngorongoro = *a crater which is the result of a massive volcanic collapse about 2 million years ago; the name comes from the pastoral Maa (Maasai) word describing the sound a cowbell makes –* **'ngoro ngoro'**, *it includes the Oldupai gorge, the site of discovery of early hominid life, and part of the Arusha district of Tanzania*

Nkokua = *heavy rains, rainy season*

Nyasi nyekundu = *red grasses of the Serengeti and other places*

Nyumbu = *wildebeest*

Olapa = *Moon Goddess; wife of Ngai in some legends, wife of another god in others, she is the mother goddess*

Oldupai = *from Oldupaai, a Maasai word for the wild sisal plant which grows in the gorge of the same name, Loduvai and Olduvai are variations borne of mispronunciation of the word*

Oloirurujuruj = *misting rains, transitional season between heavy rainfall and the beginning of the dry season*

Pemba = *one of the three large islands off the eastern coast of Tanzania*

Shuka = *lengths of cloth traditionally worn like capes across the shoulders of tribal warriors*

Ulimwengu = *the world, realm, some stories relate this as the place from which Ngai created everything; the universe*

Unguja = *the historic name for the island of Zanzibar, one of three dominant islands east of Dar Es Salaam, along with Pemba and Mafia*

Watende = *a traditional African name meaning 'there shall be no revenge'*

About the Author

LJ FARROW'S CHILDHOOD FEAR OF the dark naturally led to a fascination with supernatural beings. Curiosity about their origins was the way she demystified them as a child, although she admits that trying to understand them did not make them any less frightening. A Colorado native, she now lives and writes in rural Indiana. She is still afraid of the dark.

If you enjoyed **south**, look for **east**, the third book in the Morningstar series!

Azuma is the dragon guardian of a revered warrior tradition, cursed by the Morningstar with longevity and a taste for human blood. At the intersection of science and technology she discovers the means to unlock the fundamental code which holds the secret of life itself, but she finds it cannot be fully deciphered without the power of love.

east is the third novel in the Morningstar series, which follows the lives of four supernatural beings, each of whom must overcome a specific challenge to their humanity as part of a personal journey toward redemption. The prevention of an apocalyptic war planned by the Morningstar will only be possible if they work together to harness the unique powers that each possesses.